LET TERRY CALDER, THE SASSIEST, MOST APPEALING HERO SINCE HUCKLEBERRY FINN, TAKE YOU BACK TO THE DAYS WHEN YOU WERE A KID.

When having to wear shoes and sit in school on a hot summer day was torture.

When cigarettes were something you mooched, catfish something you learned to catch in your bare hands, and stolen tomatoes dipped in salt tasted better than anything.

When life itself was a simple thing and the only education you needed came through friendship—even if the whole world stood against it.

Set against the intriguing world of Florida's swamps, freight cars, canneries, and labor camps in the early 1940's, SUMMER LIGHTNING follows the adventures of a boy on the run deep in the Everglades, learning the important things about living and surviving from McCree, a wily old maverick who has lived outside the law for half a century. Police and truant officers are on their trail, but in this sultry summer, their trail is a vanishing wave on the water.

"The story of Terry and Mr. McCree will capture the heart of anyone . . . a rare and poignant love story, one that conveys the magical, fleeting world of a runaway boy in a country on the edge of war."

Literary Guild Magazine

SUMMER LIGHTNING

Judith Richards

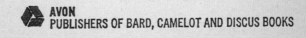

AVON
PUBLISHERS OF BARD, CAMELOT AND DISCUS BOOKS

AVON BOOKS
A division of
The Hearst Corporation
959 Eighth Avenue
New York, New York 10019

First Avon Printing, September, 1979

AVON TRADEMARK REG. U.S. PAT. OFF. AND IN
OTHER COUNTRIES, MARCA REGISTRADA,
HECHO EN U.S.A.

Printed in the U.S.A.

To My Grandparents:

Edna Thomason Anderson
Russell Anderson
Gertrude McCormick Richards
Alfred Elliot Richards

Foreword

Sometimes when an author is too close to something, he can't write it. Introspection and evaluation of others around him become elusive.

That was the case with the real Terry Calder, about whom this book is written. Today he is an accomplished writer. From him, I heard this story many times. I know his parents. I never knew Mr. McCree, but I feel as though he was my friend. So it was with everyone in this book. Those I never met are no less my friends because I listened to so many tales and warm words about them.

This book is true—and not true. Fiction and nonfiction. Asked to classify it, I am at a loss to do so. There was a Terry Calder. That much is truth, as was much of what happened herein.

—JUDITH RICHARDS

the pan onto plates heaped with soft homefries and
green onions.

"Old Crowfoot remembers well this day,"
McCrea observed.

A gentle breeze gave breath to the palms; fronds sighed, whispering, promising a good day at Lake Okeechobee. An aroma of overripe dates in the palms, and a buzz of sweat bees suckling nectar from spoiled fruit, reminded Terry that wild bananas would be a bitter-sweet reward if he bolted and ran.

"Eat your breakfast, Terrell."

"Yes ma'am."

Migratory workers were already in the fields. Voices of their children came to his ears—going to school in Belle Glade, half a mile distant. A scent of guava mingled with the perfume of poinciana and citrus trees planted throughout Camp Osceola.

"I want you to go to school today, Terrell."

"Yes ma'am."

Through the kitchen window, he saw long lines of yellow boxcars on railroad tracks above and behind the house. He heard the clink of couplings, the hiss-chug of engines as United Fruit cars were shifted according to a mysterious system that would ultimately see them filled, iced and on their way north.

"There's been enough playing hooky," Mama said.

"Mickey, the boy says he's going," Daddy answered.

"He said that last week, too."

"He said he's going," more sternly. Daddy gazed at Terry. "Didn't you, Terrell?"

"Yessir."

A huge black bee with pollen-laden legs thumped

1

the screen, bump, bump, then swerved away. A warning whistle from the tracks, two shorts. That meant the train was going to move. A brakeman had taught this to Terry.

"Hurry now." Mama reached over, wiped Terry's mouth, both corners. Flicked at a crumb, brushed hand over hair. "Time to go," she said. Daddy folded his newspaper to another page.

"I don't know what this country is coming to," Daddy commented. "Now Roosevelt wants to arm merchant ships."

"Terrell, I said it's time to go."

"Yes ma'am."

He stood on incredibly thin legs, knees knobbed, exposed by short trousers which he detested.

"Wash your face and hands."

"Yes ma'am."

"You know what that means," Daddy said. "The Germans will have a legitimate reason to sink our ships. If that happens, we're that much nearer war."

"Terrell!"

He had been standing in the hall doorway, listening to Daddy. He hurried to the bathroom, turned on the water, gingerly lifted the soap with two fingers, wet it and placed it back in the dish unused. He wiped his face and hands on a towel. He went into the bedroom to get his books, carefully bound with a belt like other children carried theirs.

"Terrell!" Vexation in her tone now. Aside to Daddy, "Lord that child is slow."

"Mickey, don't shout. You're always shouting at that boy."

"How do you suggest I get his attention? Whisper?"

"Terrell!" Daddy's voice.

"Yessir."

"Let's go, boy. Time for school."

"Yessir."

Mama gave him a brown paper sack: two potted

meat sandwiches with mayonnaise mixed with a sweet relish. An apple. A nickel for a drink.

"Milk," Mama stated.

"Yes ma'am."

"Go *to* school."

"Yes ma'am."

He eased the screen door closed behind him. He was aware of Mama's eyes as he crossed the backyard, climbed a cinder-strewn incline to the maze of railroad tracks and disappeared from her sight. The musty smell of disuse and former cargoes seeped from opened boxcars as he passed. He ducked between two stationary fruit cars, past a coupling and out the other side. He walked along the tracks, deliberately taking a path that would carry him beside the steaming locomotive. He liked coal-burners better than diesels. They had a roaring fire, activity of the coal car and a fireman shoveling black nuggets into flames.

"Can I have a ride?"

The engineer grinned. He nodded and the fireman reached down with one hand to bodily lift Terry aboard. Terry went directly to a thin, hard, padded seat opposite the engineer. The engine reverberated beneath his feet and he wished he were barefoot.

"Going to school?"

It was obvious: clean, shoes, books. Terry nodded.

Far down the track a man leaned out into view, holding a low rung of a ladder on the side of a car, waving to the engineer.

The vehicle groaned, wheezed, as the throttle was eased forward, the mighty engine creaked, wheels squealing as sand dropped on the rails for traction. Ruffer-ruffer-ruffer, pistons spun the wheels, boxcars moved and a rhythmic clack of cars rippled down the track as the engine pushed what it had formerly pulled. They didn't move far. The flagman waved again, jumped off, threw a switch and waved anew. The couplings responded to the pull, clickity-clackity-clickity-clack,

3

and they backed up, drawing a snaking curve of cars off a siding for redistribution.

"You're going to be late, little buddy."

"Yessir."

"Let me help you." The fireman lifted him over the side and down onto the cinder bed. Hot fumes blew Terry's red hair as he passed the length of the engine between tracks.

He crossed a bridge connecting Camp Osceola with the main town road. He cut between the packing houses. There was no point walking on blistering hot pavement with the wide eave and cool platform of the packing house so available. The building was a hive of activity, the vegetable smell of celery and foliage pungent and pleasing. Voices, machinery and water sounds formed a cadence that could hold him spellbound by the hour.

He climbed unbanistered steps, entering the long, open shed of the three-story building. The structure was laced with ribbons of steel-rollered conveyors, each filled with crates end to end, beginning high overhead where the cartons were assembled and stored. Women wearing rubber aprons and boots packed the boxes. Terry passed a washing machine that sprayed the produce to give it a final cleansing before green shredded paper was put over it and a top was nailed on. He approached one of the aproned women.

"May I have a piece of celery?"

She tore off a stalk, gave it to him with scarcely a glance, talking to a fellow worker.

He passed the hot-dog stand where most of the laborers purchased quick lunches of hamburgers, hot dogs, chips and soft drinks. A tantalizing lure of cooking sauerkraut tempted him to invest his nickel in a spoonful. Or better yet, he might trade away his lunch to one of the black people working here, for a dime or fifteen cents more. He had done this before. They were tired of eating the same food from the hot-dog stand

4

day after day. It was a fair exchange. But he didn't do it. He was fresh from breakfast. Besides, the best deals were made closer to lunch.

Terry saw several men taking a break, smoking. He asked one of them, "Can I have a cigarette?"

"You're too young to smoke."

"Please."

"Give the kid a cigarette."

"Stunt your growth, boy."

"Thank you." He put the Camel in a top pocket, careful to place it so it wouldn't break if he leaned over. He crossed the packing house to another group.

"Can I have a cigarette?"

The same protests, the same results. He did this four more times before he reached the end of the building. Six cigarettes of four different brands, one with a filter, the rest without. One mentholated, one overpowering Home Run, one equally potent Picayune. These he could trade away to the boys at the high school, who willingly paid as much as three cents for a cigarette, regardless of the brand.

He followed a circuitous route through several packing houses, arriving at the far end of the last one, which abutted the back way to the icehouse. Bucky Dallas was sitting on the warped steps of a shack constructed under an eave of the building. Bucky had a crossed eye. His father ran the icehouse. Bucky's parents didn't seem to care whether he went to school or not.

"Want to buy a cigarette?" Terry asked.

"I got no money."

"Want one then?"

"Sure."

Terry gave him the Picayune. It was the hardest to sell. Bucky was always good for a chunk of crystal-clear ice in the dead of summer. He'd once socked Billy Poole in the mouth on Terry's behalf, too.

"Going to school?" Bucky asked.

"Yeah."

"You're late."

Terry went across the pavement, avoiding pitch bubbles raised by the hot sun. A canal separated the school from the packing houses. It was lined with thick growths of bamboo, a source of fishing poles, anoles and occasional green snakes. It was a cool retreat for errant boys who would not be in class today.

"School started?" His question was at large to three older boys.

"Long time ago."

"Want to buy a cigarette?"

"How much?"

"Nickel."

"Shit."

"For two," Terry added.

"Forget it."

"Okay. Three for a nickel. My choice."

The deal was made: mentholated, Home Run and Camel, a nickel.

"Your mama's going to whip your ass, redhead," one of the boys said, chewing a bamboo shoot.

"How come?"

"Teacher's already been out here looking for you. She's going to tell your mama."

The realization brought a quickening heartbeat, a hurried debate of alternatives.

"I'm going to school," Terry said.

"You're late."

"I'm going." He crossed the single rickety board linking the narrow canal banks, through more bamboo and into the fenced school yard. Deserted. From an open window, he heard the Pledge of Allegiance, from another window, the morning prayer and from across the bare, burnt brown yard, a ting of flag clasps against the metal pole.

If he didn't go, Mama would be angry. If he did go, Mrs. Wright would send him to Mr. Hammond, the principal, for being late again. He heard one of the older truants laugh.

"You going, or not?" came the question.

"I'm going."

"In time for lunch," somebody stated.

"Are you inhaling?"

"Sure I'm inhaling."

"Let me see. Take a puff and open your mouth so I can see."

"He swallowed it."

"No I didn't, piss-ant. I inhaled. Watch this."

A frog plopped in the canal. Behind Terry, the bamboo stirred, settled, whispered anew.

"Hey, Red," Bucky's voice close by. "Come on. Let's go swimming."

"No."

"You really going in this late?"

"Yes." Terry turned, looking at Bucky.

Bucky studied him with one eye as the other eye contemplated the bridge of his nose.

"Come on, Terry. No point in getting your ass whipped for being late. Might as well get it whipped for being absent."

He heard a scraping of wood chairs on the floors as students settled down. An insect zurred past his ear, zurred again and darted toward the stand of bamboo.

"What you say?" Bucky prodded.

"I got to go to school." He started across the open expanse of the yard toward the red brick building. He had the uncomfortable sensation that all eyes were on him. He passed by the skeletons of playground equipment, swings inert over scoops made by thousands of pushing feet in motion, a slide hot enough to cook flesh, a maze of monkey bars.

The covered walkway between the high school and elementary classrooms was cool, red, terra-cotta tile. A water fountain on one wall was surrounded by a wet place where trickled sips had eluded the thirsty. He was trembling, clutching the paper sack.

From the hallway off which the first- through sixth-grade rooms were situated, he felt a flow of air. He smelled chalk, heard a coughing student, a teacher's voice. His room was all the way at the other end.

"Son?"

He wheeled. It was the secretary from Mr. Hammond's office.

"What class are you in?"

"Mrs. Wright."

"Well, hadn't you better get on in there?"

"Yes ma'am."

He walked down the hall, her footsteps behind him. He heard her stop, tap on a door; he kept walking.

"Aaaayyyy . . ." voices in unison. "Beeee . . ."

The door had frosted glass panes except for one in the very center, higher than he could stretch to see. He heard Mrs. Wright now. "Who knows what this is?"

"Ceeeee . . ."

The secretary had concluded her errand and was walking back the way she'd come, heels tapping the floor.

"Eeeee . . ."

He swallowed, put a shaking hand on the knob to turn it.

"Effffph . . ."

At this end of the hall was another set of doors, seldom used, leading to a large storage room beyond. The doors were open to admit as much air as possible.

"Eddy, can you open the windows for me?" Mrs. Wright's disembodied voice requested.

Across the hall, another teacher, voice booming, "All crayons must be replaced in the boxes, students. Check around your feet to be sure you haven't dropped one. Let's all do that now."

"Geeee . . ."

Terry walked back along the hall, gaining momentum

as his resolve evaporated. He hit the door at full run, bolting like an animal with a glimpse of freedom. Past the water fountain, into the yard, a shimmering wave of heat searing bare legs and arms, brushing his face, as he impelled himself as fast as his legs would move.

"Terrell!" Mrs. Wright! She was at the window. "Terrell!"

He reached the plank bridging the canal and in three racing steps cleared it, went past the smoking boys, across hot pavement and into the packing house. He dashed between conveyors, skirted stacked boxes, vaulted a dolly being pushed toward a boxcar. A rasp of metal teeth shredding blocks of ice roared in his ears as he ducked beneath a tube shooting the frozen matter into an open lid of a fruit car.

"Hey! Kid! Damnation!"

He crawled through a jumble of burlap sacks heaped in a bin, gained the far side and higher elevation to the second floor.

"Hey! Get outta here! Hey, you! Get the hell out—"

He was out, on the first floor again, settling to a slower pace. He glanced back repeatedly, as though expecting a horde of teachers led by the principal, armed with rulers and bent on dragging him to class.

"Want to buy a lunch?"

"What is it?"

"Potted meat sandwiches. Two of them."

"Nah."

"Cost you a quarter."

"Nah. I brung my own. Potted meat."

Next man. "Want to buy two potted meat sandwiches? I'll throw in a apple too, all for a quarter."

"No thanks. Look, get out of the way, son."

Next. "I'll sell you two potted meat sandwiches and a apple."

"How much?"

"Quarter?"

"Dime."

"Fifteen cents."

The man fished out coins, holding them as he inspected the sandwiches. "They're smashed," he said, but gave Terry the money.

"Thanks!"

Twenty-five cents total, snug in his pocket, trouble at home tonight, but until then— He paused at the hot-dog stand and bought one, and a big RC, and sat amid workers taking first lunch break.

He wasn't going to think about what was coming later. He savored the onions and relish, steamed bun and mustard. He took huge swigs from the RC, maintaining suction to avoid a backwash. He considered buying a pack of salted nuts to pour in his drink, but decided against it. Salt took the fizz out of soda.

He walked out the Chosen road, detouring through a cane field where black men with machetes were harvesting thick, juicy stalks.

"Peel me a stalk?" he inquired of a gleaming ebony worker.

"Sure nuff."

The man flashed startling white teeth. His accent told Terry this was an islander from the Bahamas, come to cut cane and make a few dollars American before returning to his own home. The cane dripped around Terry's hand. He had no way to cut off plugs, so he chewed from top to bottom, reducing each bite to a tough fiber sucked dry of fluid.

He ate as he walked, still carrying his books, chewing cane and wondering if he'd see McCree today. Snake man, they called him. McCree called Terrell Terry or Little Hawk and never asked discomforting questions.

Terry heard a car coming and got off the road. His second week of school had taught him about Miss Ramsey, the truant officer. She came this way every morning, gathering the unwary to haul them back to Mr. Hammond's office.

There were stories that Miss Ramsey had caused a tenth-grader to be shipped to Marianna, to the boys' reformatory, because he skipped school. And stole things.

The car passed. It was not Miss Ramsey. It was the greens keeper at the golf course, on his way to work. Dust swirled from the roadbed, settled on saw grass and temporarily colored the air russet.

Terry crawled down a bank to reach canal water, ever mindful of snakes. He pushed aside blue-blossomed hyacinths, a favorite resting place for the cottonmouth moccasin, and washed sticky cane juice from his hands.

He nearly slipped. Only a quick grab for the belt around his books saved them from total loss. He retrieved the dripping bundle and moaned. A red dye from the cover of his reader bled onto his fingers. He knew his problems had just been compounded.

He continued toward Chosen, alert to the sound of an occasional approaching automobile; dust, sweat and red dye from his book turned his hands and all he touched a dingy brown.

He followed a familiar path from the road down a canal bank, to a crossing board, through a thicket of Australian pines and into a small clearing. Here lived Eunice Washington, a stout black woman, and her sole grandchild, LuBelle.

"Hey, Eunice."

"Lord God, boy, you near scared me to death! Don't come creeping up on Eunice like that."

"You seen Mr. McCree?"

"Not yet. He'll be along directly."

"Can I wait?"

"Help yourself." Eunice poked a bleached broomstick into a boiling cauldron of lye soap, rain water and "took in" clothes, which she washed and ironed for pay.

"LuBelle here?"

"Ain't she always?"

"Inside?"

"Most likely."

The house was built on stilts, over earth packed hard by years of foot traffic. There were no windows, only holes cut in the siding with hinged shutters which opened from the bottom. No screens kept out insects, and the inhabitants shared the cool, dark, three-room building with whatever chose to enter. The house was always an odd mixture of odors. Boiling beans simmered on a wood stove, where Eunice also heated her irons, and a damp, musty aroma of fresh dirt rose through cracks between floorboards.

LuBelle was sitting in the middle of a bed, naked. A year younger than Terry, she never wore clothes. It had not occurred to him to give this a second thought. He had never seen her otherwise.

"You want some taffy?"

"No," Terry said.

"Mawmaw made it last night."

"Listen, LuBelle, you got any worms?"

"No."

"Reckon we could go dig some? I'm going to ask Mr. McCree to take me fishing."

"He ain't going. Today's his day to trade with Mawmaw. Mr. Cree don't do nothing on trading day, except trade."

"Today?"

LuBelle pointed at two quart jars on a bare table. The contents looked like kerosene. But they weren't.

"Ho, Eunice."

"There he is," LuBelle grinned.

"Look what I got you, Eunice!"

"Lord God, Mr. Cree," Eunice always dropped the *Mc* from his name, "what you doing bringing that here?"

LuBelle and Terry ran to the front porch. Mr. Mc-

12

Cree was standing in the yard, laughing, Eunice holding him at bay with her broomstick. The old man gripped the heads of two huge rattlesnakes, one in each hand, tails whirring a dry staccato warning.

2

～ ～～ ～

Mickey Calder twisted her auburn hair into a bun behind her head. She turned before a full-length mirror, examining a seam in her nylons. She tugged the hem of her skirt to cover a lacy edge of slip. Her hands were perspiring. She was still irritated from her conversation with Gerald.

"He did it again, Gerald."

"Who did what, Mickey?"

"Terrell skipped school."

A long silence on the line, background sounds of office activity behind Gerald's exhaled sigh.

"Where is he now?"

"Gerald, how would I know that? I know he isn't here. I know he isn't in school!"

"All right, Mickey. All right."

"Mr. Hammond called."

"The principal?"

"Yes. And Mrs. Wright, his teacher. Miss Ramsey, the truant officer, came by a moment ago. This is embarrassing, Gerald. That child makes us appear to be negligent parents."

"I don't see anything we can do until he comes home tonight, Mickey."

"We could go look for him."

"Look? Where? The packing houses? Chosen? Lake Okeechobee? He said he went to all those places last week."

"I don't know, but I'm not going to sit here all day worrying."

"What did the principal say?"

"He said Terrell was seen running from the school by his teacher. He said Terrell ignored her call and kept running."

A sound on the line made Mickey's nerves crackle. "Are you laughing, Gerald?"

"Clearing my throat, darling."

"There's nothing funny about this, Gerald."

"Just clearing my throat."

"There happens to be a state law about six-year-old children attending school, Gerald. Miss Ramsey made a large point of it."

"All right, Mickey."

"I would appreciate a bit of maturity on your part, Gerald, I really would. I'm at my wit's end. Do you know that boy hasn't attended but three days of classes—one of which was half a day before he ran at recess?"

"I know, Mickey. Terrell's a boy. Boys do this sort of thing."

"Gerald, really! Miss Ramsey sits here prim and proper and says the most condescending things. I must have help with that child, Gerald. He belongs to *both* of us!"

"All right, Mickey."

"I'm going out looking."

"If you insist."

"Isn't it better than sitting here doing nothing?"

"No. Frankly, no. He'll be home tonight. Deal with it then."

"I want that boy blistered for this tonight."

"Now, Mickey."

"I mean it! I want him worn out. He told me with a perfectly straight face he was going to school."

"We'll see, Mickey."

"Are you going to do what is necessary?" Her voice was trembling.

The metallic reply on the telephone, "If you insist."

"I won't be home."

"Okay."

She had hung up without good-byes. Now dressed, feeling very pregnant, she cursed the wiggly line of her hose, stray wisps of hair eluding her barrette, and the heat. She checked the calendar, a daily task. Tuesday, September twenty-third. The baby was due the first week in December.

Gerald's office was a scant two hundred yards away, in the general administration building. If he needed transportation, he could borrow one of the tan government vehicles. Mickey got into the suffocatingly hot Chevrolet they had just bought, the new-smell still strong. She backed down a long drive to the camp's main entrance, crossed a speed-break hump in the pavement, passed over a canal and turned toward Chosen.

Since Gerald had taken the position as manager of this migratory labor camp two years ago, they had seen their fortunes steadily recover from the utter deprivation of the Depression years in Birmingham, Alabama. Here a three-bedroom house was provided, two hundred a month income, and Gerald was happy. After graduating from Birmingham Southern College with a degree in journalism, Gerald had aspired to becoming a writer, and he had an overwhelming need to "help" mankind. His job here satisfied the latter, anyway.

Established to give housing and medical care to migrant workers, the camp had a steady flow of laboring families arriving and departing to tend crops. Before the camps, these poor people slept in vehicles, swamps, cane fields and beside highways. They had lacked health facilities of any kind, and disease of epidemic proportions was too often the result.

Gerald and the Farm Security Administration were doing something of tremendous importance for mankind. But at what cost to Terrell? He was smoking at four, wandering far and wide at five, and now, in his first year of school, rebelling against restrictions. Where would this child be in ten years after associating with tough, transient children? Murder, robbery, rape were almost daily occurrences in Belle Glade.

"Gerald, we must curtail that child!" she'd demanded.

"How, Mickey?" She'd made him angry. "You suggest he play with no one? Keep him at the house? Don't let him run around the camp, is that it?"

"I don't know how. But he's becoming—contaminated."

"That's a good word," Gerald had snapped. "Contaminated."

"Gerald, he's *smoking*."

"All boys do that."

"Do you know that's your standard response? Anything Terrell does, you say the same: all boys do that. Around here, his friends *all* do things I don't want Terrell doing, Gerald."

"Mickey, for God's sake! Terrell will be all right. He runs hither and yon throughout the camp and I wouldn't have it any other way. Now if you want to make that child miserable, segregate him from his peers. Make him, and them, think he's different. Then his life will be a daily hell, believe me. I grant you, he isn't running with the Duke and Duchess of Windsor. But all that he sees, good or bad, all that he experiences, good or bad, can be a growing experience. He's a fairly self-sufficient kid."

As with most of these conversations, that one had ended with sulking silence, issues unresolved, Terrell still untethered and running wild. There were evenings when the boy didn't show up until after dark.

"Where have you been, son?"

"Playing."

"Where?"

18

"Around the camp."

"*Where* around the camp, Terrell?"

A shrug of small shoulders, a wrinkling of his freckled nose. "I don't know, Mama. All over."

All over. She had an idea of the scope of that from casual comments made by camp employees.

"That Terrell's a pistol ball! I seen him over to the sewage disposal plant walking those intake pipes like a monkey!"

"Gerald, should he be allowed to do that?"

"It's probably all right."

"What if he fell in?"

Gerald's expression indicated that wouldn't be the best thing to happen, but he said, "He could get out."

A woman from the camp canning plant said, "Terrell's a sight. Comes by and charms the ladies right out of sauerkraut they're canning. All the women love him."

"Gave Terrell a ride on the mowing machine today . . ."

"That boy asks good questions . . . out with the Bahamians cutting cane yesterday . . ."

"You should've seen the size of the snake that boy caught . . . bare-handed!"

"I don't want to worry you folks, but it isn't safe really . . . to play on top of the auditorium . . . in packing houses . . . on railroad tracks . . . in cane fields where he could get lost . . . rats as big as cats, if he ever went to sleep out there . . . in the canals, even if he didn't drown, the chance of ear infection . . ."

Mickey turned toward Kramer Island Road, past the new golf course. The vehicle rose along a dike which held the waters of Lake Okeechobee in place in time of hurricane. She paused atop the swing bridge, looking out from this vantage point.

Below, hyacinth-choked, murky black water flowed. To either side, the dike wound away to infinity, a man-made molehill humping across otherwise flat terrain. Saw grass with razor-sharp cutting edges, cattails

19

higher than a man's head, snake-infested swamps and tangled growth all around. This was where Terrell had spent most of last week!

"Doing what?" Gerald had questioned gently.

"Playing."

"I know, Terrell. But playing how, with whom?"

"LuBelle."

"Who is LuBelle?"

"A friend of mine."

"Who are her parents?"

"They ran off."

"Who does LuBelle live with, then?"

"Her grandmama, Eunice."

"What is Eunice's last name?"

"Washington."

Like extracting teeth. Each question answered with an absolute minimum of words.

"Why isn't LuBelle in school?" Gerald persisted at Mickey's urging.

"She's too little."

"Younger than you?"

"Yessir. I think."

"Where does Mrs. Washington live?"

"Chosen."

"Can you tell me where in Chosen?"

"Off the road there."

Mickey had stepped in then. "What do you do with LuBelle? Where do you go?"

A twist of Terrell's thin lips, scratching under his nose with one small finger. "Just out to play."

"Terrell, I want a better answer than that."

"Mama, we just *play*."

"He should be spanked, Gerald."

Eyes widening, a stiffening of Terrell's back.

"You think you should be spanked, Terrell?" Gerald hedged.

"No sir."

"Why? You told your mama you would not skip school and you did."

"The entire third week!" Mickey snapped.

"Why, Terrell?" Gerald asked.

"I don't know."

"Don't you like the teacher?"

"She's okay."

"Are the children unfriendly to you?"

"No sir."

"Then, what is it?"

"I don't know."

"You know you must go to school."

"Yessir."

"It's a law."

"Yessir."

Gerald had studied the boy, the two of them soberly judging one another, the child a miniaturized copy of the father except for Terrell's red hair.

"You're going to school tomorrow?"

"Tomorrow is Saturday, Daddy."

"Very well. Monday then. Going to school?"

"Yessir."

So he did, Monday. Today was Tuesday. Mickey passed on over the bridge, halting at the end of a slope on the far side. A small store nestled under the shade of government-planted pines, selling snack foods and fishing supplies. Mickey set the brake and went inside. It was a masculine place, scented with shellacked fishing poles, earthy aromas from boxes marked "BAIT" and cool from the effect of water just outside. Men sat around here, for lack of anyplace else to congregate, swapping tales, trading jokes, almost all with a central theme of fishing or hunting.

"Morning, ma'am."

"Have you see a little redheaded boy, age six?"

"Terry, you mean?"

Why did that child insist on changing his name from

something as strong and masculine as Terrell to the feminine Terry?

"Yes," Mickey said, "Terry."

"Not today, ma'am." The man behind the counter stood with one foot on a barrel, meeting her eyes levelly.

"Want I should send him home, if I do?"

"Yes, please do."

"I'll sure do it."

"Thank you." She left feeling uncomfortable, huge and awkward. She bumped her stomach getting behind the wheel. "Damn it!" she whispered.

Gerald had been right, the area was hopelessly large. Nonetheless, Mickey drove out Kramer Island Road, between stands of wild grasses higher than the automobile. The heat was magnified in this hollow between vegetation, the sole breeze created by movement of the vehicle. Hundreds of black, red and orange grasshoppers blanketed the dirt road and a grisly crunch of their bodies under the wheels kept her teeth on edge.

She'd driven perhaps two miles, to the first wide place where she could turn around. It was a pumping station, motor roaring, water gushing as it was drawn from one level and emptied into a drainage canal. The air was breathlessly still. Flitting swarms of gnats buzzed around her face, into her eyes, ears and nostrils. Her efforts to brush them aside seemed to multiply their numbers. What if she got stalled or stuck out here? Almost seven months pregnant, the temperature surely in the nineties? She'd have to walk through those horrid grasshoppers for help—

Mickey leaned forward, her dress sopping with perspiration, trying to see what lay immediately beneath the wheels. She eased the car around, staying well onto packed soil. No telling what was beneath matted growth to either side of the road.

She pushed down on the accelerator and the car choked, coughed, hesitated, then lurched. She overreacted, jerking her foot from the gas pedal, and the car stalled, died.

"Dear God—"

She turned the key, heartbeat ascending, insects a living drone in her ears. The motor turned, turned, turned, quit. She smelled gas.

"Easy now. Keep calm. It's flooded."

She wiped her face with the bottom of her skirt. She caught a glimpse of herself in the rearview mirror—hair plastered to sweating flesh, skin red from the heat.

How could Terrell possibly enjoy this? The harassment of gnats, the buzz of disturbed mosquitoes ever present and constantly awaiting warm blood. She withheld her foot from the gas, turned the key. The motor caught.

Mickey didn't look any further. She went home to shower, change clothes, exhausted and miserable.

"Gerald?"

"Yeah, hey, Burrell!" Gerald clamped the receiver between ear and shoulder. Ribbons tied to an oscillating fan wiggled in the airstream.

"Gerald, what's this I hear about Eleanor Roosevelt coming down to inspect the camps?"

"Where'd you hear that, Burrell?"

"Here and there."

The Belle Glade paper, a product of Burrell Mason, was an astonishing enterprise. Agriculturally oriented, the four-hundred-pound owner had produced from his staff one syndicated columnist now working in Washington, one Pulitzer Prize–winner who had gone on to the *New York Times* and Associated Press.

"You amaze me, Burrell."

A guttural grunt on the phone. "Is she coming, then?"

"That's what they say. Rumors, mostly."

"That black camp's her pet, isn't it?"

"She has expressed a good deal of interest in it, yes."

Burrell Mason breathed into the receiver, a labored sound. "Keep me posted on it, will you, Gerald?"

"If she'll allow it," Gerald said. "And if I know she's coming. Last time she showed up with no prior announcement."

"Keep me in mind."

"I'll try."

The fan oscillated in a half-circle, stirring heated air. Through opened casement windows, the odor of freshly mowed grass came to Gerald's nostrils, the clacking of rotating blades chewing away fast-growing lawn.

"You think there'll be war?" Dr. Norman brought Gerald's mind back to his visitor.

"There already is war," Gerald stated. "Lowell Thomas said the Nazis have begun mopping up around Kiev—two hundred thousand Russians trapped there."

"Newspapers said the Germans lost a hundred fifty thousand. But I don't mean that. I mean war with us?"

"I don't know, Phillip. God I hope not. Just getting over the Depression—now this."

Dr. Phillip Norman raised himself from his chair. He accepted Gerald's signed receipts for inoculations delivered.

"I'm glad summer is over," Dr. Norman said. "Polio took its toll this year."

"You had cases?"

The doctor nodded, "Four. Sent two to Warm Springs. Maybe they'll get to meet the President."

Gerald watched the man go, his Palm Beach crinkled suit looking none too cool. He dialed home for the third time. Still no answer.

"Mr. Calder?" The admissions officer, Marilyn.

"Yes?"

"We have a family of sixteen and only two single-family metal shelters. Let them take both?"

24

"Are they next to one another, the shelters?"

"Separated by one between."

Regulations required two shelters for that many people. There was no way to keep them from sleeping all in one, overloading the limits; but it was better than the alternative—camping in swamps.

"Let them have it, Marilyn. When a larger single family dwelling opens up, move them. Tell them that."

"Yes, Mr. Calder."

He rubbed his eyes with thumb and forefinger, massaging away the pounding. He was tired. Long hours, constant worry about a hundred things. Now this problem with his family.

He stood, looking down at his desk; work aplenty. He sat again, signing documents without conscious consideration. He'd tried reasoning with the boy. Was he unhappy? "No sir." Didn't he like school? "Okay, I guess." "Punish him," Mickey insisted. For what? For being a boy? For doing what, God knows, every child truly yearned to do—run away and play? Given a choice, would he, Gerald, sit in a seething hot classroom with twenty-two other perspiring youngsters? Or go swimming at the nearest water hole?

"Mr. Calder?" Marilyn again.

"What, Marilyn?"

"Can you send maintenance over to section four? They have a plumbing problem in the bathhouse."

"All right. Make a note on it."

Gerald continued signing a seemingly endless mound of admission forms, inoculation forms, daily reports and statistical information which the Palm Beach office demanded.

He had tried to be a good father. He took Terrell up to Port Myaca fishing, over to Pahokee swimming, out to the Seminole Indian reservation now and then. Every other weekend or so they all drove over to West Palm Beach to eat at Morrison's and see a film. When Mickey got too far along to take the trip comfortably, he'd taken Terrell alone, just the two of them, to see *Bambi*.

"Did you enjoy the movie?"

"Yessir."

"What did you think was the best part?" Seeking more than a static response.

Terrell chewed his lip, thinking.

"Where the daddy deer came and saved Bambi in the forest fire."

"Yes," Gerald had said. "That was good."

"Want to play alligator poker?" Terrell asked as they turned from Palm Beach out onto the forty-five-mile-long highway to Belle Glade.

"Sure." Easy out. Count the alligators on your side. The side with the most at the end of the trip is winner. There were always hundreds of them east of Six Mile Bend. The balance of that excursion had been a series of mechanical responses.

"What did you two talk about?" Mickey later questioned.

"Oh, the movie."

"Anything else?"

"Played alligator poker."

"That's all?"

"What else is there?"

Mickey had sighed, trying to adjust her protruding stomach against two pillows to ease her back. He rubbed her shoulders, kneading away the constant tension she suffered these days.

"Being a parent is a bitch," Mickey said.

"It isn't easy."

"I hope this one is a girl. Girls are different from boys."

"I yield to that."

"Girls don't do nose dives off the roof, or set off fire alarms just to hear bells ring."

"I spanked Terrell for that."

"Girls don't leave chewing gum coated with sugar stuck to the coils of the refrigerator."

Gerald had laughed, moving lower with his massaging.

"Girls don't pull off grasshopper heads and stick them in keyholes."

"Good Lord."

"He did that and forgot about it. I found the first one when I went to unlock the storage room door."

The telephone rang and Gerald lifted the receiver, the fan swinging across his desk unsettling papers which he pinned with his free hand.

"Gerald?"

"Yes, hey, Mickey. Any luck?"

"No."

"He'll be along tonight, honey. Don't worry about him."

She hung up without another word.

3

LuBelle scratched her belly, the pupils of her brown eyes surrounded by white as she observed the ritual of slaughter. Terry watched Mr. McCree lop the heads from both rattlesnakes, letting the writhing bodies fall to bleed in a washtub.

"Don't touch the heads," McCree warned. "They still bite."

"I ain't touching nothing," LuBelle said.

"You two young 'uns stay way from them snakes," Eunice called, stirring her wash and kicking hot embers back under the blackened cauldron.

"With your mawmaw's beans, fried rattlesteaks," McCree said, his voice deep, graveled, "we got us a feast ahead."

"Mawmaw don't eat no snakes," LuBelle advised.

"Reckon not," McCree said. "But I got fish for her."

"I be of a mind to eat some fish myself," LuBelle mused.

"Plenty for all," McCree agreed. He skinned the headless carcasses, which still twisted in his hands.

"That hurt them?" Terry asked.

McCree leaned over close to a rattler's head on the ground. "That hurt you?" he asked the head.

" 'Spect his head hurts," LuBelle said, "if anything at all."

"Without a head, he's dead," McCree explained. "Dead things don't feel nothing, except pain in the soul."

"Snakes got souls?" Terry inquired.

"Like as not." McCree sliced pure white reptile flesh into wafers suitable for frying. "Seminoles think so. They think trees and grass and all manner of things have souls. I never talked to a dead man, so I couldn't rightly prove it right or wrong."

"Only folks got souls," Eunice stated.

"My dog died and went to heaven," Terry said. His wirehaired terrier had been struck by a car.

"Whose heaven?" McCree grunted. "Yours or his?"

"What do you mean?"

"Your heaven might be full of chains and locks and pens to keep a dog from running in God's backyard. His heaven might be full of rabbits and star-nosed moles and crunchy bugs to chomp on. If you was a dog, which would you want? A tether, or freedom?"

"I never tied up my dog!"

"Got killed, too," Lubelle said.

"That isn't my fault!"

"Nobody's fault," McCree responded. He lifted a quart jar with a bloodied hand, unscrewed the Mason lid and took two huge swallows. He wiped his unshaven chin with the back of a gritty sleeve.

"Mind what you teach them children," Eunice chided. "I don't want no bad dreams or long questions after you leaves."

"Boil your clothes, woman."

LuBelle laughed and McCree winked at the black girl. "Fetch some salt, child."

"Can I have the rattlers?" Terry asked.

McCree handed them to him. Terry stuck the appendages in his pocket with the two cigarettes. Feeling these, he asked, "Want a cigarette?"

"Nope. Want a plug of Bull of the Woods?"

"Nope," Terry said.

McCree took a round box of iodized salt from Lu-Belle and liberally applied it to the diced rattlesnake meat. This done, he went to his battered pickup truck, followed by the two children.

"Where's your dog?" Terry asked.

"Round about. Dog!" McCree withdrew a burlap sack from the bed of his truck and reached inside. He pulled out two catfish, considered these, pulled out two more. "Dog!" he hollered again.

Dog was the animal's name. A mongrel with one blue eye and one green, the old man's companion and "chief snake sniffer," the pup had taken refuge in a hollow under an elephant-ear plant.

"There's Dog," McCree said.

"Go stir them beans, LuBelle!"

"Yes ma'am."

"Stir to the bottom now, so's they don't stick," Eunice commanded.

"Mr. McCree, reckon we can go fishing sometime soon?" Terry questioned.

"When did you have a mind to?"

"Today."

"Not today, Little Hawk."

"You said you'd teach me how to catch fish with no bait."

"I did that, and will, too."

"When, you suppose?"

"Oh, tomorrow maybe."

"You think I can do it?"

"Anybody can."

"Them beans bubbling?" Eunice called, lifting clothes on the end of the broom handle, transferring them to a bucket.

"A little," LuBelle replied.

"Eunice knows about beans," McCree said, cleaning the catfish.

When the washing was done, they cooked the snake meat and catfish in large frying pans over the remaining embers, the odor of lighterknots burning, sap crackling, the aroma of food making their bellies churn.

31

McCree cut a green bamboo stalk, split a section into slivers, and they used these to spear meat directly from the pan onto plates heaped with soft butterbeans and green onions.

"Old *Crotalus adamanteus* served us well this day," McCree observed. He called most things by their "true" names. It seemed only proper, he said, to call things what they really were. Names meant something, Mc-Cree told Terry. *Crotalus,* big rattler, *adamanteus,* unyielding.

"Don't smack your lips," Eunice said to Terry. "If a bite's too big to shut on, make a smaller bite of it."

"Yes ma'am."

"Don't say ma'am to me, neither."

"Yes ma'am."

McCree passed his jar to Eunice and she helped herself to several small swallows, winced, handed it back.

"Can I have a taste?" Terry asked.

McCree gave it to him and Terry took a sip of the liquid, felt it sear to his innards, a lingering kerosene scent in his mouth.

"I don't like it," Terry said.

"Didn't think you would."

"I have some?" LuBelle asked.

McCree handed it to her with one hand, spearing more snake meat with the other. LuBelle put her tongue in the tilted jar, withdrew it, face contorted. "Tastes like coal oil smells."

"It does," McCree agreed.

"How come you drink it then?" Terry asked, speaking to McCree and Eunice.

"Punishing myself for long-ago sins," McCree said. Eunice laughed.

"What kind of sins?" LuBelle questioned.

"Minor infractions, mostly against the flesh," Mc-Cree stated. Eunice laughed again.

"Now and again, taking the Lord's name in vain," McCree added.

The sun was settling behind the tops of Australian pines, making tatted patterns through the topmost branches of bamboo stands. Crickets had begun the first evening serenade. They sat around the fire, lying back against a tree, bucket or stump, watching the embers pulling ashen blankets over the reddish glow below.

"I had aplenty," Eunice said, refusing McCree's second jar. McCree took noisy, sucking sips, exhaled a sigh of satisfaction and began cutting a plug from a tobacco patty he carried in his top pocket. He offered this around, the children soberly refusing, then put it away.

"I saw a wonderful thing today," McCree said, settling back. "I saw a snake eat a buzzard's egg."

"You did?" Terry slipped nearer. McCree took LuBelle under one arm, Terry under the other, sharing his leaning spot.

"Commenced to eat that egg with a head no wider than my thumb. The egg was big as this——" He showed three fingers wide. "I seen that before, but it always confounds me. Egg so smooth and that snake just unhinges his jaws, his bottom jaw stretches apart and he ain't got no place to hang a fang; still he does it and down it went. A big bulge like a tater in a long sock. He'd have eaten more, but Mrs. Buzzard came back right about then, mad with the snake, and me for letting the snake do that."

"Why didn't you stop him?" LuBelle asked.

"Ain't my right to do it," McCree said. "Snakes got to eat just like the rest of us folks. He was hungry, he found the egg and it was his to eat. People who go around trying to choose up sides with nature do no living thing a favor. But I don't suppose Mrs. Buzzard would agree."

LuBelle had her head against McCree's chest, eyes catching the last of the firelight, reflecting it at Terry, who assumed the same position and stared at her across McCree's body. The old man smelled like cured tobacco, his breath a miasma of the weed he chewed. His words came to Terry's ears two ways, from overhead in words, from within as comforting hums behind a rib cage.

"Some of these days a gator or cougar is going to feed on my bones," McCree stated.

"Hush such," Eunice said, but not firmly.

"As it should be. I been eating their kind nigh onto eighty-three years, more or less."

LuBelle's eyes fluttered, closed. Fluttered, closed.

"Go to bed, child," Eunice admonished.

"Let her be," McCree squeezed LuBelle slightly.

Bullfrogs burping, tree frogs in key on a higher note, crickets fiddling, cicadas chirping, wind whispering, bellies filled, pine smoke holding off mosquitoes, the final light of day gone, Terry sighed deeply, eyes closing.

"Where you reckon that boy's mama be?" Eunice asked, softly.

"Says he ain't got none."

"No mama?"

"Says that."

"Dressed the way he do? He got a mama."

McCree lifted Terry aside, putting him on a mat of fallen pine needles. He carried LuBelle to the house and placed her in bed, covering her over with a thin sheet to ward off pests.

"Got a daddy then," Eunice said, when McCree returned.

"Says not."

"You believing that!"

McCree gazed down at Terry, sleeping. "I tell you about believing, Eunice. I believe what he believes, even when I believe it ain't true. What he believes is what is."

McCree shook Terry gently. "Little Hawk?" He shook again. "Little Hawk, the owls are coming out to play."

Terry opened his eyes to darkness. McCree caressed

34

the child's shoulder, rubbing away knotted muscles and sleep with the same strokes.

"The moon's rising, Little Hawk."

"Yessir."

"Better flit away home."

Terry rose and accepted McCree's hand, following the old man to the pickup truck. "Dog! Let's go, Dog!" The pup bounded past Terry onto the front seat. Terry settled against the shuddering door of the cab, Dog's tail thumping him in the arm as McCree said so long to Eunice, and thanks.

He next awoke at the bridge over the main entrance canal of the camp. McCree's hand was shaking him.

"Flit away home, Boy."

"We going fishing sometime?"

"Whenever," McCree said. "You awake?"

"Yessir."

"Going to be all right?"

Terry slipped from the cab. He watched the truck go over the railroad tracks, one fender flapping noisily, the rear bumper twisted, the sole taillight flickering. He crossed the bridge. Overhead, security lights hummed and whirred with nocturnal creatures, the smell of fallen insects strong as he skirted the poles. The lights were on in the house. He halted in a small grove of guava trees, considering his next step.

He circled the house and, through a kitchen window, saw Mama washing dishes at the sink. He went to the living room and climbed up to peer inside a window. Daddy was sitting at the radio console, turning dials. Terry's body had touched the antenna, disturbing the reception.

He was suddenly aware that he had lost his books. He felt each foot with the other—shoes still on. He might survive the books, but not losing the shoes. He tried to lift his bedroom screen and could not. Mama had double-latched it.

There was nothing else to do except go in the front door. Or the kitchen door. He elected to take the front.

Daddy didn't turn until he was almost to the hall. "Terrell—"

"Yessir."

"Why didn't you go to school today, son?"

"I meant to."

"But you didn't?"

"No sir."

"Your mother has been hunting you, worrying, all day."

"I'm sorry, Daddy."

Mama, coming through the dining room, wiping her hands with a dish towel heard their voices. She took in Terry's appearance with a glance, her lips tightly compressed.

"No talk," she said. "Wear him out."

"Now, Mickey."

"Now nothing, Gerald! Do it, or I will."

"Mickey, I think I should discuss this with Terrell first, I think he should be aware of why—"

"Do it!" Mickey commanded sharply.

"Terrell, you told your mother you would go to school today. You told us both that."

"Yessir."

"You promised us, really, in so many words it was a promise, wasn't it?"

"Yessir."

"Look at you!" Mama's voice lifted. "You're filthy! Your new—those clothes—Gerald!"

"Son, breaking a promise is a very bad thing to do. It is more than a promise. It makes it a lie. You said you were going and you didn't, so that makes it a lie. Do you understand that?"

"Yessir. I'm sorry, Daddy."

"Gerald!"

"Mickey, go back to the kitchen, I'll handle this."

Mama lunged at Terry, seized his arm and shoved

him toward the bedroom. "This isn't fair, Gerald. It is not fair. I shouldn't have to do this myself."

"Mama!" Terry bumped the wall as she pushed him toward the impending punishment.

"Mickey, wait a minute, now. I'll take care of this if you will simply be patient and allow me to approach it in my way."

Mama slammed the door. The door started to open and Mama threw her weight against it, knocking it closed. Outside, slightly stunned, Daddy said, "All right, Mickey. All right. I told you I'd—"

Mama tore off Terry's pants and he stood, unresisting, eyes wide, trembling. She held him in one hand, getting a belt from the top of the dresser with her other hand. Terry threw up one frail palm, crying, "Mama! Please, Mama! I'm sorry!"

The strap fell hard, wrapping a searing thong around his nude thighs, raising blistering welts. Whap! "Mama! Please, I'm sorry." Whap! Whap! Whap!

It went on—and on—and his screams choked to shattering sobs, his legs fiery red and aflame with pain. Mama stood over him, her stomach heaving, glaring down, face flushed.

"You will go to school tomorrow, Terrell," Mama said, her voice quivering. "You will go to school or I will wear you out every evening you don't. Do you understand that? I will wear you out every day you don't go."

"Yes ma'am."

"Get up. Go take a bath and go to bed."

"Yes ma'am."

She guided him across the hall, belt still in hand, into the bathroom. "Use soap, too," she ordered. "Wash that filth with a washcloth, get yourself clean and come let me see you before you go to bed."

Daddy stood at the end of the hall, in the living room, his face hidden by shadows, his body a silhouette unmoving.

"Mickey, I told you I would take care of——"

"Shut up, Gerald! I don't want to hear it."

"Mickey, I was going to do that, but in my own——"

"Just shut up! I don't want to hear it."

Water rushing in the tub drowned their voices, now hushed, but still speaking in the kitchen. Terry closed the spigot with shaking hands and eased himself into the water, flesh searing. "Oh, oh, oh, oh——"

"I mean use soap, Terrell!"

"Yes ma'am."

"Oh, oh, oh——"

Mama suddenly appeared in the bathroom door, "Stop that! Bathe and stop that."

"Yes ma'am."

Mama threw a washcloth in the tub. Terry squatted, ankles, wrists, hands and buttocks below water, all else dry.

"Get at it, Terrell!"

"Yes ma'am, Mama."

"Now!"

"Yes ma'am, Mama."

He forced himself to sit, wincing. Mama glared at him. He wet the cloth, rubbed soap against it and began smearing it across his dry chest. Mama's expression altered slightly.

"It would be easier if you got wet all over," sharply.

"Yes ma'am, Mama."

"Well. Do it."

"Yes ma'am."

He ladled water up his chest, over his arms and shoulders. He began anew, watching her with wide eyes, body jerking as he muffled involuntary sobs behind closed lips.

"I don't want to ever do that again," Mama said.

"Yes ma'am."

"I don't want to ever have to hit you——" Her lips pulled at the corners. "I don't like having to do that to you."

"Yes ma'am, Mama."

"I want you to go to school. From now on. Every day."

"Yes ma'am, Mama."

She knelt beside the tub, looking at him, water brimming in her eyes.

"I love you."

"I love you, Mama."

She tried to smile and it slipped, lips turning. She busied herself scooping water onto his back, taking the washcloth from his hands. He saw her examine his legs. She began to cry, bathing him gently, helping him towel-dry, then holding him tightly, each clutching the other, sobbing quietly.

She dressed Terry in long pants. Breakfast was a tasteless, uncomfortable time.

"I'm taking Terrell to school," Mickey said.

"Why?"

"He lost his books. I'll have to get more. He will probably have to see Mr. Hammond. In case they're considering spanking him, I want to make it clear he's been spanked."

"Good idea," Gerald said.

Terry rode past the packing houses, the montage of machinery, conveyor belts and human forms weaving, working, the sounds pulsating in his ears. From the Last Dollar Café came the recorded voice of Hank Snow, "Moving On."

The high school was where they parked, amid faculty and student automobiles. Mama led him up the long concrete walk, through the front door and to Mr. Hammond's office.

"I'm Mrs. Calder, to see Mr. Hammond."

"One moment, Mrs. Calder. Please sit down."

"Listen," a high school girl implored to another, "if the Rams are going to be like all the other crappy years past, forget it, I don't want to be a cheerleader. But if we're going to do some new yells, okay."

"I said I agree," the reply, walking out. Sounds of morning rush seeped through from the hallway even after the door was shut.

"Mrs. Calder! Good morning. Come in, come in."

Mama's stomach pooched, her skirt higher in front than back. She went through a swinging counter gate that Mr. Hammond held open. Terry followed.

Mr. Hammond's office had football players' pictures on the walls. And a paddle with holes bored in it. Terry had been told the holes created blisters.

"This is our recalcitrant child?"

"Yes. I think he and I have an understanding. Terrell will be in class hereafter."

"That right, Terrell?"

"Yessir."

"Good! A man needs his education this day and time."

"I thought it best to come with Terrell this morning," Mama said. "He also managed to misplace his books."

"No problem, I'm sure, Mrs. Calder. Mrs. Wright—that's his teacher, Mrs. Wright, isn't it? She'll get a new issue for Terrell."

Mama stood as Mr. Hammond stood. Terrell had never been seated. "I'm sure Terrell will be a good student," Mr. Hammond said, smiling, putting a hand on the boy's shoulder and shaking him slightly.

"Thank you, Mr. Hammond."

Two high school boys slouched in the waiting room, expressions sullen. Mr. Hammond's voice changed sharply, "Go in there," he commanded. Then to his secretary, "Call Mr. Endley as a witness."

"Yessir."

To Mama: "If it isn't one thing it's another, Mrs. Calder."

"I'm sure, Mr. Hammond. Thank you."

The office door closed and Terry heard Mr. Hammond's voice as he spoke to the two young men. "I warned you, didn't I? All right, boys, today is your day. I'm going to beat your . . ."

They walked the hall, as alien as zoo animals in the pushing, laughing, echoing ensemble of students opening and closing lockers. Mama walked very straight, her pocketbook held almost in front, as though to hide her protruding stomach. Her steps were so fast Terry had to almost trot to keep up.

They left the high school, following the covered walk to the lower grade levels. Mrs. Wright stood at the door, watching them approach. She was not smiling.

Terry's heart was slamming so hard his ears rang. His muscles were cramping, taut from the whipping, an overwhelming urge to run controlled only by willpower and Mama's presence.

"So this is what he looks like," Mrs. Wright said.

Mama laughed. "Door-to-door delivery, Nancy."

"Did you bring a lock and key?"

"That," Mama said, suddenly serious, "had better not be needed. Right, Terrell?"

4

The blackboard reflected sunlight. Outside, at recess, the fourth- through sixth-graders ran, yelled, the swings squeaking as students pumped ever higher. A ball thumped against the wall near Terry's desk. He glanced out, saw a tousled head just beneath the sill, the bamboo stand beyond the yard, the roof of the packing houses. Faintly in the distance, a train groaned on the rails.

"Slanted lines go up and down, up and down . . ."

A breeze fragrant with canal scents and the odor of fetid vegetation tantalized Terry, drawing his eyes to the outside.

"Terrell!"

"Ma'am?"

"Pay attention."

A wolf spider appeared on the window, hairy legs holding the iridescent body aloft, multiple eyes glistening.

"Do not use your wrist, students. Move your entire arm. See how this part of your arm should be on the desk? Move your whole arm and make big, round *O*s."

Moaning from afar, the low wail of a whistle. A train coming from the north. If Terry could see the cars—a trainman had taught him to decipher the coded chalk marks on the sides which told where the freight was going.

"Terrell! *Terrell!* Will you sit down, please? Sit down."

"I can't see the blackboard."

"There's nothing on the blackboard."

Several students giggled, turned to stare at him.

Recess was carefully structured, the teachers standing in the cooling shade of the covered walk, watching boys run and throw themselves about, clothes clammy with perspiration. The girls dominated the swings, skirts flying, voices screeching. Terry eased toward the bamboo stand. He had his two cigarettes from yesterday. A casual glance at the adults, quick dart, and he was across the canal into the shade.

"Hey, Terry." Bucky Dallas lounged in a well-hollowed spot, leaning against the bamboo. He was smoking.

"Got a light?"

Bucky offered his butt, holding it as Terry lit a crumpled Lucky Strike.

"How's school?"

Terry stared at the teeming school yard pensively.

"Rough, huh?"

"I hate it."

Bucky examined his pinched Pall Mall, made one last effort to secure another puff and dropped the remnant, shaking his burnt fingers.

"I hate it," Terry repeated.

"Frig it. Let's go get some ice."

"I can't. Got to go."

"Dump it," Bucky urged, calmly. "Let's go."

"No."

"You scared?"

Terry studied his companion, unbuckled his trousers and pulled down his pants, exposing bruised welts above the knees.

"Jeeze."

Terry rebuckled his trousers as a hand bell announced recess was over. He gave his cigarette to Bucky and without another word retraced his steps to the yard. He pulled a handful of pine needles to chew, to kill the

44

odor of tobacco on his breath. Munching the bitter foliage, he joined the others and, after a file was formed, marched dutifully back to class.

Burrell Mason wore a broad-brim Panama hat which he dropped on a corner of the table. The large man looked oddly balanced on the twisted wire legs of the soda-fountain chair, his body engulfing the seat portion. Perspiration soaked his collar, the white suit he wore. He patted his forehead and cheeks with a handkerchief.

"Gerald, do you realize the consequences of this new camp?" Burrell asked.

"I know it will be good for the area, good for the cane growers."

"That's General Dextrose and nobody else," Burrell huffed.

"Anything good for General Dextrose is certain to be good for the entire area," Gerald argued mildly.

"Bullshit. I mean it. Opening up a black labor camp is going to bring darkies in here by the thousands. It's going to freeze wages where they are for the whites who compete against them. There's going to be resentment, Gerald. Gut resentment."

"Listen, Burrell, I don't make policy for Washington. They have purchased the land, construction is in progress and the camp will be, that's all there is to it."

"I'm against it, not because they're black. I'd be against it if they were whites. The only way to raise wages is to squeeze management where it hurts—manpower supply."

With a sudden shift in subject, Burrell Mason grunted, "You see the *Miami Herald* yet?"

"No. What?"

"A seven-thousand-ton U.S.-owned tanker under Panamanian registry was torpedoed and sunk in the south Atlantic."

"Dear God."

"Roosevelt is sitting on his duff in D.C. saying one

45

thing with his mouth, doing another behind our backs. He's putting us into this war, Gerald. You know why Washington is building that new camp, don't you?"

"For more laborers."

"No. Well, yes. But it goes deeper than that. The whites—and blacks—are going to be overseas before you know it, fighting Hitler and Tojo. This new camp is for Bahama laborers, Gerald. Specifically that. To get the cane crops in come hell or high water."

"Burrell, assume that's true. If the Americans are at war, we'll need those Bahamians. Be reasonable."

"I'm going to fight it, Gerald. With my little newspaper, right here in Belle Glade."

"You're looking for a bee to put under somebody's saddle. You always are."

The truth of that was reflected in the editor's eyes, a flicker of amusement. "That," he labored to rise, "is what it's all about, Gerald. Bees make the mule buck. Bucking mules make headlines. The Democrats are the mules. Nothing personal. Have they asked you to manage that black labor camp?"

"What makes you think they'd ask me?"

Burrell gazed at him a moment. "Who else would be fool enough to take such a thankless, godawful job, Gerald? Who else in this entire nation would be so hell bent on curing the ails of mankind, rectifying the racial inequalities and giving sustenance to the indigent?"

Gerald watched the thickset publisher move with astonishing agility through the drugstore toward the door.

"Who indeed?" Gerald thought.

Mickey rebuttoned her blouse, waiting for Dr. Norman to speak. When he did not, she asked, "How am I?"

"Retaining too much fluid. Stay off your feet."

Mickey laughed.

"That's what I thought you'd say," Dr. Norman stated.

"Other than the fluid?"

"Everything seems to be normal. Good heartbeat—yours and the baby's. I do want you to hold down on your salt intake and standing. Walk if you must, but don't stand in one place, ironing, for example."

He ushered her to the door of the clinic, through a waiting room full of migrant workers, pregnant women with gaunt, expressionless eyes, children with muck sores daubed with gentian violet.

"Mickey, I'm worried about Gerald."

"Oh?" A tingle of alarm twisted her innards.

"He's working too hard, Mickey. He's distracted, overwrought. He needs a rest."

"And I should stay off my feet."

Dr. Norman lifted his eyebrows, nodded acquiescence. "Do what you can on both counts, yours and his."

"I will. Thank you, Doctor."

Mickey strolled from the clinic toward the house. It was unseasonably hot for late September, and the humidity permeated everything. She crossed the road into her backyard. The sounds of tractor-drawn mowers droned, fighting the fast-recovering Bermuda grass which was Gerald's pride and joy.

"Mrs. Calder!"

Through shimmering waves of reflected heat, Mickey saw Marilyn at the administration building calling between cupped hands.

"Mrs. Calder!"

Now how could she expect to communicate at this distance? Irritated, Mickey waved.

"Mr. Calder . . . there?"

Mickey shook her head in exaggerated motions.

"Where?"

Mickey pretended not to notice the second question,

going into the house. Roaches skittered across the back porch. God, she hated those. She dared not try anything tricky to step on them. She couldn't see below her waistline. The phone was ringing.

It was Marilyn. "Mrs. Calder, do you know where I might find Mr. Calder?"

"No, Marilyn, I don't. Something wrong?"

"Yes. No. I mean, Mrs. Roosevelt is coming."

Mickey's heart skipped a beat. "Today?"

"No ma'am. Next week."

"Keep it under your hat, Marilyn."

"Oh, I *will*."

Mickey hung up. "Sure you will," she said aloud. She mentally scanned possible places where Gerald might be. Lions Club met tomorrow. On camp dealing with any one of two dozen problems. Out inspecting new construction at the black camp. Mickey felt slightly faint. She sat on the couch and let her head fall back, both hands on her belly .

Her eyes touched on a petrified wad of toilet paper which Terrell had wet and thrown up to see it stick. There had been hundreds; Mickey had somehow missed that one. "Please be a girl," she whispered.

Perspiration trickled down Terry's sides, absorbed at the waist by his trousers and underwear. He was fighting a desire to close his eyes and sleep. Last night's spanking had left him aching and stiff, resentment festering with each passing minute.

"One plus one," Mrs. Wright chanted, then put a hand to her ear.

"Equals two," the class response.

"Two plus one—"

"Equals three."

Terry's mind numbed, staring without seeing. He wondered if Mr. McCree had been looking for him out at LuBelle's. The prospect of learning to catch fish with his bare hands was so exhilarating he smiled.

"What's funny, Terrell?"

"Ma'am?"

"What's so funny?"

"Nothing."

"I don't hear you answering, Terrell." Mrs. Wright looked hot, cheeks red, hair coming unknotted. "All right, class, let's have Terrell answer this by himself."

All eyes on him now.

"What is six plus one, Terrell?"

"Seven."

"Eleven plus one."

"Twelve." Stupid bitch.

"Seventeen plus one."

"Eighteen."

Her expression hardened. "Eleven plus three."

Imperceptibly, his fingers came down on wood, a pause. "Fourteen."

"Fourteen plus seven."

Long pause. "Twenty-one."

"Twenty-one plus thirteen."

He ran out of fingers, confused his toes. No reply.

A hand wagged insistently in the air, the student lifting as high as he could without actually leaving his seat. Curly hair, white shoes, wide freckles, Eddy Kent.

"What's the answer, Eddy?" Mrs. Wright asked.

"Thirty-three!"

A softer, forgiving tone, "Thirty-four," Mrs. Wright said. Then to Terrell, "Pay attention!"

He went home by way of the packing houses.

"Look out there, kid!"

He sidestepped a hose being dragged along the floor, a booted man washing down the platform. He approached a woman on the line, sorting tomatoes.

"May I have a tomato?"

She gave him one, eyes instantly returning to the concentration required for grading. Terry walked on to the hot-dog stand. The salt shakers were gone.

"May I have some salt, please?"

"No. Beat it. You kids ain't using up free salt on snitched tomatoes. Beat it."

Terry stood by waiting for a customer. When one arrived, he asked, "Will you get some salt for me?"

"Sure, hold on. Jake, gimme two dogs and a Pepsi."

These on the counter, the customer asked, casually, "Got any salt?"

He stalled, unwrapping his hot dogs until the owner turned away, then handed down the shaker to Terry. Terry shook furiously until one palm was filled. He grinned up at the man, who winked at him. Terry proceeded toward home, dunking the vegetable into his cupped hand, savoring the juice with each bite.

Mama was sitting on the couch when Terry arrived. She scrutinized him as he stood just inside the door.

"You went to school today?"

"Yes ma'am."

"How was it?"

"Okay."

"Not so bad after all, was it?"

He shrugged his shoulders.

"Were the children nice to you?"

"Okay."

"Please don't say okay to Mama." She sat forward, eyes squinting. "What's that all over your shirt?"

He looked down, chin on chest. "Tomato juice."

"Go take that shirt off and put it in the sink with cold water to soak."

"Mama, can I go play?"

"Not until you change clothes."

"Then can I?"

"Yes." *Please do.*

He did as told, ran out shouting good-bye and was gone before Mickey's call could stop him. "Terrell! Where are you going—Terrell!"

He raced across the yard, past the clinic, through the area of one-family dwellings where he seldom played. These were the most transient of the camp residents and few friendships ever came from there, for lack of time to nourish them. He ran the quarter-mile distance to the back side of the camp, where most of the boys hung out, around a playground erected for migrant kindergarten children.

"Hi," he came to a breathless halt and flung himself on a bench.

"Got a cigarette?" somebody inquired.

"Yeah, but I'm saving it."

"Come one, Red, we need a smoke."

"No. I need it for trading tomorrow. Unless you promise to pay me back."

"Pay back when?"

"Tomorrow."

"Piss on it."

Vera and Darlene, two daughters of the camp foreman, sauntered past.

"I'd take some of that," Lonny said. He was the oldest of them, nearly eleven.

"Sure you would," one of the others sneered. "Vera's thirteen and Darlene is twelve. Besides, their old man is camp foreman and he'd pinch off your weewee if he heard about it."

Deliberately making the passing girls as uncomfortable as possible, they stared. Lonny issued a low whistle. Everybody laughed.

"What say, Terry, how about that cigarette?"

Terry withdrew the now-stained cigarette and smoothed it between thumb and finger.

"Got a match?" Terry asked.

"Happens I do," Lonny grinned. He struck a long-stemmed stove match against the seat of his pants, an act Terry had struggled to duplicate in private with no success. Terry took two quick puffs to secure the igniting, then a mouthful which he held behind closed lips, offering the cigarette to Lonny.

Lonny puffed, inhaled, puffed anew, blew smoke

51

through his nose, another puff inhaled atop the first. It was beautiful!

"You're going to hotbox it!"

"Pass it around, Lonny."

He did so, slowly exhaling, eyes focused down at his nose, watching smoke spew. Finally, with rounded lips, he blew a perfect ring, to the utter awe of his companions.

Terry let smoke trickle between his lips.

"Hey, listen," Lonny said, "let's go over to the sewage plant and shoot rubbers."

He was speaking of the prophylactics which appeared in the treatment pools, mysteriously bloated like jellyfish, floating atop the scum.

"Got any BBs?"

"No, but I got the gun. You got any?"

"No."

"Nobody?"

Terry felt a bit giddy. He waved the cigarette past.

"Gimme another drag," Lonny said, taking the cigarette from the hand of an obviously inexperienced puffer. He repeated his performance of a moment ago.

"Know what I've been thinking about?" Terry said to nobody in particular.

"What?"

"Running away."

They looked at him with varying degrees of skepticism, but with mounting respect.

Their interest was not in why but how. Terry wove a fantasy of plans, as though he'd been giving the matter long consideration.

"I'd pick a fruit car going to Kissimmee," he said. "There's lots of fruits and vegetables this time of year, so I could get all I wanted to eat from packing houses and orange groves. Or maybe beg from a house or two, if I had to. I'd sleep nights in the hobo jungles."

"How would you know where they'd be?"

"Just like the one out at the train trestle, everybody

knows where that is. I'd find them. There'd be coffee and trading for cigarettes, just like the one here. I'd get along."

"Yeah, but where would you go?"

"Out west, maybe. North. I don't know. Wherever I had to go. Maybe somebody along the way would want to adopt me for a little while. I know where I wouldn't go."

"Where?"

"School."

"Cops'd getcha."

"No they wouldn't. So what if they did? Eldridge Hopkins said the state school at Marianna had tennis courts and swimming pools. He said it was real nice."

"He ran away from it twice," Lonny reminded.

"I would too, if I didn't like it."

"You'd have to steal things," somebody noted.

"That's okay. I'd look in unlocked cars, like Eldridge said he did. People always leave things in the pockets of their cars. Money, Eldridge said. Once he found a gun. Lots of cigarettes."

"What if somebody tried to stomp on you?" a voice shrouded by dark.

"I'd carry a sock with sand in the toe, tied in a knot. It makes a blackjack. It doesn't leave any cuts or scars, either." That had come from a Dick Tracy comic book. He had lots of good ideas for committing crimes he garnered from that source.

"You'd have to come home someday."

"I would. Someday. Maybe when I'm fifteen or twenty."

"What about your folks?"

"What about them?"

"They'd get unhappy, wouldn't they?"

"They got another baby coming."

"Yeah."

"Besides," Terry concluded, "I wouldn't come back until I was too big to whip."

He walked toward home, winding between shelters, the family sounds of crowded tenants in his ears, an angry male and a rejoining woman. People sat on concrete steps outside open doors, trying to escape the ovens of their dwellings. The odor of cooking heavily mixed in the air: cabbage, beans, fatback. He passed the auditorium where movies were shown every Thursday night; it was closed now.

He wished he could, really. Run away.

5

Saturday came at last.

"You may go with me to the store, Terrell." Mama was huge, stomach taut, bulging.

"I want to go play, Mama."

She almost looked relieved. "Be home before too late."

"I will."

He trotted all the way to LuBelle's.

"Seen Mr. McCree?"

"No."

"Is he coming by?"

"Didn't say so." Eunice tested a flatiron for heat with a moistened fingertip. The sizzle satisfied her and she pushed the iron hard against fabric stretched over a board.

He took a rutted, narrow back road that dwindled away to nothing. The swamp out here where McCree lived was a constantly moving thing. From tens of thousands of sources came sounds without apparent cause. Sounds which alone might go undetected came together to form the voice of the glades. The hum of insect wings, the crunch of gnawing teeth; serrated blades of saw grass rasping as a breeze swept a sea of vegetation. Serpents slithered, dragonflies hovered before alighting on the tips of cattails, ratlike nutria scurried through impenetrable underbrush. Rabbits rustled through tunnels from warren to burrow, frogs leaped in long arcs from lily pads to water retreats, and over it all, the distant cry of birds in flight.

Terry halted, eyes alerted to a somnolent coil of water moccasin sunning at the edge of a pond. He scanned the scene for others and, seeing none, circled the motionless snake. He stood a moment watching the reptile. The forked tongue did not flick. McCree had taught him that this probably meant the snake was asleep, despite unblinking eyes behind immovable scales.

Water oozed underfoot, Terry stepping where he was most sure of solid support. On higher ground again, he walked past tremendous beds of ants that were almost as high as his knees. To stir one of those was to ask for agony. He saw ant workers laboring to bring a bird's feather through grass, twisting, turning, dozens pulling this way and that, yet working in harmony.

He reached a small lake, a clearing of growth, and stood gazing toward a shack on the far side. He saw McCree's battered truck.

"Ho, McCree!" As loud as he could. His voice bounced here, there, rippling away in echoes.

"Ho, McCree!" The swamp was abruptly silent, creatures transfixed by the alien call. Gnats buzzed Terry's face. He thrust out his lower lip and blew up at his nose to fend them off.

"Ho! Ho! Ho! McCreeeeee!"

The old man appeared in the darkened doorway of the shack, barely visible through wiggly waves of heat and moisture evaporating from the lake.

"Hey! Boy!"

Terry began circling the body of water. He weaved his way through mangrove trees poised like vegetable spiders on exposed roots, forming a hammock over which he climbed. He paused now and again to shake interlocking webs of growth, the sounds of watery escape reassuring him of the wisdom of this maneuver as serpents dived for cover. Birds beat skyward, squawking in protest as he encroached on nesting areas of cattle egrets, blue herons and roseate spoonbills.

Below the matted root system of the mangroves lay pitch-black water, swirled now and then by startled minnows, most prolific of the fishes and food aplenty for the denizens of this jungle. Terry pushed out into the open, ducking under the symmetrical web of a black and yellow "dancing" spider. The owner of the web promptly vaulted back and forth on his homemade trampoline, shaking it vigorously.

McCree was still in the doorway, waiting, when Terry arrived, grinning.

"Skeeter-bit and thorn-tore," McCree said. "Better suck on them scratches, boy, else they'll get sore."

Terry did this, the saline of his own blood pleasant to the taste. He followed McCree inside where it was dark, noticeably cooler and exciting.

There were no electric lights. No toilet, except the all-outdoors when the need called. The furniture was never furniture in fact; the table was two orange crates topped by a flat piece of plank McCree had found somewhere. The seats were more crates bottom-end up and covered with "croker" sacks for padding. McCree's source of evening illumination was one of several kerosene-burning lanterns, but these were seldom lit. His house was filled with enviable items of never-ending curiosity. Bleached skulls of beheaded snakes were strung on strings to dry; windowsills were piled with the rattles from *Crotalus adamanteus*. Shells of turtles in various states of disassembly cluttered shelves, boxes and floor. Crocus sacks stuffed with pine cones seeped coniferous aromas that gave the dwelling a continuous feel of Christmas. A huge round paper wasp's nest hung from the rafters. Bushel baskets of various seeds were stacked according to a system only the old man understood.

From nails driven into exposed wall studs, vacated

skins from molting snakes hung as diaphanous reminders of past inhabitants.

From these things the old man earned a living. Seeds, cones, rootstocks and dried cattails he shipped to wholesale nurseries and florist supply houses. Skeletons, 'gator skulls and snake rattles went to biological laboratories. Poisonous serpents he sold to Ross Allen's Reptile Institute in Silver Springs and others who milked venom, canned meat or used the snakes as tourist attractions. Bobcats, raccoons and an occasional bear cub were purchased by animal dealers from Miami.

McCree held up a spiral-shaped object the size of his thumb. "If you see any of these, I have an order for a thousand."

"What is it?"

"Cocoon. The Cecropia moth."

"I see them now and then."

"Save them for me, will you."

"A thousand?" The number was incomprehensible to Terry.

"If I can find them."

McCree shuffled through some papers he kept in a pasteboard carton. "Got an order for three hundred bushels of Australian pine cones. Easy to fill. Good pay, too."

Terry had helped with that chore once before. The cones had to be harvested from the tree green and unopened. It was the seeds they were buying; the cone was merely a carrier.

"Three hundred bushels?" This was nearer his scope of understanding.

"Yep. Three hundred. You know what ten is."

Terry held up both hands. McCree nodded. "Ten times ten is a hundred. Thought I taught you that."

"I forgot it."

"Show me."

Ten flicks of both hands. One hundred.

"A thousand?"

Uncertainty. Then remembering, "A hundred times ten."

"I need that many cocoons."

"A lot of cocoons!"

"It is that. Want coffee?"

There was no coffee like McCree's. At first, Terry thought the flavor came from the boiled swamp water he used to produce the beverage. Or from the process of dumping grounds in a pot of that water and boiling the mixture until it "smelled right." But he had since learned the delicious difference was from a blue-flowered weed which McCree uprooted and stored.

Cichorium intybus, McCree called it. "The leaves make a fine salad. Roots can be boiled and eaten with butter. Or, dried, ground and used as coffee. Came to this country about a hundred years ago, brought from Europe. First as a garden flower, it spread out so now folks think of it as a weed. Truth is, it is what it is to you. To me, and a heap of other folks, it's good old chicory."

The mixture was well diluted with liberal squirts of condensed milk, sweetened with honey stolen from a hive in a hollow stump.

"Sweet enough?" McCree questioned.

"Just right. Hot."

"Scald the hair off your tongue," McCree agreed, sipping.

"Reckon you could take me fishing today?" Terry asked.

"Might as well, as not," McCree said. "When it gets cooler."

"Will you show me how to fish with no bait?"

"I can try."

A flutter of inner excitement. Terry nodded, wincing as he sucked cooler surface liquid from his heavy mug.

"Know what I'm thinking, Little Hawk?"

"What?"

"I'm thinking, the best place for such fishing lies south of here about half a day away. Might be, if we waited until tomorrow early, we'd do better going down there."

Seeing his opportunity slipping away, Terry couldn't mask his disappointment.

"On the other hand," McCree said, "we might have some luck this afternoon before nightfall, if you want to try."

"I'd like to try."

"You had something to eat?"

"No sir."

"Hungry?"

"A little," Terry said.

McCree kept gallon jars on a shelf. In these, he put his foodstores, gathered from what he called the biggest garden in the world: the swamp. Other than salt, an occasional sack of flour and sugar he traded for from a mill, he seldom bought anything.

"Cheaper," he explained, adding, "and tastes better to boot."

When he went on treks in search of seed, he seldom took food with him, relying instead on his ability to harvest something near at hand. Terry had seen feasts formed from the tips of palms—"swamp cabbage," McCree said. He had observed the old man producing pancakes from cattail roots, sweetened with blackberries and covered with cane syrup. Venison, smothered in mushrooms and bamboo shoots, was often followed by sapodilla gum for dessert and to cleanse the teeth. From wild lime trees came flavoring for pan-fried fresh-caught catfish or bass.

"City frills," McCree often said, "can best be done without."

In an abandoned washing machine with no motor, McCree kept live rattlesnakes. When his fortunes ran low, the truck needed repairs or another used tire, the venomous snakes were his most readily turned cash item.

"Got any big rattlers on hand?" Terry queried.

"Couple. Bunch of small ones."

"Mind if I see them?"

"Help yourself. Mind not to get bit on the nose looking."

If McCree watched, he did it so casually Terry was unaware of it. The boy lifted the lid of the washing machine, as McCree had taught him, ever wary for a serpent creeping up the side in search of freedom. On the bottom, beneath a bed of straw, the snakes lay inert.

"Don't make them rattle," McCree warned. "A rattling snake is a dying snake. A rattler shakes his tail because he's afraid, like a human shivering with fear. The more he shakes, the more nervous he is. Pretty soon he rolls over, dead. Cut him open and his three-chambered heart is busted. Three-chambered hearts aren't as good as our four-chambered ones. That's how come a reptile gets tired so quickly, I reckon."

Gingerly, with a stick, Terry pushed away straw and looked down at the head of a snake as wide as his hand. McCree said, "He can't see you."

"Why? Is he shedding?"

"No. Because the scales over a rattler's eyes stick out. Makes him look like this," McCree pulled his thick eyebrows low in a menacing scowl. "So naturally, he can't see straight up without turning his head.

"He can feel the heat from my hand though," McCree was almost whispering. "In the darkest burrow, the old rattler, and the water moccasin and copperhead, too, can sense heat from a mouse's body. He strikes at that heat and whap! Got himself a meal."

Demonstrating, McCree reached into the tub, after making certain the other snakes were covered and unaware of his presence. The old man's gnarled, discolored hand opened slowly, with thumb and forefinger extended. He eased down on the back of the snake's neck, close behind the skull.

"Have to be careful with loose skin," he intoned, "else old *Crotalus adamanteus* might twist around and hang a fang in your hand. I learned not to do that after it happened the first time."

The thumb and finger clamped the snake, other fingers working beneath the elongated body. Then, without protest from the snake, McCree lifted the reptile up and out of the barrel. It was longer than Terry was tall.

"Beauty, ain't he?" McCree said.

"Sure is."

"Magnificent snake. Male, too." McCree had shown Terry how a male's tail suddenly tapered in at a certain point, whereas the female's tail tapered off evenly to the segmented scales of the rattles.

"That snake'll bring me fifty, maybe sixty cents," McCree said, lowering the snake back into the enclosure again. A lolling black tongue licked the air. "Tasting what we smell," McCree called it. "Pulls in dust particles and puts them against the roof of his mouth, tasting the way things smell."

The sun was a fuzzy ball of flame still a half-hour above the horizon when they arrived at a selected spot in the backwaters of a canal. Here McCree tamped down grass to give them a place to sit, lie or squat as the need be. With a finger to his lips compelling silence, McCree knelt and stared down into black water.

Terry tried to see what the old man saw. Nothing. Except the reflection of McCree's unshaven face. Then, on the old man's parched lips, a fleck of foam appeared. Slowly, it gathered volume, bubbly spit, drawing downward as gravity pulled it from McCree's mouth. Terry knew to sit absolutely still and this he did, mesmerized by the silvery thread drawing longer and longer from McCree's lips, closer and closer to the water. It dropped. Tiny ripples moved in ever-expanding circles away from the disturbed surface.

Again, more spit, the old man staring straight into the water, making a gurgling sound as he worked up saliva which drew long, suspended.

One hand lifted, moved unhurried, outward. The spit dropped. McCree reached down and picked up a tremendous catfish. The surprised fish at first did not even thrash. McCree sat back, drool on his chin, looked at Terry's open astonishment and laughed.

"Nothing to it, Little Hawk. That's big enough for both our suppers, agreed?"

"Yessir!"

"You see how I did it?"

"Yessir, Mr. McCree."

"Think you could do it?"

A shiver of ecstasy. "I don't know."

"Want to try?"

"Yessir."

"Good. Be real still. The spit's got to be full of bubbles. If at first the fish don't come, keep at it. Look straight down, and soon enough that old fish thinks you belong up there. When you go to reach for him, don't do it sudden; move slow. Put your hand in the water like a knife, slicing down, and grab him gently. Otherwise he'll slip away. When you have him, hang on and get him up over the bank. Think you can do it?"

"I'll try."

"Take my place."

Terry leaned out, staring down. He saw a murky figure pass below, too deep to reach. His own blue eyes stared back at him in the glasslike surface. He worked spit, pushing and pulling it between his teeth, creating the necessary bubbles. As he had seen it done, the spit drew out, not so long as McCree's, then dropped. He began again. Unbelievably, rising in the water, unafraid and unaware, another catfish came nearer and nearer the surface. More spit, dropped!

His hand eased out, quivering with excitement. He kept his fingers together as McCree had shown him, eased into the water; cold flesh, alive, fingers closed. He had him!

Terry threw himself backward, the fish flopping wildly, McCree's roaring laughter booming in his ears, the flick of water from the catfish tail flung into his face. Still he held that fish for all his life was worth!

"Don't choke him to death!" McCree cried. "Drop him behind you."

"I did it!" Terry shouted.

"Did it the first time, too."

"He let me reach in and grab him."

"Did right good."

"He came up there and let me put my hand right down on him!"

"Bigger than the one I caught," McCree said, cutting a green, pliable switch which he ran through the gills of both fish so they could make a handle by which to carry them.

"Did you see him slinging water and flopping?" Terry was so excited his words were a jumble, face flushed, scarcely able to contain himself.

"Whipped water like a snapped limb," McCree smiled. "But you held him tight enough."

"Boy he was—he was so *big!*"

"Going to make some good eating tonight, too."

"He was so big, wasn't he?"

"Bigger than the one I caught."

"I did it," Terry said, awed, "I really did it."

"Kind of surprised me, to tell the truth," McCree drawled, walking now back toward home and frying pans. "Never saw anybody catch on quite so quick as that."

"Really?" Chest bursting with pride.

"I once taught a Seminole kid to do that. Later grew up to be a chief, that boy. But you know, it took him nigh twenty times to catch on to it. You know what *twenty* is."

Two quick flicks of the hands.

"Well sir, I thought he'd never get the knack of it. He'd stick his head in too fast, or try to grab too quick; excited, I reckon. He'd try to snatch that fish out of the water, or his hands would shiver and the fish felt him coming before he reached it. Or his head moved. Or something! It took him nigh on to twenty times."

"A Indian? It took him twenty times? A Indian?"

"He became a chief."

"A chief?"

"Yessiree, a chief. Smart boy. But I never saw anybody catch on so fast as you did. First try!" McCree's hand rode easily on Terry's shoulder, both of them walking faster than necessary.

"That was something," Terry said.

"Sure was that. Something. Beat the Indian chief."

"Really was. Something."

"Bigger than the one I caught."

When McCree delivered Terry to the entrance of Camp Osceola, they were still talking about the catch, and the flavor. "Best catfish I believe I ever tasted," McCree had said, of his. "But that bigger one was better yet."

It was, too, or so it seemed. Sopped in the juice of a bitter lime picked green, simmered in a sauccepan of "secret" juices, eaten with a potatolike bulb dug from a place on high ground under a particular tree where such things grew—the meal was unforgettable.

"Think you'll be out tomorrow?" McCree asked.

"I don't know."

No further questions. McCree nodded in the dark. "Enjoyed it, Little Hawk."

"Me too. Mr. McCree?"

"Ho boy?"

"Thanks for teaching me."

"You sure learned in a hurry, Little Hawk."

"Thank you."

McCree pulled the door of the truck shut, slammed

65

it again, slammed it a third time before it caught. The motor grumbled, faulty muffler coughing, and the vehicle went over railroad tracks toward the packing houses and disappeared.

"Where have you been, Terrell?" Mama. Angry.

"I went out to Chosen."

Daddy looked over his newspaper. The Cities Service Band of America was on the radio, faint sounds of music in the living room.

"I am at my wit's end, Gerald. I am. Really. Supper comes and goes and this child—"

"Are you hungry, Terrell?" Daddy asked.

"No sir, I ate."

"Where?" Mama demanded.

"I caught a fish and—Daddy, I caught a catfish this big!"

"Hey, that's a big catfish."

"Yessir! And—"

"Go in there and get bathed," Mama said.

"Mama, I caught the fish with—"

"You smell like fish. What *is* that I smell?"

Fish? Lime juice? Chicory coffee? The cigarette he'd smoked? "I don't know."

"Whatever it is, it smells rotten! Get in there and bathe now. I made some banana pudding. Do you want some?"

"Yes ma'am!" He ran to the bedroom and got his pajamas, began running a tub of water. He heard Daddy laugh.

"You can't say he's a sissy, Mickey."

"Granted that."

"I like it, Mickey. Makes the boy self-sufficient. It's a good lesson for him. Drop the matter, why not."

He strained to hear a reply. Mama had gone to the kitchen.

Terry was in the tub when Daddy's head appeared in the door.

"How big?" Daddy asked, his expression and tone intentionally skeptical.

Terry carefully held out his hands, adjusting to the truest dimension he could recall.

"That was a whopper."

Terry nodded, eyes growing vacant, remote. "Sure was," he said, softly. "It was something."

6

Bucky Dallas was sitting on the back steps when Terry finished breakfast. "Tomatoes are coming in," Bucky noted. "I got a box of salt. Want to go to the packing house?"

"Sure!"

Mickey stood at the kitchen window, listening to the exchange.

"Mama, may I go to the packing house?"

"I suppose so."

She watched them walk across the yard, Bucky's arm around Terry's shoulder. They halted at a hibiscus shrub, pulling off blossoms and sucking nectar from the exposed base of the flowers.

"Gerald, do you think it's all right for Terrell to run around with that Dallas boy?"

"I don't see why not."

"He's at least five years older," Mickey said.

"So much the better. He looks after Terrell."

"You think he does?"

"Didn't Terrell say the Dallas boy once had a fight with the Poole kid? Over Terrell, as I recall. Bucky is like an older brother. I imagine that's a good thing, don't you?"

"I guess. I suppose I worry too much over nothing."

"Yes," Gerald said, gently, turning to his newspaper. "Lord, did you see the paper this morning? 'Rome, Berlin and Tokyo have formed an axis,'" Gerald read the headline. "'Aimed at creating new order for the world, the Japanese minister said, celebrating the first anniversary of the tripartite pact.' The bastards. In the same column, the Nazis claim to have captured 665,000 Russian troops in the battle of Kiev! Stuka planes strafed Serbian guerrillas while they razed the city of Uzice to put down a rebellion. Some 'new order' they're creating."

Mickey washed dishes, her hands in tepid water which intensified the heat of the morning and the flashes of internal warmth she was already experiencing. She saw Terrell and Bucky top the railroad tracks and pause, standing close together facing one another. A puff of smoke rose between them.

"Terrell is smoking," Mickey said.

" 'Nazi firing squads shot three Czech generals and twenty-one others who conspired to restore Czech independence—' "

"Where do you suppose that child finds cigarettes?" Mickey asked. "I've been buying a single pack at a time, hiding those."

"Damn Washington," Gerald seethed. "Averell Harriman has pledged U.S. support to the U.S.S.R. at the opening of the Anglo-U.S.-Soviet parleys in Moscow. Maybe Burrell is right, they are leading us into that mess."

Mickey dried her hands, pushing hair from her forehead with the back of one wrist. She mechanically marked off another day on the calendar. Gerald had turned on the radio, seeking the football games.

"Charles Lindbergh said the three most important groups pressing the U.S. toward war are the British, Jewish and the Roosevelt administration."

"Um-hmm," Mickey said.

"He was speaking at an America First rally in Des Moines."

"Gerald, have you been leaving your cigarettes lying around lately?"

70

"I don't think so," Gerald patted his top pocket. "They're here someplace."

Mickey sighed. She left him to his football game and went to lie down. She briefly debated a cooling shower, then wearily abandoned the idea as she propped her stomach against a pillow, lying on her side.

"Mickey, you want to listen to the ball game?"

"No."

"What?"

"No!"

She heard Gerald grumble, something about, "Not as much fun by yourself."

Bucky led the way, the two boys walking unhurriedly. Bucky retrieved his box of salt from where he'd hidden it under the platform of the Blue Goose Packing Company ramp.

"Hey!" Terry pointed. "There's Mr. McCree's truck."

The old man was selecting hampers from a refuse pile. To ship his goods, McCree scavenged damaged crates and boxes from this area, repairing them with brads, nails, bailing wire and slats from other smashed containers.

"Hey, Mr. McCree!"

"Ho, Little Hawk. Who's your friend?"

"Bucky Dallas."

McCree extended a hand to the cross-eyed stranger and soberly shook Bucky's hand. "Pleased to make your acquaintance," McCree said. "What're you two up to?"

"Going to eat tomatoes, Mr. McCree. Want to go with us?" Terry glanced at Bucky for permission. It was Bucky's box of salt.

"Where to?" McCree asked, examining a broken hamper, then tossing it onto the bed of his truck.

"In the loft," Bucky replied.

"Sounds fine to me," McCree said. "I got a jug of sassafras tea. Reckon we'll get thirsty?"

A moment of hesitation from the boys and McCree added, "With some wild mint in it."

"I like it," Terry said.

McCree reached behind the seat of his vehicle and brought out a gallon vinegar bottle, holding it by the glass ring-handle. He gestured for Bucky to lead the way and followed behind.

"Mr. McCree taught me how to catch catfish with my bare hands," Terry said.

"Caught one the first time, too," McCree noted.

"Bare hands?" Bucky snorted.

"Really! No bait or nothing."

"Come on!" Bucky laughed, sensing a joke.

"He did," Terry said, then to the old man, "didn't you?"

"Sure enough did. Big catfish you caught, too, bigger than mine."

Because McCree was an adult, Bucky pursued the matter no further, but he clearly didn't believe the tale.

They climbed two long flights of stairs to the third-floor storage area of the packing house. Here, stacked almost twenty feet high, were hundreds of crates of freshly picked tomatoes ready to be delivered down below, where women would sort and grade the harvest for packing.

Bucky clambered up a service ladder, stretched far to one side and secured a precarious hold on the mountain of boxes. Safely atop these, he waved Terry up behind him. McCree followed. Ensconced amid crates of tomatoes fresh from the fields, Bucky lifted several lids and they selected the juiciest, almost overripe vegetables and passed around the salt.

"Delicious," McCree said, tomato seeds in his chin whiskers. "I believe we can lower this heap a little, if we try."

"I mean to do it," Bucky agreed.

They ate until their stomachs bulged, aching. Falling silent only when footsteps sounded below, they thereby avoided the patrol of an occasional employee en route from one point to another. For the most part, their whispered exchanges were drowned in the normal rumblings of machinery on the first and second levels.

"You ever shoot the shoot?" Bucky asked Terry.

"Sure! We did it together, remember?"

"We did? Oh, yeah. We did."

They peeked over the top edge of the crates, watching for interlopers, then eased out to grab the ladder and climb down.

"Want to do it?" Bucky asked.

"What's this?" McCree inquired.

"Shoot the shoot," Bucky said, dubiously. "It's kind of scary."

"Too scary for me?" McCree asked.

"I don't know."

"Not for Mr. McCree," Terry stated. "He's not scared of anything. He picks up rattlesnakes with just his bare hands."

Bucky looked off into space, but his cocked eye was studying McCree. "That really true?" he questioned.

"Yep. Show you sometime, maybe."

"Want to shoot the shoot?" Bucky offered.

"Might as well as not," McCree said. "Show me how?"

They walked through the cavernous building to a far end. Here, packing crates and hampers were constructed and stored. To send the finished product down to packing lines three floors below, crates were placed end upon end into a spiraling chute that turned like a polished corkscrew from here to the main floor. At the bottom, the chute straightened and became a series of rollers over which the crates passed down a fifty-yard-long incline. Having reached the bottom of the dizzying corkscrew and passed the steep incline of rollers, the remainder of the exhilarating trip was a flat track where women usually packed fruits or vegetables into the boxes. Beyond this, the ultimate joy, the washing

73

machine. Triggered by the passing of each crate, the machine blew stinging jets followed by misty sprays, from all four directions eventually, and the box cleared the washer at the far end, ready to be labeled, capped and shipped.

Listening to this, McCree nodded seriously. Bucky completed his explanation and stood, jaw twisted, his expression unquestionable: he expected McCree to decline.

"Who goes first?" McCree asked.

Bucky shrugged his shoulders. "It don't matter. But whoever goes last has to be ready to run for it, because by the time the third one gets out of the washing machine, the guard is usually on his way, hopping mad."

"I don't run fast as I used to," McCree said. "Might be I ought to be first, then?"

"Second would be best," Bucky advised. "That way you can see how it's done and still have time to get away from the guard."

"Sounds about right," McCree said. "Who's first?"

"You run fastest," Terry told Bucky. "I'll go first."

"What about your sassafras tea?" Bucky asked McCree. "You're so big, it's going to be pretty crowded in that crate."

"I'll take the jug," Terry said.

"Remember, don't let your elbows or hands stick out over the sides," Bucky warned. "You might lose a finger."

"Okay." Terry got into a crate, knees pulled up, his elbows wedged inside the box, prepared for the initial spiraling, headlong fall. Bucky pushed Terry's box to the edge of the chute.

"Ready?"

"Ready!"

With McCree pulling up another box, Bucky shoved Terry forward, the box tilted and zoom—he was falling. Round and round, heat from friction causing the wood slats to leave a smoking trail behind him, gathering momentum, thrown by centrifugal force against the back of the box, the jug clutched between his knees, Terry roared out of the corkscrew and hit the slanted ramp. Gaining speed, Terry shot the length of the building over the heads of startled workers, a whine of rollers stretched out behind. Side rails narrowed, constructed to slow the projectile. The crate bumped two protruding wires, jolted, halted a second, then a conveyor drew Terry through the washing machine, soaking him thoroughly. Bumped this way and that by mechanical guides within and finally pushed out the far side, the journey ended. Breathless, head spinning, he jumped out, pulled his box further along to make way for McCree and waited. He heard the old man coming.

"Aiyeeeee!"

He knew by the sounds of the rollers McCree had reached the ramp—zingggg! Thump! Water sounds. In the distance, a cursing male voice and running feet. The guard was fat. There was time. Behind McCree the squeal of another crate coming down the chute—zoom!

McCree appeared between strips of hanging mats hung at either end of the washing machine to keep spray from blowing out. The old man was drenched, grinning, eyes wild.

Terry seized the box, yanking, pulling, getting it out of the way for Bucky, who had now entered the far end of the machine.

"Hurry, Mr. McCree!"

"That was something else," McCree said, still not moving.

"Hurry, Mr. McCree! Here comes the guard!"

McCree started to stand and had to grab for support. He stretched his legs, unknotting muscles. "Something else!" McCree said.

"Hurry! Hurry!"

The old man stepped off the conveyor, legs wobbly, holding Terry's shoulder for support. Terry urged greater speed, heading for a tunnel route they often used for escape. McCree barely made it as Bucky landed on the far side of the conveyor and decoyed the guard away, his harsh cursing voice and shaking fist adding zest to the adventure.

"That was really something," McCree said. He followed Terry more by feel than sight, crawling between crates toward a point of light at the end of the tunnel.

Terry turned, standing, and helped McCree to his feet. They stood looking at one another, grinning, eyes sparkling, laughing.

"This way," Terry instructed. He went down the exit steps, ducked beneath the platform and, with McCree at his side, traversed the entire width of the building with the spatter of water seeping from above, soil moist, the clatter of equipment and stomp of feet overhead. They emerged near McCree's truck, where Bucky waited.

"You did it right," Bucky said, with respect.

"Thank you," McCree replied. "You taught me how. The credit rightly belongs to you. I'm glad you told me to keep my hands inside. That box gets hot!"

The boys laughed. "Sometimes the nails wear the heads off rubbing the rails on the way down," Terry said. "Then the whole box falls apart before it gets to the washing machine."

"My fanny got a mite warm," McCree confessed. He took his jug of tea from Terry, uncapped it and offered it around.

"Ugh!" Bucky cried. "That tastes terrible."

"Better when it's cold," McCree admitted.

"Let's go to the icehouse and get a chunk, then," Bucky said. Terry explained that Bucky's dad ran the icehouse.

They rode in McCree's smoking truck, followed Bucky into the cold refrigerator and there chipped ice into pieces small enough to be pushed through the neck of the bottle.

Outside, they swirled the contents to hasten cooling and the jar was passed again.

"Not much better to me," Bucky protested.

"I like it," Terry said. He took a larger swallow.

"You boys want to go out to my place?" McCree asked.

Bucky shook his head. "I have to mind the plant while my pa and ma go to town this afternoon."

"Well, Little Hawk," McCree asked, "how about you?"

"Yeah!"

They left Bucky watching them depart, his disappointment somewhat salved by McCree's repeated promise to teach the boy how to pick up a rattlesnake with his bare hands, sometime.

They went to LuBelle's, actually, where they consumed green beans McCree had traded for, cooked with pigs' knuckles he'd also traded to get. While McCree and Eunice sat on the porch chewing Bull of the Woods, talking, Terry and LuBelle played a form of hopscotch they'd worked up together.

McCree delivered Terry to the camp entrance shortly after dark.

"Did you like shooting the shoot?" Terry asked.

"Don't know when I've liked something so much," McCree said. "Tomatoes were good, too."

"Mr. McCree—"

"Ho, Little Hawk."

"I sure do have fun with you."

McCree's throaty chuckle came in the dark. "You keep an old man young, Little Hawk. Come see me when you can."

Tonight, Mr. McCree sat in his pickup, motor idling, watching Terry walk across the bridge. Terry deliberately went away from the house, not forgetting his fib that he had no home, no parents.

He didn't really know why he'd told McCree that. Perhaps to avoid worry about the hours he kept, or probing questions about do your folks know where you are. The lie came from his lips before he was aware of its forming and McCree had looked at him a long time, without blinking, then nodded. The deception had been carefully reinforced ever since, a patch in the tale here, suggestion of deprivation there. This was not truly required—McCree had never brought up the subject a second time.

Terry recognized a car belonging to Burrell Mason, local newspaper publisher and editor. He halted on the porch, voices coming through the living room windows.

"What do you think the eleven allied governments hope to accomplish?" Mr. Mason's tone was intense. "This so-called Roosevelt-Churchill Atlantic Charter— what do you think that will accomplish, Gerald?"

"It will set up a food pool to rehabilitate Europe during the postwar years, Burrell, just like they said."

"Crock o' shit! You believe that? Mickey, you hear that crap? People like Gerald believing what they hear on the radio—they're dupes of propaganda, all of them!"

"Then, Burrell, what *is* it for?" Mickey asked, so Gerald wouldn't have to.

"It is an alliance getting ready to fight the Axis, Mickey. You can believe they aren't thinking about *after* a war that hasn't really got going good. There'd be a rebellion in this nation if Roosevelt announced it for what it really is: an alliance to *fight!* Food for the postwar years. Godamighty!"

Terry walked in and the mood altered noticeably.

"Have fun today?" Mama asked.

"Yes ma'am."

"Been over at the packing house all day," Mama told the men. "If you want to know doing what, take a look at his clothes."

Tomato seeds had dried like burrs to the fabric of Terry's shirt. Mama was unbuttoning it.

"Mind you don't lose a toe in a fan belt over there," Mr. Mason said. Terry secretly despised him for that.

"You are careful, aren't you?" Mama asked, her face showing instant alarm.

Terry exhibited his bare feet. Daddy laughed.

"He has all his toes, Mickey," Daddy noted.

"Supper will be in a while," Mama said. "Mr. Mason is having dinner with us tonight."

Terry took his cue from a slight jerk of Mama's head that sent him to take a bath.

"If we stay out of this war," Mr. Mason continued, his voice pitched lower than before, "it'll be despite Roosevelt, believe me."

"Let's change the subject to something more cheerful," Mama urged.

"One last point," Daddy said, before yielding. "Roosevelt declares we are not going to war, Burrell. He ran for office on that and I believe the man."

"Ye gods and golden minnows!" Burrell snapped. "You'd believe anything that comes from Washington, Gerald!"

"Let's talk about something else, please," Mama persisted. Her voice lifted, "How about that bath, son?"

"Yes ma'am." Terry closed the bathroom door and started the tub. He stood gazing into the swirling, greenish water. He wasn't quite sure what war was, but the tone of the word, the expressions it elicited, brought a quicker beat of the heart and a shortness of breath.

Gerald sat at the kitchen table, tapping his fingernails against the porcelain top. He had offered to help Mickey with the dinner dishes, but she'd refused. Outside, unseen insects thumped the window screens trying to get in to the light.

"You know if we have war, I'll have to go," Gerald said, softly.

"Please, Gerald, not tonight. After that blood-and-guts discussion over supper, I'm not sure my stomach can take more tension."

Gerald went behind her, reaching around to clasp his hands atop her belly. "I'm sorry, darling."

"Really," Mickey said, "Burrell is so depressing. Why do we have that man out here? He belittles your work, insults your intelligence, practically calls you a government lackey and rings a doomsday bell the entire time. I honestly don't think he tastes a bite of what I cook."

"He consumes enough of it," Gerald laughed.

"Quantity consumed does not attest to quality," Mickey said. "He never says he enjoys it. Have you ever noticed that?"

"Noticed what, darling?" Gerald was back at the table, one ankle crossed over the opposite knee, fingers drumming again.

"Burrell never says he enjoys my cooking."

"He eats enough of it," Gerald said, his eyes distant.

Mickey stared at her husband a moment, went back to dishwashing. "Gerald?"

"What?"

"We are going to have a war, aren't we?"

"I don't know." She had his full attention now.

"But it looks that way, doesn't it?"

"Roosevelt says—"

"Forget Roosevelt," Mickey said. "I'm not Burrell. I want to know your honest opinion. Are we going to war?"

Gerald said nothing. When Mickey turned, he wore an expression which frightened her. They gazed at one another a very long time. Mickey dried her hands and walked to Gerald, pulling his head against her stomach, holding him like a child.

"I love you, Gerald."

Terry had paused in the hallway on his way to the

kitchen for a drink of water. He turned, on tiptoe, and quietly returned to bed.

In the dark, eyes unseeing but open, he lay thinking about the slight tremor in Mama's voice, his father's lack of reply.

Suddenly, for a reason Terry didn't fully understand, he was afraid.

7

"Terrell, are you going to school today?"

"Yessir."

"Straight to school?" Daddy persisted.

"Yessir."

"Good."

Not satisfied, Mama added, "You had better get there this morning, Terrell."

"I will, Mama."

He accepted the brown paper sack. "What kind of sandwiches?"

"Two liver-cheese," Mama said. "Several cookies. A banana. Five cents for milk. *Milk,* understand?"

"Yes ma'am." It was a good package for trading purposes. Knowing what made it better, Terry asked, "May I have a dill pickle?"

Mama wrapped one in waxed paper and put it in the sack. Terry kissed them both and ran out the back door. He climbed a steep cinder path to the railroad tracks, looked both ways and crossed to the far side. Out of Mama's sight, he checked his top pocket—two cigarettes from a package Daddy left on the bedroom dresser last night. Terry trotted toward the packing houses.

"Want to buy a lunch, two liver-cheese sandwiches, a dill pickle, a banana and some cookies."

"How much?"

"Thirty cents."

The man dug for coins and Terry instantly wished

he'd asked for more. He knew better than to raise the ante at this point; that could kill the whole deal. He waited as the buyer checked the contents, accepted his money and walked hurriedly toward the icehouse.

"Can I have a cigarette?"

"Hell no. Your mama would kill me."

"No she wouldn't."

"She know you smoke?" All the men were looking at him.

"She catches me now and then."

Laughter. Somebody pulled out two cigarettes from a package of Old Golds and handed them to him. Terry thanked them and hurried on.

"May I have a cigarette?"

He got it without protest. Again, another group. Another from a lone man at the end of the packing house. His quota reached, Terry spoke to Bucky in passing.

"That old man really catch snakes bare-handed?" Bucky asked.

"Sure does."

"You think he'd really teach me how?"

"Said he would. He will."

"He taught you to catch catfish bare-handed?"

"Yep."

Bucky halted at the perimeter of the school yard. "Hey, Terry!"

Terry turned, midway over the crossing plank.

"I'll be waiting here at recess."

"Okay."

Terry ran into the school yard, all the way to his room. Mrs. Wright met him at the door.

"You're late, Terrell."

"I'm sorry."

"If you can't get here on time, you must get up earlier and leave sooner."

"Yes ma'am."

Mrs. Wright stepped aside, allowing him to pass.

He went to his desk and sat. Without speaking, hands clasped atop the desk, the students waited. The bell rang, a whir in the hallway. Everybody stood, to the right of his or her desk. All eyes on the flag, hands over hearts, they pledged allegiance. Afterward, heads bowed, the morning prayer. Everybody seated. Terry's posterior itched from perspiration caused by his running. He squirmed, positioning his rump against the rounded edge of the seat to create the most friction.

"Sit still, Terrell."

"Yes ma'am." Now it really itched.

"Quiet, students," Mrs. Wright said mechanically. She was marking math problems on the blackboard. Four plus 3; 3 plus 4. Across the entire width of the board, neat white marks low enough for the children to reach them.

"Guess what I got?" a whisper behind Terry's head.

"What?"

"A jar full of tree frogs."

Terry turned, looking at Cooty Jones. The dark-skinned boy was the son of an attorney. He had a habit of lifting one corner of his upper lip, his nose rising at the same time, clearing his nares which were never truly cleared.

"Lemme see," Terry whispered.

"Know what I'm going to do?"

"What?"

"Put them in Mrs. Wright's desk."

"Quiet students," Mrs. Wright, still writing problems.

"You are?" Terry saw the boy in a new light.

"Yep. Recess. Want to help?"

Terry grinned, nodded. Remembering Bucky, "Second recess," he instructed.

"Why?"

"I have something to do, first recess."

Obviously in need of moral support, if not assistance, Cooty agreed.

The morning went slowly, one after another of the students going to the board to work a problem. Terry counted off his position in the line of sequence, the problem that would be his, and worked it out ahead of time. He went to the board, pretended to study the numerals, then wrote the answer and returned to his desk.

"Second recess," Cooty whispered.

Terry nodded, smiling.

He met Bucky as planned. "Listen, Bucky, you got a cigar box?"

"At the house."

"Can I have it? Get it for me, will you?"

"Yeah. Got a cigarette?"

Terry paid the bribe, waited impatiently. Bucky reappeared with the box. Terry accepted a few quick puffs, tore off pine needles to chew and dashed back in time to join the line going to the room. He had the cigar box under his shirt.

"Where're the frogs?" he questioned Cooty.

"In a jar, my desk."

"Let me have them. I got a box."

"She'll never see them in a box," Cooty protested.

"She will the way I'll fix it. Give them to me."

Mrs. Wright halted them outside the rest-room doors. "Hurry along, children."

Cooty scooted into the room, got his jar and returned. Terry looked at the mass of pale-green, sticky-footed amphibians and took the jar into the toilet. The frogs were transferred to the cigar box with much grabbing, cramming, grabbing for escapees and more cramming. At last, the task was done, the lid closed, all captives inside and accounted for.

"What's that for?" Eddy Kent asked.

"None of your beeswax," Terry said. Then to Cooty, "Don't tell him nothing."

They left Eddy Kent, curly head high, covering the sting of his rebuff with haughty sounds of superiority.

On the way to their seats, Terry detoured by Mrs. Wright's desk and quickly snitched a rubber band and a thumbtack. Meeting Cooty's eyes, Terry grinned with satisfaction.

Terry attached the rubber band to the lid with a thumbtack. He then pulled open the center drawer of Mrs. Wright's desk, placed the box inside and, by reaching up in the top, tacked the rubber band to the immovable desk. This done, he carefully cut the paper which acted as a hinge for the box lid.

"When she opens the desk drawer," he reasoned aloud, "the rubber band is going to yank off the top."

"Then what?" Cooty asked, none too certain this was better than frogs turned lose initially inside the drawer.

"What's a tree frog do when light hits him?" Terry asked.

"Jumps."

Terry grinned. "Yep."

Several times they thought she was about to open the drawer. Her hand touched the handle twice, but then went to other drawers instead. She bumped the drawer with her hip as she leaned against the desk for support toward the end of the day. The final bell rang and school was out.

"Now what?" Cooty wailed.

"I don't know."

"What if she opens the drawer and there's nobody there to see it?"

"I don't know," Terry confessed.

"You wasted my frogs," Cooty accused.

"Maybe she'll open it tomorrow. Yeah, she will. She has the attendance book in her desk. She'll open it tomorrow."

"She better," Cooty said.

Terry forgot the incident overnight. He'd traded well for his sacked lunch on the way to school the next morning, and rarity of rarities, actually arrived at the school grounds with a few minutes to play before class. Cooty was absent. So nothing made him think about it.

The students took their seats, hands on their desks, awaiting the signaling school bell. Mrs. Wright pulled open her center desk drawer.

Terry, like everyone else, was quietly sitting with eyes forward. Suddenly Mrs. Wright threw herself backward, swatting the air, bumping the blackboard. Tiny flecks of green dotted her dress, neck, hair and arms. Then Terry remembered.

Mrs. Wright drowned the bell with a scream, and, to the amazement of her students, she clawed her hairdo to a shambles and began tearing off her clothes.

Another teacher peered through the door. "Nancy?"

Mrs. Wright was busy. She jolted as though struck from behind and began slashing at her bare backside.

"Nancy!"

"Who did this?" Mrs. Wright demanded, voice quivering.

"Nancy, what's going on?"

Mrs. Wright lifted her dress from the floor, at arm's length, between two fingers barely pinching enough material to hold it. Something caught the corner of her eye and she leaped sideways toward the other teacher, who was now standing so the only clear pane of glass was covered.

"Nancy, honey, what is it?"

"Watch it!" Mrs. Wright shrieked and the second teacher mounted a nearby chair.

Mrs. Wright shuddered, shook her dress, shivering.

"What *is* it?" the visiting member of the faculty was holding her own skirt above the knees.

"I demand to know who did this," Mrs. Wright said, her blush now complete.

"I know!" Eddy Kent's hand, waggling, on tiptoe to lift his signal higher. "I know, Mrs. Wright!"

She transfixed the curly haired tattler and Eddy Kent turned with malicious pleasure to point at Terry Calder.

Terry felt small sitting in a chair where his toes didn't quite touch the floor. The arms of the wooden structure were so far spaced only his elbows reached, and then his hands couldn't touch one another. He elected to sit with his hands in his lap.

"What are we going to do with you?" Mr. Hammond asked.

"I don't know."

"You have stayed out of school, you are constantly late, Mrs. Wright tells me. Now this."

Terry watched the ominous man circle from his chair and sit on one corner of the desk, glaring down at him.

"Are you unhappy at home?"

"No sir."

"Is there a problem you'd like to discuss with me?"

"No sir."

"You may, you know. If you have a problem, you can come to me anytime and I'll try to help you with it."

No reply.

"Why do you stay out of school, Terrell?"

Shrug of the shoulders.

"Why?"

Another shrug.

"Do you dislike Mrs. Wright, is that it?"

"No sir."

"You must not like her very much! You don't come to class, or come late when you do. Then this morning you scared her half to death."

"I'm sorry, Mr. Hammond."

"What?"

"I'm sorry."

"I can't hear you, Terrell."

Terry cleared his throat. "I'm sorry," he said, louder.

"You should be. I want you to tell Mrs. Wright

you're sorry. You understand? I want you to tell her and I want you to apologize to the entire class for disturbing the Pledge of Allegiance and morning prayer."

"Yessir."

"I can't hear you."

"Yessir!"

Mr. Hammond stood and opened the door. "Tell Mrs. Wright you want to apologize. Then do it. Apologize to the entire class."

The hall was a roar of activity. High school students jostled, called, laughed, their voices echoing from floor to ceiling. Terry hugged the wall opposite the lockers, easing between bodies, dodging unseeing boys pushing and shoving one another playfully.

He reached the exit unscathed and started down the walk toward the elementary section. He was shaking in nervous relief, from his release from the punishment he'd geared himself to accept. His arm was a little sore where Mrs. Wright had dragged him to the office, her fingers pinching into the muscle.

He felt all eyes turning toward him—students on the playground, teachers sitting on benches under the covered walkway. Terry approached Mrs. Wright, who lifted a hand to keep him silent until the teacher speaking had finished.

"What is it, Terrell?" Icy cold.

"Mr. Hammond told me to apologize."

"Did he spank you?"

"No ma'am."

The teachers looked at one another.

"I'm sorry, Mrs. Wright."

She stared at him, eyes hard.

"Mr. Hammond said I ought to apologize to the class."

"I told you he wouldn't do it," another teacher said to Mrs. Wright. "That's part of the problem around here. If they're fifth grade and under, forget it."

"Then he wonders why they act the way they do in

90

high school. Listen to the bedlam in that hallway right this minute!"

"Go play," Mrs. Wright commanded.

"Yes ma'am."

Terry dared not try to make it to the bamboo stand. But he got as near as he could, hoping to see Bucky. He didn't. That afternoon he left school carrying a note from Mrs. Wright, sealed in an envelope.

"I expect a reply from your mother, in the morning, Terrell. Don't come to school without it, either."

Terry stopped at Bucky's, joining the other boy on the steps to the one-room dwelling that was Bucky's room.

"Will you read something to me, Bucky?"

"Sure, what is it?"

Terry gave Bucky the note. Bucky tore it open. He stared at the flowing blue-ink script. It was signed, "Nancy."

"Dear Mickey," Bucky hesitantly translated. "Your one and only robbed me of ten years today. He planted a cigar box full of small frogs in my desk. I opened the drawer and they plastered themselves to me and I'm afraid I gave the children an impromptu peek at a mature female form undressing in class. The reaction here has been, for the most part, great humor at my experience or utter relief that Terrell isn't theirs! I report this for no other purpose than sympathy, actually. Mr. Hammond put the fear of God into Terrell and I trust that will suffice until he reaches the second grade. Best regards—"

Bucky tucked the note back into the envelope. Terry took it, discarded the envelope and put the note itself in his top pocket. The two boys lit cigarettes and smoked without speaking.

Finally, Bucky said, "Your mama will probably blister your ass."

"I know it."

"What if you didn't show her the note?"

"Mrs. Wright said don't come to school without an answer."

Bucky nodded, considering this. "What if we get somebody to write a note and you say your mama wrote it?"

Terry looked at Bucky, heart ascending. "Who'd do it?"

"Renée, at the Last Dollar Café."

"How come she'd do that?"

Bucky stood. "Maybe she won't. It's worth trying, ain't it?"

Terry walked with Bucky, and just as they started to enter, asked, "Would it help if we spent some money? I got a quarter."

"It might. Come on."

The jukebox blared, wailing groans of hillbilly music pounding the listeners. Men with shirtsleeves rolled above the elbows sat along a counter drinking coffee. In booths, all filled, other men and women laughed, talking loudly to be heard over the recorded din.

"Hey, Renée!" Bucky stood at the end of the counter, yelling. "Hey, Renée!"

"Hello, Bucky baby!" Renée carried cups of coffee stacked up her arm, swinging open the counter gate with one hip.

"Can I see you a second?" Bucky inquired.

"Minute, Bucky. Be back, hold on."

Water in glasses atop the counter formed tight circles of sympathetic ripples in time with the throb of music. The Wurlitzer had columns of lights going up each side, with bubbles traversing the length of the box and merging somewhere inside to reappear from the bottom, or so it seemed. Between recordings, in the abrupt silence, the human contribution to the pandemonium temporarily reigned, then subsided, then lifted anew as another record was seized by a mechanical arm and placed on a rubber table the size of a dinner plate, where it awaited the needle.

"Whatcha need, Bucky?"

Bucky told her. She read the note and threw back her head laughing. "You did that, kid?"

"Yes ma'am."

"Ma'am? He's got manners, ain't he, Bucky?"

Bucky nodded.

"Okay, why the hell not," Renée agreed. She got a piece of paper from a back room, sharpened her pencil and, with smoothly gliding strokes, wrote: "Tough shit, baby. I got a real man for a kid."

Bucky read it aloud. Then to Renée, "I don't think that'll fool her, Renée."

"That's what I'd say was it my kid," Renée declared.

"Yeah, but Terry's mom wouldn't. You got to sound like Terry's mom would sound."

Renée's mouth turned down, her head jerked in a twisting motion and she went for another piece of paper. This time she transposed more thoughtfully.

Bucky read the results: "Dear Mrs. Wright: I am truly sorry my boy caused all the truble. If he does such again, let me know and I will ware him out. Signed, his mother, Micky."

They watched Terry for judgment. He grinned, folding the note. "Two cups of coffee, please," he said, grandly. Renée laughed and the two boys slipped onto stools.

"Think it'll work?" Bucky asked.

"Sure! Thanks, Bucky."

But it didn't. Mrs. Wright opened the note the next day and something in her eyes told Terry he had been betrayed even before she asked, "Did your mother write this?"

He couldn't afford another trip to the office. Tears welled in this eyes. "No, Mrs. Wright."

"Who did, then?"

"A friend of mine."

"How old a friend?"

"Forty or fifty, maybe."

"An adult!"

"Yes ma'am."

"Where is this—friend?"

"She works at the Last Dollar Café."

Mrs. Wright's eyes closed and stayed closed a long time, her hands slowly sinking to her sides. When they opened, she said quietly, "Go sit down, Terrell. Let's forget the whole thing, shall we?"

"You want me to apologize to the class?"

"No, that won't be necessary. Please sit down."

The day was excruciatingly long. Only a quick smoke at recess helped him get through it all.

"Did it work?" Bucky inquired when Terry appeared among the bamboo stand.

"No."

"It didn't?"

"No, she must not write like Mama. Mrs. Wright knew it wasn't Mama. Tried to trap me in a lie, asked me who wrote it."

Alarmed, Bucky asked, "Did you tell her?"

"No," Terry lied now.

Bucky's shoulders lowered in relief. "I'd hate to make Renée mad. She writes notes for me all the time. My teacher can't tell the difference."

"Gotta go," Terry forefeited his butt and raced for the school yard.

Bucky was waiting at lunchtime. Several other older boys were there, too. Bucky and Terry huddled together after Terry sold off four cigarettes for a total of fifteen cents, an all-time high: a pack didn't cost but eighteen cents.

"You think she'll go to your mama?" Bucky whispered.

"I don't know," Terry said. "Give me another puff."

"If she goes to your mama, it may be double trouble."

"I don't care. I'm thinking about running away, anyway."

"Running away? Don't be stupid! The cops'll throw your butt in the hoosegow."

"I don't care."

"You'd care," Bucky said. "One of those lifers cornholes you and you'll care."

"What?"

"My brother did three months on a road gang once," Bucky related. "He said they cornholed him every night."

Horrified, Terry stared at his companion.

Bucky took advantage of the moment, had another puff before handing back the cigarette.

"Ev-ur-ree *night!*" Bucky said.

Terry stood as the school bell called. He snatched pine needles, chewing them. He couldn't take that. Not ev-ur-ree night. Maybe he'd better think of another way out.

Or, he vowed, assuming his place in line, maybe he'd better have a way to stay clear of cops, if he did run away.

"You wasted my frogs," Cooty hissed, close behind Terry.

Terry turned slowly. "So far," he warned, "I took all the blame alone. But I'll be glad to ask Mrs. Wright it we can get back *your* frogs."

Cooty shrank.

"Terrell!" Mrs. Wright's voice. "Face front, please."

8

Mama stood suddenly. She rushed from the breakfast table to the bathroom. Daddy followed her. Terry heard the sound of retching. Disturbed, he went to the bathroom door. Mama was on her knees in front of the commode, one hand holding hair away from her face. Daddy was wetting a washcloth in the sink.

"Are you sick, Mama?"

"Mama's all right, Terrell. Go finish your breakfast."

A violent, explosive sound came from Mama's throat.

"Terrell, I said go eat your breakfast."

"Yessir."

Terry got his lunch sack, paused at the back door. More noises of illness came to his ears. He closed the screen door behind himself, a leaden feeling in his own stomach. He plucked hibiscus blossoms, sucking nectar and discarding them as he walked toward the railroad tracks. Mockingbirds traded insults with blue jays as Terry climbed the incline. On the far side of the tracks, in a cluster of tenement houses, screeching black children chased one another in a game of catch-can.

A long, narrow store on stilts served this group of houses. The place was owned by a burly ebony man who sold Terry a full pack of Pall Malls. These in his pocket, Terry took a slightly different route toward school, skirting the packing house. It was somewhat cooler this morning. The aroma of cut cane came to him, and the whack of descending machetes. The laborers were chanting, voices melodic, their Bahamian accents lending flavor to the work songs.

"Black mon got it!"

Others answered, "Gonna keep it!"

"Black mon want it!"

"Gonna keep it!" The whacks of curved blades cutting cane kept cadence.

"Po' mon got it!"

"Gonna keep it!"

"Po' mon want it!"

"Gonna keep it!"

Terry could imagine succulent juices seeping from freshly hewn stalks, sweat glistening on bare backs, the masculine odor of overheated bodies.

"Whatcha gonna tell me?"

"We gonna keep it!"

"Whatcha gonna keep mon?"

"Fayyyth in the Lord!"

The voices ebbed as Terry put a packing house between himself and the chanters. An automobile passed, scattering gravel, a cloud of dust swirling around him. He plucked a dandelion, blew the snowy globe of seeds and watched them spread like miniature parachutists before landing. He heard adult laughter from somewhere afar, the jukebox at the Last Dollar Café, mechanical throbs from packing houses, a train spinning wheels for traction.

He had stopped without realizing it. His mind was dumbly repeating the chant, "Black mon got it; po' mon got it; everybody got it; fayyyth in the Lord!" A caterpillar wearing a prickly jacket of black and yellow bands rippled past his feet, scurrying to safety. On electric lines above, birds twittered, preened, rustled their feathers. Below, in hollows of dust, sparrows bathed themselves, shivering their plumage to get the lice-chasing sustance next to their skins.

"Black mon got it; po' mon got it—"

He began running, no conscious decision made, his

legs doing that for him. He paused at a particular place
he'd used before and discarded his shoes and socks.
Now that his legs were well again, he was once more
wearing the despised short pants. He wiggled his toes
in hot dust, began running again, his lunch sack tightly
gripped in one hand.

Borer wasps building nests in stems of hollow reeds
zipped and darted, oblivious to Terry. He turned out
Chosen Road, his gait steady, a pace he could hold for
an hour without overexertion. The soles of his feet
were toughened and thick. He did not feel the mounting heat from the pavement nor the jagged shells and
stone imbedded in asphalt.

He met McCree as the old man's truck reached the
road and halted, checking for cross traffic.

"Ho, Little Hawk!"

"Can I go with you?"

"Sure enough. Hop in."

McCree never drove fast and seldom in third gear.
With his radiator boiling and the smell of hot oil in their
nostrils, he most often traveled in lowest gear, bumping
over and through back roads or on the embankment
beside a highway. In the rear of his vehicle were stacks
of hampers, burlap sacks and long bamboo poles with
metal hooks attached to the ends.

"Going to get those pine cones, Little Hawk," Mc-
Cree said. "Out Tamiami Trail would be about the best
place, don't you reckon?"

"Most likely."

Planted by the government along the ubiquitous canals, the trees served two purposes: they kept sleepy
drivers from a watery death and acted as windbreaks on
an otherwise flat terrain.

"I knew a man drove into one of those canals once,"
McCree said. "He fell asleep driving, him and his wife.
All of a sudden he wakes up in pitch dark with bubbly
sounds in his ears, and his wife screaming like a mad
woman."

Terry listened intently.

"Now he knew, this man did, if enough time passed, the hyacinths would slowly come together again over the car. The tubular roots on hyacinths grow six to ten feet. He tried to roll down a window and it wouldn't budge. It was wintertime, as I recall."

Terry nodded, twisting to hear better over the clatter of fenders and racing motor.

"Doors wouldn't open either," McCree continued. "Water pressure pushing in on them. He knew the car was most likely sinking into mud and chances of ever opening them doors was slight. Know what he did, Little Hawk?"

"No sir?"

"Kicked holes in the windows. So the water would come in faster. But the windows in a car are different from windows in a house. Know why?"

"Two pieces of glass stuck together so they won't shatter," Terry said.

"Have I told you this before?"

"I like to hear it."

"I have? I don't recollect telling you this before."

"I like listening to it," Terry urged.

"Well sir, the water commenced to pouring in, his wife was having a conniption right then and there. He said she near about deafened him."

Mr. McCree pronounced it *deef-ened*.

"She couldn't swim." McCree pulled across the road to the far side and looked up out the window at thickly needled trees. He drove along more slowly, gazing up as he talked.

"Finally, when they didn't have any more room to breathe, almost, he was able to roll down a window. Dark, cold, didn't know how deep he was or what was out there . . ."

McCree halted, cut the motor. "He told his wife to take a big gulp of air and he snatched her out, dragging her on top of the car and lo and behold! Standing on

100

the car, his head was clear. He somehow got his wife to the bank of the canal. She was hurt. Legs hurt. He pulled her up and she couldn't walk."

The next part had given Terry nightmares for weeks. He waited with macabre anticipation.

"Man went to fetch help, walked several miles to town and woke somebody up. When they got back his wife was dead, Little Hawk."

"Yessir."

"Rats killed her."

A shiver.

"Don't never lie down in a swamp or cane field and go to sleep, Little Hawk."

"No sir."

"Reckon we can get some cones along this stretch?"

They walked the row of trees, estimating the yield they could expect. "Looks good," McCree said. He got one of his bamboo poles with a hook on the end and began snaring the cones, snapping them off. Terry climbed the tree itself, to the uppermost limbs.

"Break them off and throw them down," McCree instructed.

"I will."

"Mind you don't get swallowed by a giant red bug."

Terry laughed, wedging himself in a fork between two scaly, rough-barked limbs. He worked fast and expertly. Cones showered down as occasional traffic zoomed by.

"We'll have those three hundred bushels before you know it!" McCree hollered up.

"Sure will!"

"That-a-boy!"

They stopped for drinks of sassafras tea and finally ate Terry's sandwiches for lunch.

"Must've made these yourself," McCree observed.

"No, my—" that was close, "friend made them. Her name's Renée. She works at the Last Dollar Café."

"Right nice of her to do that."

"Yessir." Terry chewed a bite gone dry with his near-slip.

They worked until the dark made it difficult to see cones on the ground. The ride back to town and then to Camp Osceola was passed with few words.

"Want to join me at my place for supper, Little Hawk?"

"No. I better go."

McCree reached across Terry's lap and helped with the jammed door handle. "See you again, Little Hawk. Many thanks for your help."

"I enjoyed it."

"Night," McCree said. Terry was trotting away.

Terry expected retribution the moment he stepped through the door. Instead, Mama greeted him mildly. "Get ready for supper, son."

Daddy was on the telephone. "Burrell, Mrs. Roosevelt has said you can join us for inspection of the Negro migratory labor camp when she arrives. Tomorrow. About nine o'clock. She's having lunch at the camp and you're welcome. Some of the women—what? Of course they're black, Burrell. It's a black camp!"

"Terrell, get washed up."

"Yes ma'am."

When Terry returned to the table, Mama was seated, waiting for Daddy to get off the telephone. She tapped Terry's hand as he reached for a biscuit and he withdrew, also waiting.

"She's coming here first, Burrell. Then we'll drive over for the inspection."

"Mama, who's coming?"

"Mrs. Roosevelt. The President's wife."

"Tomorrow?"

"Yes."

"Can I meet her?"

Gerald came in as the question was posed. "Sure you can," he said.

"What about school?" Mama asked.

102

Gerald's expression was still set from his phone conversation. "How often does a child get to meet the wife of a President of the United States, Mickey? Let's have the blessing."

Eleanor Roosevelt was taller than Daddy. She wore a dress that fell halfway between knee and ankle. Her purse was woven white raffia. Her graying hair was piled atop her head in a rolled, bushy effect. She spoke with an odd accent.

"Mrs. Roosevelt, I'd like you to meet my wife, Mickey."

"How do you do, Mrs. Calder? When is the blessed event?"

"Hopefully the first week in December," Mama said.

"At least, perhaps, by then the heat will have abated."

"And this is my son, Terrell."

Mrs. Roosevelt's hand extended, taking Terry's and holding it as though in mid-shake. The backs of her hands were laced with purple and red veins, her skin was smooth and waxen. She smelled good.

"That child ought to be wearing shoes," Mrs. Roosevelt said.

Mama laughed nervously. "In south Florida, Mrs. Roosevelt, that is a losing battle all mothers fight."

"Yes. I imagine."

"This is our camp foreman," Daddy continued, "Randy Adams."

"Mr. Adams," Mrs. Roosevelt said everyone's name after hearing it.

"Our administrations officer—"

"Can I go play?" Terry whispered to his mother.

"We're planning lunch at the other camp, Mrs. Roosevelt," Daddy was saying.

"Can I go play, Mama?"

"This is our publisher and editor, Burrell Mason."

"Yes, I know of Mr. Mason."

"You do?" Daddy was astonished.

"Mama, can I go play, now?"

Mama had a silent, effective and positive way of letting her displeasure be known when they were in public. With a smile on her face, she simply grasped Terry's wrist and her fingernails dug into flesh. He had learned to counter this with pained expressions and blood-curdling shrieks. He had also learned that to do this was inviting far greater punishment later, when they were alone. He felt her nails dig, not too severely.

"The lawn looks lovely," Mrs. Roosevelt commented.

Daddy's face was flushed, pleased.

"How many men are required to keep it that way?" Mrs. Roosevelt inquired.

Terry saw Daddy's instant alertness, a silence falling over the listeners.

"We use tractors," Daddy said, "pulling seven mowers. Two men can mow it in a couple of days. You know, Mrs. Roosevelt, so few of these families have ever had a lawn upon which to play. This is their yard here, actually."

She nodded, now smiling. "I hadn't considered that. Of course it is, isn't it? Very nice. Shall we go?"

Mama and Terry were left standing with Marilyn as the others returned to duties or climbed into automobiles for a trip to the south side of Belle Glade and the new camp. Mama waved as they drove away.

"How many times do I have to tell you about interrupting people while they're talking?"

"I'm sorry."

"Change clothes. Then you may go and play."

Mama put a quivering hand on the side of her stomach.

"You all right, Mrs. Calder?" Marilyn asked.

"It must be a boy," Mama said.

"Why?"

"He kicked and turned through that entire introduction. I'm sure it must've shown to anyone who was looking."

Marilyn laughed. Terry ran ahead of Mama to the house, to get out of the stiffly starched white pants and shirt he wore. The entire day still lay ahead.

"Thought I'd missed you, Little Hawk!"

"I had to meet somebody."

"Oh? Who?"

"A lady named Roosevelt."

Mr. McCree looked at Terry steadily. "Was she nice?"

"She has buckteeth."

McCree chuckled. "Get in, Little Hawk. I'm going after the rest of my Australian pine cones."

The first structure completed at the new camp was an administration building. Then came the huge recreation center, which served a multiple purpose: grocery store, movie theater, sports arena, town meeting-hall and refuge for residents of the camp in time of storm.

The black women, wives of junior administrators and construction personnel, had placed long tables together as Gerald had suggested. In the center of each table were dozens of blue hyacinth blossoms someone had picked from the canals to give the setting more cheer and color.

Mrs. Roosevelt inadvertently hurt their feelings by commenting on the flowers. "I detest hyacinths," she said. "They are a bane, aren't they? We're fighting a losing battle trying to eradicate them, I'm afraid."

Throughout their walk over the expansive camp, Burrell Mason had taken meticulous notes, asking pertinent questions. All the while, Gerald had held his breath in a state of tension for fear Burrell would suddenly throw an embarrassing query at the First Lady.

As he had at the white camp, Gerald took care to

introduce the black people, each of whom had an opportunity to shake Mrs. Roosevelt's hand.

"These people have a great deal of respect for you, Mr. Calder," Mrs. Roosevelt commented.

Ignoring Burrell's knowing glance, Gerald replied, "And I for them, Mrs. Roosevelt."

Through the several hours they were together, Gerald had expertly handled her questions, readily admitting it when he wasn't sure of the answers.

During luncheon, the prayer was delivered by an elderly lay minister who droned on far too long, blessing everything from the food to the President and his administration.

It was on their way back to Camp Osceola that Burrell let the hammer fall:

"Mrs. Roosevelt, isn't the purpose of this new camp actually to meet the manpower needs of the impending war?"

"War, Mr. Mason?" Mrs. Roosevelt asked. "It isn't impending, Mr. Mason. We've been fighting poverty and deprivation since men assembled in caves. Did you see the distended bellies of some of those black children?"

"Yes, Mrs. Roosevelt, but—"

"That's a dietary deficiency, Mr. Mason. My husband is pushing for federal standards which will require the bakers of America to enrich their products with nutrients. The sole purpose is to correct such things. Impetigo, pellagra, pyorrhea all have a common denominator, Mr. Mason—poverty. But the laborer is the greatest victim of all. Don't you agree?"

Gerald listened in absolute satisfaction as Burrell did the only thing he could do: agree.

"What is that old man doing there?" Mrs. Roosevelt leaned over the seat, speaking to Gerald.

"Gathering pine cones, apparently," Gerald said. He slowed so the President's wife could see for herself.

Something high up the tree caught Gerald's eye, but traffic diverted his attention.

"My word," Mrs. Roosevelt said, "if that child fell it would break his neck!"

"Mrs. Roosevelt, with war looming on the horizon," Burrell began anew, "wouldn't we be inundated with Bahamian laborers?"

Gerald cast a glance in the rearview mirror. He saw Mrs. Roosevelt's toothy smile.

"Mr. Mason, you should be working with the Washington newspapers, not here in Belle Glade."

"Why is that, ma'am?"

"You are asking questions best directed to my husband. Not me."

Terry had seen the familiar tan government vehicle coming and attempted to shield himself. The car slowed, a face at the rear window, then picked up speed again.

"That was them, Mr. McCree!"

"That was who, Little Hawk?"

"That lady. Mrs. Roosevelt."

McCree stepped around his truck and gazed after the sedan. He looked up at Terry, face solemn, but too far removed for Terry to catch the expression.

"How many bushels we got now?" Terry called down.

"All told?"

"Yessir."

"Fifty or sixty, maybe. Getting tired?"

"No sir!"

They worked through the afternoon, the distance between the old man and boy reducing all conversation to a minimum. Terry plucked what McCree couldn't reach from the ground, scooting out limbs over canals where cones had to be hand-picked, because they'd drop into the water otherwise.

"Join me for supper tonight, Little Hawk?"

"No sir, Mr. McCree. I better go."

The old man followed their ritual at the entrance to Camp Osceola and Terry scampered away home.

"Burrell says they're going to ask you to manage the new camp, Gerald," Mickey said.

"Burrell doesn't know that. He says a lot of things to get a reaction."

"What if they should ask you?" Her tone was conversational, but something had Terry taut in his chair at the table, eating, listening.

"I don't know, Mickey."

"Would you do it?"

"I don't know."

The adults ate without looking at one another. Terry stuck a finger into a biscuit, twisting the appendage to make a hole large enough to hold butter and syrup.

"Don't play with your food, son."

"Yes ma'am. Pass the syrup, please."

"Gerald, I don't want you taking that job."

"Could I have the butter, too?" Terry asked.

"We have enough problems right here, without suffering the additional problems we'd encounter over there."

Daddy sighed, dropped his fork on uneaten food. "Excuse me, please," he said, rising.

"You know," Mama's tone sharpened, "just once I'd like to talk something all the way through with you. Just once."

Daddy turned in the doorway. He stood there a moment. He came back and sat again. "All right, Mickey."

"I don't want you to take that job over there."

Daddy stared at Mama.

"Well?" she asked.

"Well what?"

"Well do you have anything to say about that, Gerald?"

"Yes. I said I *don't know* what I would do. That is the truth."

Mama shoved back her chair. She slammed Daddy's plate on her own, a fork skittering to the floor. Terry got down and retrieved it.

"Ten thousand things to worry about," Daddy followed Mama into the kitchen. "Ten thousand . . . damned things. Then you want to talk about something that is not, notice I said *not,* even happening yet. It may never happen. If they ask me, I will then sit down and we'll discuss the matter from start to finish. Until then—"

"Go away, Gerald."

"Mickey, this is ridiculous, you—"

"Go away! Do you hear me?"

The food in Terry's stomach curled into a knot. He lifted his fork with a shaking hand and mechanically took a bite of the spinach he knew he must devour. Daddy walked past, into the living room, and turned on the radio.

". . . Chase and Sanborn brings you . . . Edgar Bergen and Charlie McCarthy!"

Mama took Terry's plate, the spinach not finished. Over her shoulder, she said, "Go to bed, Terrell. No argument. Just go to bed."

9

Randy Adams, camp foreman, was sitting with Daddy at the breakfast table when Terry entered. Mama motioned Terry to his seat, her face compelling silence. He looked with distaste at the oatmeal she placed before him. She began slicing a banana into the bowl.

"What should we do with them, Mr. Calder?" Randy asked.

"What is the objection to having them take a house somewhere on camp?"

"Hell, Mr. Calder, they're *Japs*. Black folks don't think of them as black and white folks sure don't think of them as white."

"How many are there?" Daddy questioned.

"Seven."

"Seven? I don't think any of our tenants will complain about seven people, Randy."

Randy grunted, rising. "I don't want no trouble, that's all."

"Neither do I, Randy. Tell Marilyn to put them in the best possible location to avoid that."

The two men went onto the porch talking as Terry pushed oatmeal this way and that with a spoon. Terry caught a vulgar word, spoken by Randy Adams, and Mama glanced his way to see if Terry understood it.

"Do I have to eat this?"

"You certainly do."

"I hate oatmeal."

"Eat it."

He fished out a slice of banana, scraping oatmeal off the fruit before putting it in his mouth. "Mama, can I have four sandwiches?"

"Four!"

"I've been mighty hungry lately."

"Then eat your oatmeal and maybe you won't be so hungry."

Well, he'd walked himself into that one. Terry eased out the drawer on the porcelain kitchen table. With Mama at the sink, her attention on the talking men, he raked his oatmeal into the receptacle and shoved it closed.

Mama handed Terry his lunch sack. "How many sandwiches?"

"Three," she said.

"What kind?"

"Mashed prunes and peanut butter."

"Aw, Mama! I hate prunes and—"

"Go to school!"

"The Nazis executed fifty Frenchmen because a German officer was murdered," Randy Adams was saying. "They said if the killers aren't turned over by midnight October twenty-second, they're going to execute fifty more."

"I heard H. V. Kaltenborne's report on that," Daddy said.

"They're killing them off like flies over there, Mr. Calder."

"I know, Randy."

Terry squeezed past the men and out the front door. He left camp by the main entrance and, with little attempt to hide himself, began trotting toward Chosen and Mr. McCree.

"Mr. McCree, what's a Nazi?"

The old man was filling hampers with cones, then capping them. "I don't rightly know, Little Hawk."

"They kill people, right?"

"That's what I hear. I wouldn't know for sure."

Terry dragged a burlap bag of cones over for Mc-Cree to empty into another hamper. "What's a war?"

"Well, a war is when a whole country gets into a fight with another country. They use guns and try to kill one another off."

"You ever been in a war?"

"Nope. Not likely to, either, at my age."

"You think we're going to have a war?" Terry asked.

McCree halted his work, looking at the boy. "I ain't been keeping up with it much, Little Hawk. Why do you ask?"

Terry shrugged his shoulder. "I don't know."

McCree indicated Terry's lunch with a pointed finger. "What you got there?"

"Something awful."

"Don't say. What is it?"

"Mashed prunes and peanut butter sandwiches."

McCree winced slightly. "I think maybe I could find something better around here. Why don't we give your prune sandwiches to my friends the birds?"

"Okay."

They walked outside and McCree unwrapped one of the waxed-paper parcels. "Be real quiet now," he cautioned.

The old man held his arm straight out and pursed his lips, making a warbling, low note. Terry stood to one side, transfixed. McCree warbled again. He did this for several minutes, making no motion, the sandwich held in an open palm, calling with his whistle. Suddenly, from a nearby tree, a titmouse flew down and landed on McCree's fingers.

Enthralled, Terry watched the old man continue calling until dozens of the tiny birds were hovering around him, landing on his arm, shoulders and head. Other kinds of birds began arriving then, some taking a peck at the sandwich in passing flight, others clearing

113

a place on his arm where they could light and dine in leisure.

When all the food was gone, Terry followed McCree back inside again.

"Why did they come?" he asked.

"Hungry, Little Hawk."

"But they don't come for me, or anybody else."

"How many times do you feed them?"

"Never," Terry confessed.

"Might be that's the reason, then."

"Did you charm them?"

"Your sandwiches were all the charms we needed, Little Hawk."

"I never saw anything like that before. Do they always come when you call them?"

"Most always."

"Wow. That was really something, Mr. McCree."

"Now let's you and me find something decent to eat," McCree said.

"Oh, dear God," Mickey cried.

"What is it?" Gerald stuck his head out of the bathroom.

"Terrell dumped his oatmeal in the table drawer."

Gerald laughed and Mickey's temper instantly flared. "You wouldn't think it quite so funny if you had to clean this mess!"

"I will clean it," Gerald offered, "as soon as I finish shaving."

Mickey dumped the contents of the drawer into the sink. "I'll have to wash all that silver," she seethed. She ran scalding water into the fixture, rinsing away oatmeal.

"This isn't the first time he's done this," Mickey stated. "I wore him out for doing it once before."

"You know how he hates oatmeal," Gerald appeared in the door, patting his face with a hand towel.

"Gerald, that is absolutely beside the point! That

child is deliberately defying me. He smokes, he lies, he—"

Gerald took the drawer from her hand and nudged her aside. He began cleaning the sticky mess.

"Honestly, I am at my wit's end, Gerald. I feel positively guilty for whipping him. The last time I tore his legs up, and it hurt me to do it. It really hurt me. Most things he does wrong, I've gotten to where I let them go by as though I hadn't noticed. I found two snake rattlers floating in the washing machine yesterday. If there's such a thing as marking a baby, Gerald, this one will be born with a forked tongue and a tail with a green tuft on it."

"Don't worry about it. He's going through a phase."

Automobile tires on the driveway drew Mickey to the living room. She recognized the vehicle with a sinking heart, even before the driver stepped out.

"Gerald!"

"What, Mickey?"

"Miss Ramsey the truant officer is here."

"Who?"

Mickey opened the door, mustering a smile. "Good morning, Miss Ramsey."

"Good morning, Mrs. Calder. How are you feeling?"

"Very large."

Miss Ramsey smiled sympathetically. She entered to find Gerald coming from the kitchen.

"Oh, good, Mr. Calder. I'm glad I caught you. I need to speak to both of you."

"Don't tell me," Mickey said.

"I'm afraid so, Mrs. Calder. Did you know Terrell has been out of class for the past three days?"

"I knew about yesterday, I kept him home."

"I see. Was he ill?"

"No, my husband wanted Terrell to meet the President's wife, Mrs. Roosevelt."

Miss Ramsey accepted a seat. Gerald and Mickey sat across from her on the couch, side by side. The truant

115

officer opened a folder she carried, withdrawing several papers.

"Mr. and Mrs. Calder, I have some rather unhappy news."

The parents waited.

"The law in Florida is very explicit about truancy. Until a child is sixteen, by law, he must be compelled to attend a recognized school."

Mickey looked at Gerald, her face flushed.

"Terrell has been absent from class forty-three of the fifty-five days thus far this year. In your position, Mr. Calder, I'm sure you can appreciate this. There's been so much parental abuse of children in years past, making them laborers for a few dollars, which go to the family coffers."

"Child abuse," Gerald said, numbly. "Miss Ramsey, I assure you we aren't abusing Terrell."

"No, of course not. Judge Franklin said the same thing this morning."

"Judge Franklin?" Gerald's face warmed. "What has Ike Franklin to do with this, Miss Ramsey?"

"All truancy reports which persist go to him, Mr. Calder." Miss Ramsey sat, her trim legs touching at ankle and knee, nylons straight. Mickey felt obscenely obese.

"You see," Miss Ramsey continued, "we aren't handling Terrell very well, are we? We've tried reasoning. Mrs. Calder tells me she administered corporal punishment. Mrs. Wright has told me Terrell is difficult to control in class. Mr. Hammond, the principal, recently talked to Terrell about the incident with the frogs."

Mickey made a small, involuntary sound which stopped the conversation.

"Are you all right, Mrs. Calder?"

"Frogs?" Mickey asked, hoarsely.

Miss Ramsey affected an understanding, benevolent manner, "Yes. I'd forgotten you didn't get Mrs. Wright's note on the matter."

"No," Mickey whispered, "I didn't."

"Terrell had a waitress at the Last Dollar Café attempt to forge a reply but the tone of the letter was obviously uncultured and Mrs. Wright saw through it immediately."

"What about the frogs, Miss Ramsey," Mickey asked, "as much as I dread hearing it."

Miss Ramsey's laugh almost sounded genuinely amused. She told how Terrell had placed a cigar box of amphibians in Mrs. Wright's desk. She mentioned Mrs. Wright's hysterical fear of such creatures, telling how the hapless teacher had disrobed in class, thereby subjecting herself to considerable teasing from other faculty members.

"I personally suffer the same reaction to scorpions and spiders," Miss Ramsey said.

Gerald now had his hand on Mickey's wrist. She sat, hands clasped so tightly her knuckles were white.

Miss Ramsey lifted her glasses from their place hanging around her neck, put them on. "The problem is, we are fast approaching a court action that would be of no benefit to Terrell. It would prove embarrassing, at the very least. We're all caught up in the mechanizations of our structured society in this case. The laws were created to prevent child abuse, and in the eyes of that law, Terrell looks like the son of a migrant worker who refuses to educate his children. Do you see what I'm saying?"

"Yes," Gerald said.

"Judge Franklin has asked me to defer the matter awhile longer. I agreed. He suggests a meeting with the teacher, principal and both of you, with the child. I will be there, also. Whatever Terrell's underlying problem, his point of contention, we should try to seek it out, resolve it and get him started on a normal childhood existence."

"I see," Gerald said, coldly.

"Do you know where Terrell is?" Miss Ramsey asked. She had a pencil poised.

"No."

Miss Ramsey made a note. "Has he exhibited any signs of maladjustment other than skipping school?"

"Such as what?" Gerald demanded.

"Such as pilfering minor objects, perhaps."

"Stealing? He'd better not!"

Another note. "Have you noticed any indication that Terrell might need glasses or a hearing aid? Sometimes these problems are as simple as that."

"No."

Miss Ramsey made two checks on her paper. "Does the child in question seem interested in family matters?"

"Yes."

"Have there been any problems in the home? Fighting, tensions, that sort of thing?"

"No, Miss Ramsey."

"Would the family like the services of a professional counselor? Appointments can be made Monday, Wednesday or—"

"No!"

Miss Ramsey's young face hardened slightly. "Mr. and Mrs. Calder, I know how acutely uncomfortable this is for you. But there seem to be several facets of this which you might not have considered."

Mickey stared at a point in space somewhere beyond the open front door.

"Children who are truant follow a dismally predictable path. Out of school, without proper supervision, many—most—ultimately resort to criminal activities. This begins in the most innocuous manner—taking candy from a store, trinkets at the five and dime. But study of hardened criminals has shown us the importance of nipping these things in the bud. Now. Right now while the case is merely that of a carefree boy who wants to go swimming and fishing, rather than learn his ABCs."

118

Gerald stood. Neither woman moved.

"A few more minutes of your time, if I may, Mr. Calder."

When he did not sit again, Miss Ramsey said, "If the child were any other child . . . that is to say, Judge Franklin would tell you, if you were not the parents involved here—Terrell would be in court tomorrow and subject to court-supervised restriction until this matter is solved. If need be—and let's hope it doesn't come to this—they will send the truant away to state-supported schools."

"Reformatories," Mickey said, flatly.

Miss Ramsey started to amend that, then nodded.

"Thank you, Miss Ramsey. My wife is not feeling well. We'll discuss this and see what we can do."

"I'm afraid it has gone beyond that, Mr. Calder. You are being asked to a family-school meeting, as I said. Terrell should be there. Would tomorrow afternoon at three be acceptable?"

"Yes. Fine. At the school?"

"Mr. Hammond's office. Shall I put it down as three, then?"

"Yes, Miss Ramsey. Thank you." Gerald held her arm, gently but insistently pushing her toward the door.

Mickey pulled herself to her feet.

"We'll see you tomorrow then, Miss Ramsey."

"Yes. Mr. Calder, I'm sorry it has come to this."

"Thank you, Miss Ramsey."

Gerald left the young woman even before she entered her car. He returned to find Mickey gone. He walked through the kitchen, dining room, then back to the bedroom. Mickey was in bed, lying on her side, an arm over her face.

"Mickey, don't worry about this."

"Gerald—Gerald—"

"The nerve of those bureaucratic sons of—"

"Gerald, for God's sake! To them, it looks like we

have an unmanageable recalcitrant on our hands! We can't control our own six-year-old child!"

"I'll control him," Gerald snorted. "When that boy comes home this evening, I'll control him all right."

"No you won't." Mickey pushed up to a sitting position.

"No? First you complain because I won't wear him out, now you complain because that's precisely what I am going to do!"

"You should have done that weeks ago."

"I'll call and cancel that meeting with the principal and teacher first thing in the morning."

"No," Mickey said, "do no such thing. We are going to be there. Terrell will be there."

"Go through that—"

"Yes! The same thing I've been going through all alone for some time. Tomorrow at three, mister. We'll be there. If together—teacher, parent, truant officer— if we can't handle it, you may see Terrell become a ward of the court, Gerald."

"You're suggesting I have neglected my responsibility as a father."

"Haven't you?"

"I didn't think I had."

"The court may disagree."

"This isn't going to court, Mickey!"

"What are you going to do? Call Washington? Ask for a Presidential pardon! Gerald! We are about to lose our child!"

"Mickey, take it easy now."

"Take it easy?" She whirled, facing him. With the flat of her hands, she slapped her abdomen. It was no harder than she'd done to make the baby kick on cue, but to Gerald it must've sounded like blows designed to maim and kill. He seized her arms and pinned them, eyes horrified.

"Mickey! What's happening here? What's happening to us?"

She glared at him, gasping for breath. "What's happening?" she said. "We are parents, Gerald. That's what's happening. What's happening with the world? Who but God knows? I just know I'm hot, breathless, unhappy, stuffed tighter than a blood tick and I'm worn out with worrying about it all. I wish—I wish to God I were dead."

"Mickey!"

"Let me go, please."

"Where're you going?"

"To the bathroom."

He still held her.

"Let me go, Gerald, or I'll pee all over you."

"Know what I wish, Mr. McCree?"

"What do you wish, Little Hawk?" They were picking an unusually late crop of blackberries, their fingers stained purple, the bucket bleeding juice from a crack in the bottom.

"I wish you were my daddy."

"Hmm-m. That'd be something, all right."

"We could go hunting and fishing every day. I could help you get your Australian pine cones and chicory coffee. I'd learn to pick up old *Crotalus adamanteus* and *Agkistrodon piscivorus* with my bare hands. We could do that together, couldn't we?"

"Watch for old *Crotalus* around these palmetto thickets," McCree warned. "Might be under there keeping himself cool."

"What do you think about that, Mr. McCree?"

"Mmm-hmm."

They walked toward his truck, each carrying two buckets, dodging briars which plucked at their clothing.

"You think you'd like to have me for a little boy?"

"Put your bucket so it won't tip, Little Hawk."

"I could learn everything you know, sometime or another."

"Mind you don't get berry juice on my croker sacks."

121

"I'd get up early every morning and make the coffee so you could sleep late."

"I never minded getting up early."

"Yessir, but if you were to want to sleep late, I'd get up early and do it."

McCree started the engine and it roared through the rusted muffler. A covey of water birds took flight all around them, startled.

"See," Terry said, lifting his voice, "the truth is, I think they're about to kick me out back at the camp."

"Don't say," McCree commented.

"I think they're getting tired of having an orphan kid around, to tell the truth."

"To tell the truth," McCree repeated.

"See, Mr. McCree, Renée—she's the one who makes my sandwiches, remember?"

"I remember."

"Well, even Renée said she was getting a little tired of having to sack up food for me every day. I told her it was all right and how much I appreciated her doing it all this time. I told her I knew how to find something to eat all around me, just like you showed me. I told her about how bamboo was something you can eat, if you know what to look for and how to cook it."

"That appeal to her?"

"Didn't seem to. I think she likes hamburgers."

McCree nodded.

"Anyhow," Terry said, watching for clues in the old man's eyes, "I was thinking about it."

"Thinking about what, Little Hawk?"

"About—I don't know."

They jostled toward McCree's shack. Terry stared out the opened window of the pickup, his seat stabbing with each bounce, a wild spring in the upholstery poking at him.

"I got some venison for supper, Little Hawk."

"Good."

"You like venison."

"Yessir."

"I'm out of limes, though. Reckon you could pick a few?"

"Yessir."

McCree detoured along a dike, following a road only his eyes seemed to see, the front bumper of the truck pushing through tall weeds.

"Best roll up the window awhile," McCree said, cranking his shut. Terry did this.

"Why?" he asked.

"Remember that bull we saw die?"

Terry remembered. They'd been in a marshy bog out toward Kramer Island. Several huge Brahma bulls were grazing, and the unexpected appearance of two humans spooked them. The bulls dashed away, and suddenly the sky was dark with a swarm of disturbed mosquitoes. The insects swirled like dust, covering the bulls in a living, writhing mass. McCree had snatched Terry up and run instantly, seeking the upwind side of the roaring cloud. From a safe point, they had turned to see one of the bulls go down, his eyes, ears, nostrils filled with mosquitoes. The suffocated steer lay covered with undulating waves of insects.

They reached the lime trees, stunted, abandoned by somebody years before. They picked all they wanted and drove away. They didn't raise any clouds of mosquitoes.

10

Gerald sat in the living room, posed as though reading the newspaper, but his mind wasn't on the headlines. From the radio came short bursts of laughter and Molly's voice digging at Fibber McGee.

Mickey rocked gently, knitting booties. She gasped as a fetal foot jabbed her ribs, taking her breath.

"Gerald, do you think we should call someone?"

He turned his paper, refolding it. Mickey's hands flicked by rote, without conscious thought to her handicraft.

"Gerald, do you think we should call the sheriff?"

"What?"

"Please turn down the radio, Gerald."

"Oh. I'm sorry."

In a lower voice, Mickey restated her question, "Should we call the sheriff, Gerald?"

"No. He'll be along. He's been later than this many times."

Mickey put her knitting aside. She rose with great effort, pausing to gain her feet and recapture normal breathing. She went into the kitchen, aimlessly. Had she marked today's date off the calendar? She couldn't remember.

"What is today?"

"I can't hear you from in there!"

Louder, "What is the date?"

Gerald appeared in the door, paper in hand. "Mickey,

why do you walk into another room and then start a conversation?"

"What day is this?"

He checked the paper. "Thursday, November nineteenth."

She crossed off the date. Two weeks more. She put water on the stove to heat. Somewhere far back in the camp a radio blared, too loudly. Raucous laughter came from the same direction.

"Mickey, do you realize how many labor strikes there've been this year?"

"Gerald, where could he be? It's almost eight o'clock."

"He'll be along." Gerald read from the paper, " 'Executives of the Big Five operating railroad brotherhoods have set December seventh as the date of their scheduled strike.' That's going to hurt the vegetable growers around here. It'll probably cut down on migrant workers arriving, too. I must remember to mention that to Marilyn."

"Gerald," quietly, "please put down the paper."

"Don't worry, Mickey. He'll be along. What time is it?"

"Almost eight." Mickey pushed past him to the living room. She grabbed up her knitting and walked toward the bedroom. The radio garbled as Gerald changed stations. Mickey flicked on the bedroom light and started to enter when something across the hall caught her eye. She stared into the dark. By turning on the hall light she saw more clearly—a huddled form in Terrell's bed. She went in and pulled back the cover slightly.

A sound of even breathing. Mouth open, face filthy, Terrell was asleep. His clothes had been discarded, lying in a heap on the floor at the foot of the bed. Mickey shuddered, relieved. She placed her feet far apart, held the bedstead for support and picked up the dirty clothes. These she put in a hamper in the bathroom. She doused the hall and her bedroom lights.

Drew Pearson's staccato delivery held Gerald, head close to the radio speakers, elbows on his knees. Mickey returned to the kitchen and made a cup of weak tea.

When the news was over, she said, "Terrell is home."

"Send him in here, Mickey."

"He's asleep."

Gerald moved toward the hallway.

"Don't wake him, Gerald."

"Why not?"

"He's been here long enough to be sound asleep. There's no telling when he came. I keep latching his window, but he must have unlocked it before leaving today. He sneaked in. Anyway, he'll need his strength for tomorrow."

"Mickey, I think I should spank that boy."

"Not tonight. Another night. Let him sleep."

Gerald stood there a long time, looking at her. Finally, in a low voice, he said, "I suppose you're right. I'm going to take a bath and go to bed." Mickey nodded, sipping tea.

"Terrell, so far as I'm concerned, you should be worn within an inch of your life."

"Yessir, Daddy."

"You have lied to your mother. You have lied to me. You put those frogs in Mrs. Wright's desk, then had someone else write a note about it, pretending it was your mother's note."

"Yessir, Daddy."

"Your mother is having a hard enough time, expecting the baby, without this nonsense from you. This morning you are going to school. I am going to drive you there. When school is over, your mother and I will meet you at Mrs. Wright's room and we're all going to the principal's office to see Miss Ramsey."

"Yessir, Daddy." Terry sat, back straight, both hands

127

holding the seat of his chair at his sides; he followed every move Gerald made with wide eyes, made every response in a trembling, small voice.

"Now, Terrell, I want to tell you, if I did what I think I ought to, you wouldn't be able to walk for a week."

"Yessir, Daddy."

"Get your teeth brushed, comb your hair and get ready for school!"

Terry slipped off the chair and ran to the bathroom. Throughout breakfast, Mama had said nothing. During Daddy's angry statements, she did not speak. Terry wet the soap, put it in the dish, wiped his hands on a towel. He wet his toothbrush, replaced it, then smoothed his hair with a brush and ran back to the dining room.

"Are you ready?"

"Yessir, Daddy."

"Get in the car."

"Yessir." He ran to the automobile and got in. When Daddy arrived, he tossed Terry's lunch on the seat. Daddy rammed the car into reverse and backed out, peering through the rear window. Terry kept swallowing, although his tongue was tinder dry, the effort producing odd gurgles in his ears.

Daddy circled the school building, pausing as students lowered yellow flags on poles to hold traffic back as other children crossed the street. Arriving at the rear of the high school, Daddy reached across and opened Terry's door, face grim.

"When school is out, Terrell, wait in Mrs. Wright's room. Do you understand that?"

"Yessir."

"What did I just say?"

"Stay after school. In Mrs. Wright's room."

"Your mother and I will meet you there."

"Yessir, Daddy."

"Terrell!"

He turned, almost to the covered walkway, quivering.

"You are forgetting your lunch."

Terry returned, accepted it. He hesitated.

"What is it?" Daddy demanded.

"Do you know what kind of sandwiches these are?"

"No. Go to class."

"Yessir." Terry ran up the walk. When he had not heard the engine start, he turned and glanced back. Daddy was watching him. Terry saw that most of the students were still in the school yard. The teacher assigned for early-hours duty was observing them stoically. Terry entered the building. Inside the door, he stopped, listening. The motor started, tires crunched on gravel.

Instantly, Terry stepped out and saw Daddy's car circle away. Terry broke for the yard, running as fast as he could. He ran between girls doing double jump rope, shoved aside Eddy Kent and was happy to see the curly haired tattler spill headlong in the dirt, screeching in protest. Terry hit the crossing board as two older students were coming over it.

"Hey!" Terry's momentum carried him through the flailing boys and he heard cursing, water splashing. He spun as another boy grabbed him. He heard his shirt rip.

"Catch him!" one of the boys in the canal cried.

He reached the packing-house ramp, his legs churning. Behind him, a clatter of planks told him older feet were in hot pursuit. Terry ducked for the escape tunnel near the washing machine, crawling, shins skinned but the pain ignored. He reached the far side, heard panting sounds in the dark behind him. He looked up and an older boy came around the mountain of crates. He was trapped.

Terry leaped from the platform into an open boxcar, ran through it, out the other side, ducked back and darted beneath the car and under the packing house. Across a feeder track, into another packing house. This

129

one was primarily for storage, heavy with musky odors of dry sacks, dusty floors, the cavernous building momentarily blinding him until his eyes adjusted to the faint light filtering from tiny windows several stories up.

"There he goes!"

Terry recognized one of the students from the dunking, heard a squish of water-filled shoes. He ran behind some machinery, clambered atop crates, crouched, heart pounding.

"Where'd he go?"

"Up there, I think."

"You circle around that way. Somebody climb up and knock him down."

Terry squeezed between a thick I-beam and a huge box. A button snagged, pulled loose.

"There he is!"

"Where?"

"Up there. Get him!" Terry counted four of them. He jumped an astounding span between crates, the dizzying distance to the floor a flash beneath him.

"Get him! Get him!"

There was no way to double back; they had him blocked. His only escape now lay in the yawning door at the building's end, past an office from which adults were now appearing to chase them all away. Outside, Terry would be no match for the older, stronger boys. He was about to be—

He burst into the open like a hunted rabbit, ducking, dodging past two warehouse men who were now shouting to the building at large, ". . . trespassing . . . get out . . . out . . . out . . ."

He vaulted the loading ramp and wham! He heard wind go from a man's lungs, arms involuntarily thrown around Terry as he sank into the man's belly.

"What the—"

"Please," Terry cried, "four boys—going to beat me up."

"Four boys?" The man's automobile was filled with
130

black suitcases on rollers, pamphlets, the gear of a salesman.

Over the ramp came the pursuers, intent for the moment on eluding the warehouse guards, jumping blindly, and finding themselves fenced between the warehouse wall, the salesman's car and the large man himself, who was pulling off a wide, thick leather belt.

"Be ashamed of yourselves," the salesman said, grabbing one sopping boy, the others too stunned to move. Whap! The belt fell across the boy's buttocks and he screamed. Whap! Terry stood behind the salesman, not daring to move, whap!

"Hey, mister, wait a minute, we—"

Whap! The second boy tried to walk on air and was lifted bodily, the strap falling with a well-placed and forceful delivery.

Two crying, the third snared as he tried to scramble over the hood of the car. Glimpsing freedom, the fourth boy was off and running. The salesman hauled in his next victim and Terry heard a squeak of palms on metal, fingernails screeching as he clawed for a hold. Whap! Whap! Whap!

The salesman let them go, crying all of them, rubbing their legs and bottoms. He began to pass his belt through the loops of his trousers, turned and looked at Terry. He winked. Terry grinned and winked back.

"We got 'em, partner."

"Sure did. Thanks."

"Anytime."

Terry trotted toward the Blue Goose Packing Company grinning, laughing to himself, and slightly fearful of what another day might bring.

"Gerald."

"Yes, Mickey."

"Terrell didn't go to school."

"Mickey, I took him myself. I saw him enter."

"He's not there." Mickey's breathing sounded short on the telephone.

"I can't believe this," Gerald said. "Mickey, can you believe this?"

"No."

"Well," Gerald kneaded his forehead. "Well, Mickey. Damn. I don't know what to do."

"What about the meeting this afternoon?"

"Oh—"

"Miss Ramsey thought perhaps we'd kept Terrell out on purpose this morning, because of that."

"What did you tell her?"

"I didn't tell her anything. I let her believe it. What was I supposed to do? Admit we lost him somewhere between your car and the classroom door?"

"No. No. You did right on that. Good Lord, Mickey. I don't know what to say. I—I'm stunned."

He thought he heard her laugh.

"Are you laughing?"

Calmly, "I think I'm getting hysterical."

Gerald laughed now.

"Are you laughing?" Mickey asked.

"I think *I'm* getting hysterical."

Mickey sighed, a rush of air in Gerald's ear. "Gerald, you realize what this is probably going to bring about, don't you?"

"I'm afraid so."

"My mind is numb," Mickey said. "Do you have any suggestions?"

"We could go look for him."

"You'll never find him."

"I know that. Hell, I don't know. I guess I'd better call the principal and Miss Ramsey. You wouldn't do that for me, would you?"

"No," Mickey said, "I wouldn't."

"I'll have to tell them something."

The truth was out of the question. Mickey said, "How about this: Miss Ramsey, we slaughtered the little
132

criminal before he went on to something serious like stealing candy and trinkets from the five and dime."

"Mickey," Gerald was serious, "let me see if I can get the meeting postponed, at least. I'll say we sent Terrell to Tampa to see a—a psychiatrist."

"Are you kidding?"

"Why not?"

"Why not," Mickey said.

Mr. McCree was not at his shack when Terry arrived. The boy dawdled around the building for a while, peeked in at the rattlesnakes and then trudged back to LuBelle's place.

"Look what we got for Mr. Cree," LuBelle gloated. She held up a wide-mouth gallon jar almost filled with Cecropia-moth cocoons.

"You and Eunice got those?"

"LuBelle, mostly," Eunice said. She was folding laundry and placing it in neat stacks for delivery to the owners.

"Where'd you find them all?" Terry asked, envious of the praise he knew the cocoons would bring from McCree.

"They hang on a limb," LuBelle said. "There's a heap of them, mostly on citrus trees back along the dike."

"Yeah? Listen, LuBelle, will you show me where?"

The black girl looked at Eunice. Eunice was putting the clothes into a tremendous woven basket.

"I got to go to town," Eunice said, by way of reply to the unasked question. "If you two stays together, I'm of a mind to let you go. Watch for snakes, though."

"Yes ma'am, we will."

"Boy, don't say *ma'am* to me!"

"Yes ma'am, Eunice."

Eunice twisted a bandana around itself until it was one rolled, thick strand. She tied the ends together, forming a ring, and placed this flat atop her head. It

133

was on this that the basket of clothes would ride as Eunice walked along, both hands free, nearly four miles to town.

Terry followed the naked girl, weaving her way through thickets, crawling under matted webs of vegetation, artfully skirting areas known to be infested with sand spurs, bogs, mosquitoes, chiggers, ticks or thorns.

"If you picks them by the juicy parts," LuBelle tutored, speaking of the cocoons, "they sometimes squishes right in your hand. Best to pick it by the stem. You can feel them wiggling inside."

"You can?"

"Sure nuff. Wait until we find one and I'll show you."

They walked, heads down, vigilant for the lurking threat of inert reptiles. Gnats swarmed constantly, the drone of tiny wings multipled as the pests darted for eyes, saliva on the lips or wax in the ears.

"See here!" LuBelle indicated a stalactite of living pupa as long as Terry's little finger, but thicker. It hung, motionless, beneath the branch of a wild lime tree. LuBelle demonstrated the necessity for grasping the cocoon by the stem and snapped it off. She put it in a paper sack they'd brought. Then, remembering, she withdrew it and squeezed it slightly.

"Feel," she whispered. Terry put his fingers against the cocoon and the dormant creature pulsated, twisting in the cell of its own making.

"Wonder what's inside," Terry mused.

"Gushies."

"Gushies?"

"Guts and stuff. Dont look like nothing but guts. Want to break it open?"

"No. I reckon it hurts the moth."

"Must be, but he don't say nothing. Not a peep."

"I don't want to break it, though."

They spent the entire day gathering cocoons. Fearful that those on bottom would be crushed, they made a mistake and spread several dozens of the cocoons under a shade tree. When they returned, ants had infested the harvest and the cocoons were writhing and lost.

"You think Mr. Cree be happy with what we got?" LuBelle asked, walking now back toward her house.

"Ought to be."

"Reckon maybe he give us something for picking all them coons?"

"I don't know," Terry said. "Some sassafras tea, maybe."

"Sassafras tea! I mean something *special!*"

"I don't know, LuBelle."

McCree didn't show up that day. When evening came, LuBelle poked fresh kindling into the stove and expertly sloshed kerosene over it before striking a match. Flames belched and Terry heard LuBelle's kinked hair sizzle.

"You hurt?" Terry asked.

"Ain't got no eyebrows left."

"Did it hurt you?"

"No." LuBelle pushed at the open stove lid with a lift-handle and, having recapped it, maneuvered a pot of leftover beans into place.

"Ain't supposed to let the fire die down nohow," she said. "Mawmaw gets mad when I do."

"She ought to be back before now, shouldn't she?" Terry asked. He was looking out the window at the setting sun.

"Sometimes early, sometimes late," LuBelle intoned.

They lit a lantern, ate beans at the bare table, watching insects bump the glass cover over the flickering wick.

"Can I spend the night here, LuBelle?"

"Sure nuff."

"Reckon Eunice will care?"

"No. You can sleep with me."

"Did you latch his window screens?" Gerald questioned.

"Yes." Mickey washed the last of the dishes and put them in a drying rack.

"Then he has to come through the door."

"If he comes at all."

"What does that mean, Mickey?"

"I don't know. I just said it."

"You think he might not come home?"

Mickey gazed at her husband evenly. "Would you?"

Gerald sipped cold coffee. "He'll be home."

They sat in the living room until the last radio program ended and an announcer gave blue, then red network time checks.

"Has he ever stayed out this late before?" Gerald asked softly.

"No."

"Any idea where he might be?"

Mickey controlled her voice. "None whatsoever."

"He knows about—things—"

"Things like what?" Mickey's hands had stopped knitting.

"You know. Canals. Sleeping in the cane fields. He knows about that."

"How do you know he knows?" Mickey questioned.

"He told me."

"What?"

"He told me a horrible story about a woman who got eaten by rats when she couldn't get up after an accident. Out by a canal somewhere, I think."

"Dear God, Gerald."

"I mention that to reassure you, Mickey. He knows about such things. He told me never go to sleep or even lie down in cane fields or swamps."

"Gerald, for God's sake!"

Gerald stood abruptly and went into the kitchen to prepare fresh coffee. He noticed his hand was shaking when the lid of the pot tinkled rhythmically.

"I think we should call the sheriff's office, Gerald."

"Let's wait awhile longer."

"I know why you say that," Mickey reasoned. "That's my first inclination, too, frankly. But what if he's lost, or kidnapped?"

"Nobody kidnaps anybody anymore. Not since they executed Bruno Hauptmann for the Lindbergh baby."

Gerald took Mickey's arm and eased her into a chair at the kitchen table.

"Let's be realistic," Gerald said hoarsely. "If Terry is with a friend, afraid to come home, the fear will pass. When it does, he'll come in here expecting to get his little fanny worn out. Which, I swear, he will get. If we call in Sheriff Lambert, Ike Franklin and Miss Ramsey will hear about it and we'll be in court fighting for that boy. Now Mickey, I still stand by Terrell on all this. That boy is all boy. He's going to have to be punished, but my Lord, Mickey—he's just a Tom Sawyer and Huck Finn kind of kid, that's all!"

"Remember that," Mickey said, "when you try to explain all this to Judge Franklin."

11

Gerald had been watching through the bedroom window for Marilyn's automobile. When she drove up, parking at the administration building, he dialed the phone. It was ringing when Marilyn unlocked the office door.

"Marilyn, I won't be in today."

"All right, Mr. Calder. What should I do about Randy Adams?"

"What about him?"

"He said that Japanese family has been camping on his back porch all night. Several of their neighbors threatened them."

"Tell them—tell them to go home!"

"Home where, Mr. Calder?"

"Back to the house. Tell them—never mind, I'll call Randy."

He hung up, lifted the receiver and dialed.

"Randy, this is Gerald Calder."

"What'm I going to do with these Japs?"

"What's the trouble?"

"Their neighbors chased them out last evening."

"Send them home, Randy. Tell their neighbors if we have any more trouble from them, *they* will have to leave, not the Japanese."

"If you say so, Mr. Calder."

"Can you handle it, Randy?"

"I don't want to. But I can."

"Good man. Thanks." A mental note to check the

other camp for the first available house. Gerald went to bathe, shave and dress.

He swirled his shaving brush in a cup, working up lather. He started to apply the soap and stood looking at his reflection. Was he getting gray? He turned his head aside, looking. His face was lined, and even to himself, he looked weary. He covered the wrinkles with suds.

Dr. Norman was right. He needed a vacation. His hands were shaking. Letting things get to him. Gut-knotting worry over the damned world, more worry about community repercussions from the new camp. There'd been isolated incidents on the construction site—a boulder in a water main that required digging up a quarter-mile of pipe. He couldn't be sure it was deliberate. But he suspected as much.

Gerald pulled his cheek taut, razor scraping, burning his flesh.

If there was war, he was sure to be called up. Overseas duty was likely. He had become obsessed with getting things in order for Mickey's sake. He had told her nothing about it, in fact, had tried to minimize his concern so she wouldn't worry. Now this business with Terrell. When he found that boy—

"You want me to answer that, Gerald?"

"What, Mickey?"

"You want me to answer the phone?"

He grabbed a hand towel and took the call in the living room.

"Mr. Calder, this is Bert Arthur, Washington."

Gerald's stomach twisted. "Morning, Mr. Arthur."

"Mrs. Roosevelt has taken an interest in your work down there. More precisely, the President is aware of your work."

"I see."

"They want you to manage the new migratory labor camp there, Mr. Calder."

"The black camp."

140

"Yes. Is that acceptable to you?"

Gerald's long pause made Bert Arthur add, "There's a twenty percent raise in pay."

"Mr. Arthur—I wonder if I could have time to think about this?"

"Jesus, man, don't tell me you don't want it! Mrs. Roosevelt practically assured us you were the man for the job. Furthermore, she—at least we thought—she assured us you wanted it!"

"It isn't that I don't want it," Gerald said. "I would like a day or so to discuss it with—"

"I'm afraid you don't understand, Mr. Calder."

"Understand what?"

"A news release has already gone out on this."

"Isn't that irregular, Mr. Arthur? Before notifying me, I mean?"

"Jesus, Calder! This could be very embarrassing for the administration. We bypassed several people with seniority to do this."

"Bullshit," Gerald snapped. "Nobody else wanted it and you know it. This news release crap is to box me in."

"Not true, Calder. Not true. Mrs. Roosevelt came back here glowing about your rapport with those people, the high respect you've earned in the community, your press relations—"

"Listen, Mr. Arthur," Gerald interrupted, "all I want is a day—I'll call you tomorrow morning. Is that all right?"

"Mr. Calder, perhaps I can wring a few more dollars out of the budget. This camp is important."

"I know it's important."

"No, I mean *important*. Politically. We need a man who can make a model of it. We think you're the one for this job. It could boost you right along with everybody here in Washington, if you know what I mean."

"I'll call you in the morning, Mr. Arthur."

"Calder!"

"Yes?"

"This is very important, Mr. Calder."

"I understand. Don't worry about it. I'll probably take it."

"That's what I want to hear."

"Call you tomorrow."

"Good man!"

Hadn't he just said those same words to Randy? Gerald hung up.

"Who was it, Gerald?"

"The office."

"What's the trouble?"

"No trouble. Get some rest, Mickey."

"Do you want breakfast before you go to the office?"

Gerald walked into the bedroom. "I'm not going to the office, Mickey. I'm going to find Terrell."

"You know you won't find him, Gerald."

"Nonetheless, I'm going to try."

"Want me to go with you?"

"No. No need in that. I'm going to try to locate that Bucky boy—what's his name?"

"Bucky Dallas. I think he lives near the packing house. His father sells ice, I seem to recall."

"I'll start there."

Mickey looked tired, her complexion pallid, circles under her eyes. Gerald took her shoulders, maneuvering her back onto the bed. He sat beside her.

"You have shaving cream on your face."

"I got interrupted."

The phone rang again. Gerald snatched it up. "Hello!"

"Mr. Calder, this is Marilyn. There's some trouble in Section Four. That's where the Japanese family is."

"All right, Marilyn. I'm on my way."

"Shall I call the police?"

"Not until we're sure they're needed, Marilyn." He hung up, wiping lather from his face. "I have to go,
142

Mickey. I'll call later in the day. You rest. You need it. Please. Rest."

He was almost running to his automobile.

The disturbance was over when Gerald arrived. A small group of angry men and women shouted insults from the street at the asbestos-siding dwelling assigned to the Japanese.

"What's going on here?" Gerald demanded.

"Is this a white camp, or not?"

"It is."

"Then what're them Japs doing here?"

Gerald spoke with a calm he didn't feel. "Those people are here because they have nowhere else to go. The man has a wife and small children. They can't sleep in the swamps any more than you can. He is like all of you—he needs a roof, sanitary facilities, a place to launder his clothing, a way to cook his food. Now I want you people to get back to your homes and leave this family alone."

The authority in his tone brought them up short. Gerald lowered his voice to a growl, "Any more trouble and you will be packing your bags. Do I make myself clear?"

They left, sulking, talking in low voices. Randy Adams stood beside Gerald. "That ain't the end of it, you can bet on it."

"One day at a time, Randy. Have Marilyn get these people relocated at the other camp when the first house is completed."

"There won't be enough houses over there for the families trying to get in now. I asked Marilyn about that, yesterday."

"Why didn't you call me about this yesterday, Randy?"

The foreman's expression softened. "You got enough troubles, Mr. Calder, one thing and another. I tried to handle it long as I could."

The two men regarded one another for a long moment. Gerald managed a smile and put a hand on Randy's shoulder. "Thanks." He returned to his car, drove home and finished shaving.

"Gerald, Miss Ramsey called. That woman! She asked me for the name of the doctor we sent Terrell to see. As though she didn't believe us."

"Don't worry about it. I'll call her."

"The nerve of that woman!"

"Mickey, don't lose sight of something here."

"What?"

"We did lie. Terrell isn't in Tampa at any doctor's office. I suggest we handle Miss Ramsey with care until I get Terrell back in this house. Don't get snippy with her."

Mickey sank into a kitchen chair.

"I'll find Terrell," Gerald said. "Try to get some rest, will you?"

Mickey nodded dumbly.

"What's for breakfast?" Terry questioned Eunice. The black woman stood with feet planted apart, the back of one hand propped on a hip, stirring a saucepan with a wooden spoon.

"Tater pancakes," Eunice said.

"Great! I love tater pancakes."

"Boy, your mama know where you was last night?"

"I don't have a mama."

Eunice turned, pointing her spoon at Terry. "Don't come telling Eunice no lies, boy!"

Terry shrank internally, struggling to hold his ground. "I ain't got no mama! I ain't got no daddy!"

"Who looks after you then?"

"Lots of people. Like you're doing right now."

Eunice glared at him, black eyes sparkling. She began stirring the potatoes again, mixing in chopped onions before putting patties in a hot skillet.

"Get on some clothes, boy."

"Yes ma'am."

"And don't say ma'am to me!"

"Yes ma'am, Eunice." Eunice studied him a moment, walked to a pile of clean clothes and selected a shirt and trousers. She thrust these at Terry.

"Don't reckon they'll ever know you wore 'em once," she rationalized. "Get dressed. You and LuBelle wash some of that muck off your faces and hands."

"Yes ma'am, Eunice." Terry and LuBelle went out to wash up in a dishpan of water on the back steps. The brown soap was strong, burning scratches on their arms and wrists.

"Eunice mad with me?" Terry whispered. LuBelle's eyes widened as her shoulders lifted, then dropped, expressing a lack of certainty.

"Reckon I ought to go?"

Another shrug.

"Boy?"

Terry jumped, startled. He hadn't known Eunice was standing at a window listening.

"Yes ma'am, Eunice?"

"Finish up the washing and get yourself in here. I ain't mad with you."

She was standing at the table putting potato pancakes on their plates when Terry and LuBelle sat down. LuBelle reached for a fork and began eating. Terry sat looking at her.

"What's the matter?" Eunice asked.

"Aren't we going to have the blessing?"

LuBelle held a fork halfway to her open mouth, eyes cutting at Eunice.

"Certainly, we going to have the blessing! Put that food down, LuBelle! Ask it, child," Eunice said to Terry.

"Heavenly Father give us thankful hearts for this and all other blessings, we ask in Christ's name. Amen."

He lifted his head to find Eunice staring at him with an odd expression.

"Can I eat now?" LuBelle asked, voice low.

"Help yourself."

Gerald pulled up the emergency brake and stepped out of the car. He was acutely aware of the mounting heat. He glanced at the packing houses where men were taking a cigarette break, talking. He approached the icehouse.

"Is Bucky here?"

"Who're you?"

"I'm Gerald Calder," Gerald extended his hand. "Terrell Calder is my son."

The man contemplated the outstretched hand, then hesitantly and limply shook it.

"I was hoping Bucky had seen my son," Gerald said. "He—he didn't come home last night."

The overt distrust slowly melted. "Excuse my manners, Mr. Calder. I thought you was some of them meddling school folks again. They've been sticking their noses in and around here of late."

Gerald nodded. The man went to a thick insulated door and pulled it open. He hollered into the refrigerator, "Bucky! Bucky! Come out here."

The cross-eyed child appeared wearing a heavy apron, oversized rubber boots and gloves. A set of tongs hung from a rope tied around his waist.

"Hi, Mr. Calder."

Satisfied, the man walked away, calling back, "Don't be long, Bucky. We got six thousand pounds to shred and blow this morning."

"Yessir, Pa."

"Bucky, have you seen Terrell?"

"Who?"

"My son, Terrell."

"Terrell!" Bucky laughed, pulling off his gloves. "I'll tease him plenty about that."

"What do you call him?"

"Terry."

"Have you seen him?"

"Got a cigarette, Mr. Calder?"

"Cigarette? Oh, yes, of course. Your father doesn't—"

"He don't give a shit, long as they ain't his. Thanks; got a light?"

The boy inhaled deeply. "Terry gone?"

"We haven't seen him since yesterday morning."

"He's something else, that kid. He said he was going to run away, but I didn't believe he'd really do it. I tried to scare him a little, telling him how kids got cornholed in the hoosegow."

A chill traced Gerald's shoulders, rippled down his spine, erupted on his arms. He watched the child take another experienced puff, inhale, hold it.

"Would you have any idea where Terry might be, Bucky?"

"Ain't no telling. I haven't seen him today or yesterday."

"Could you make a guess, perhaps? I thought he might have stayed with a friend."

"He ain't got no friends. Except maybe me."

Bucky examined his cigarette with the cocked eye, head turned. He made a spitting sound, as though tobacco was stuck to his lip.

"He could've got a freight going anyplace," Bucky said. "He knows all the train men. Knows how to read the codes on the cars."

"You think he did that?"

"There ain't no telling. You know he whipped three boys from the eighth grade yesterday?"

"Whipped three boys!"

"Got them whipped, anyway."

"Then you did see Terrell—Terry—yesterday."

"I didn't see him. I heard about the fight. That's all the kids been talking about. Wait until they hear that little shit took off."

"Bucky, the less people who know about this, the easier it will be on Terry when he returns."

"Maybe with teachers. With kids around here, he'll be a foot taller. Besides, if Terry ran away, chances are he ain't coming back."

Gerald fought an irrational compulsion to vomit. He reminded himself this was a *child* he was talking to.

"You could throw him in the swamp buck-ass naked and he wouldn't go hungry. He learned that from the old man."

"What old man?"

Bucky's tone was suddenly wary. "An old man he knows. I forget his name."

"I'd appreciate it if you could remember."

"I forget. Listen, can you spare another smoke for later?"

Gerald held out the entire package.

"How many?" Bucky inquired.

"All of them. You sure you couldn't remember the old man's name, Bucky? Terry's mother is not well."

"About to drop a baby, ain't she?"

"Yes. Soon. She's having a tough time of it. She's worried about Terry, of course."

"Don't worry about him."

"But we do, Bucky. He's only six years old. His mother—I—we are very worried. I'd like to find this old man, or anyone else who may know where Terry is. Just knowing Terry is all right, not hungry, not sick—"

Gerald wasn't sure whether Bucky was gazing into space pensively or at him directly.

"Mac something," Bucky said. "I met him only once, a week or two back. Mac somebody."

Gerald nodded, Bucky pocketed the cigarettes.

"Godamighty, Bucky, get your ass on it! Here come them fruit cars now and you ain't even got the ice out here!"

Gerald watched Bucky put a foot against the ice-

148

house wall, gaining leverage to pull open the heavy refrigerator door.

"Dear God," Gerald whispered. He returned to his car, drove directly to a grocery store and bought another package of cigarettes.

Terry spent the day with LuBelle, both of them going to seek more cocoons. He wanted as many as possible when he approached Mr. McCree.

"Reckon I could spend the night with you again, LuBelle?"

"I don't know. We can ask Mawmaw."

"You think she'll care?"

"I don't know." LuBelle scratched her belly with long pulls of her small hand, nails digging.

Terry's heart was pounding when he confronted Eunice. "Reckon maybe I could spend the night again, Eunice?"

"You going to get me in trouble, white boy?"

"No ma'am."

"I don't want no trouble, understand me?"

"No ma'am."

"I'm going to ask you again. You going to get me in trouble?"

"No ma'am, Eunice. I promise."

The sizzle of fatback in a skillet and the bacon smell of it brought saliva to Terry's mouth. Eunice lifted the meat, flipped it, pressed it down.

"One more night ain't going to hurt nothing."

"I can stay?"

"Might as well. You here, ain't you? It's dark, ain't it? Might've asked me earlier in the day."

"I will tomorrow, Eunice."

Suddenly she was on his level, bending, her face close to his. "You can't stay here forever, boy. It ain't cause we don't like you. We do."

"We do," LuBelle's voice came from the bed.

"But boy, there's got to be somebody out there

149

looking for you, worrying about whether you stepped in a quicksand bog, or got 'gator ate, or snakebit, or drowned in a canal. When they find you and you tell them it was Eunice and LuBelle who had you, Lord God, child! There ain't no guessing what they'll do!"

She was holding Terry's shoulders, shaking him gently for emphasis. Her breath smelled like snuff, or chewing tobacco, maybe.

"I'll go tomorrow, Eunice."

"Oh, child."

"If I can stay the night, I won't tell anybody I was here, I promise."

"Oh, child, bless your heart, child, Eunice don't want to drive you away—I wish—I wish to God I could help you."

"Yes ma'am."

She pulled Terry to her, his body mashing her flaccid breasts flat. She stroked the back of his head, his arms pinned by hers.

"Boy," she said, brusquely, "don't say ma'am to me!"

12

It was that twilight time between night sounds and daybreak, the swamp hushed and peaceful. Terry awoke beneath a sheet he and LuBelle had pulled over their heads to ward off mosquitoes. When Terry moved, LuBelle inched closer, seeking warmth. He sat up and peered through a partially closed shutter. Etched against a dawning sky, a spreading poinciana glistened with beads of dew strung through thousands of spiderwebs.

He slipped out of bed, shivering. On bare feet, he quietly found his clothes. *His* clothes that Eunice had washed and pressed, not the borrowed ones from yesterday. From a dark corner came the nasal sounds of Eunice softly snoring.

He moved in a cloak of ground fog, a disembodied red head in a liquid gray field. He ran all the way to McCree's. He found the old man applying a poultice of crushed boneset leaves to Dog's neck.

"What happened to Dog?" Terry questioned, without greeting.

"Snakebit. Dog's not smart about playing with snakes."

"Is he going to die?"

"Reckon not."

"Need some help."

"There's water boiling inside. Suppose you could pour it over some camphor leaves in a bowl?"

"I think so."

"Mind you don't get burnt. I don't have time to tend two hurt critters."

Terry carefully poured the bubbling liquid over fragrant leaves McCree had prepared. The aroma was similar to that of salves Mama rubbed on Terry's chest when he had a cold.

"What do I do with it now?" Terry called.

"Leave it awhile to cool. Later I'll put a little on Dog's neck. It holds down pain and soreness."

Terry squatted, knees under his arms, hands clasped beneath his chin, watching.

"LuBelle and I got a lot of Cecropia cocoons."

"Did you?"

"Couple hundred."

"How many is a hundred?"

Ten flicks of ten fingers. "Times two," Terry added. "I asked for permission to stay with you tonight," Terry said.

"That a fact?"

"Tonight and tomorrow night, if you want me."

McCree tied the poultice to Dog's neck with a bandana. He lowered the animal to the ground and Dog went to a favorite hollow under the shack.

"Can I stay tonight—and tomorrow night?"

McCree cut a plug of Bull of the Wood. "If it's all right with everybody."

"Like who?"

"Oh," McCree pushed against his knees, standing, "the folks you stay with. I wouldn't want them worrying."

"They won't worry," Terry said. "I told them where I'd be. It's okay."

McCree nodded. "You can go with me down in the glades then."

"Yeah!"

"Don't reckon you've had a bite to eat."

"No sir."

"Come on, Little Hawk."

McCree loaded a wide, flat-bottomed boat into his truck. He threw in a long, slender pole he favored for pushing the craft through shallow water.

The last traces of lingering fog were burning away under a rising sun when they drove through Belle Glade. The sight of the school yard gave Terry a secret shiver.

"I'm glad I don't have to go to school," Terry commented.

"I expect you'll like it when the time comes," McCree said. "You'll learn some interesting things."

"Like what?"

"About the world. Other countries. They teach you history."

"I wouldn't like that."

"Know how many cups of seeds make a bushel?"

"It's a basketful."

"Baskets aren't all the same size, Little Hawk. Two cups make a pint. Two pints make a quart. Eight quarts make a peck. Four pecks make a bushel. So how many cups of seeds make a bushel?"

"I don't know."

"That's what you'd know by going to school."

"How many cups make a bushel?"

"A hundred twenty-eight."

"Tell it to me again."

McCree repeated the dry measures. Terry whispered them to himself before asking. "Tell me one more time."

McCree did this, then said, "Now you tell me."

"Two cups make a pint. Two pints make a quart. Eight quarts make a peck. Four pecks make a bushel. There are one hundred and twenty-eight cups in a bushel."

"How many in a pint?"

Hesitation. "Two?"

"A peck?"

"I don't know."

"I thought you was pretty smart."

"I don't know how to figure it. I get mixed up."

"Write it down."

"I can't write!"

"You learn that in school."

They drove along, jolting, turning, leaving the paved road finally to push through an endless sea of grass tipped brown from lack of rain.

"Thirty-two," Terry said.

"What, Little Hawk?"

"There're thirty-two cups in a peck."

McCree laughed, his stained teeth flashing a moment. "Thirty-two it is."

"Reckon I could drive awhile, Mr. McCree?"

"Might as well as not," McCree said. "Come on over."

He had done this several times, always in the open glades where there were few obstacles to hit. Terry climbed between the old man's bony legs, gripping the shuddering steering wheel with both hands. McCree worked the gas, gearshift and clutch when the need arose, Terry steering with a face-stretching smile.

"Mind you don't run over the Spanish bayonets, boy!" Terry barely missed the spiked yucca plant, the vehicle bouncing as it struck an unseen hole. He heard the boat clatter in the back. McCree grunted but didn't reach for the wheel.

"Go a little to your left," McCree instructed. A moment of thought, which hand, then Terry did as told.

"That-a-boy! We have to go a bit faster now, so we don't stall and get stuck. You ready?"

"Ready!"

McCree's foot pushed down and the swish of grass intensified as the vehicle lunged through the glade, tires spinning now and then as they hit wet places, then

154

throwing them back against the seat as traction was regained.

"Faster?" McCree said, in Terry's ear.

"Faster!"

The passing vegetation was a blur, the wheel vibrant in Terry's hands. The floorboard beneath his bare feet shimmied with the efforts of the motor, relaying the impact of the tires over rough spots.

"Faster?" McCree yelled.

"Yessir!"

Terry felt McCree's leg tighten as the old man's foot pinned the accelerator to the floor. Breathless, the scream of the engine drowning all else, Terry turned this way and that as McCree shouted orders. The truck lurched, wheels slipping, and a wall of water rose before them and doused the windshield. The unexpected obstacle made Terry jerk back, and McCree's breath was warm on his neck as the old man laughed loud and hard.

They came to a halt beside a stand of cabbage palmettos towering high above the truck. "Good growth of zamia over there," McCree commented. "Indians made flour from the roots of zamia years ago."

Terry scampered onto the truck bed, getting the pole as McCree put his boat into water. They threw in several burlap sacks, a jug of tea and camping supplies.

"Best rub mud on your arms and face, Little Hawk. Otherwise you'll spend your energy fighting mosquitoes and gnats."

The smelly mud, scooped from underwater, dried to a cracked glaze on face, neck and arms.

"Makes us look like alligator skins," Terry said.

"Can't say it improves our looks," McCree agreed. "Climb in and don't stand up, Little Hawk."

The old man stood toward the rear of the craft, his pole jabbed down, pushing away, then retrieved in long, flowing movements that sent them gliding over mirror-smooth waters. Behind, in a widening vee, the wake rippled under lily pads and rafts of watercress and disappeared in water grasses. As they moved, the truck grew smaller and smaller in the distance.

"Mule-ear orchid over there, Little Hawk."

Terry examined the tall stalks indicated, yellow blossoms spotted brown.

"Won't see many of those," McCree said. "They're getting rare."

"What's happening to them?"

"Folks coming. Like us now. Fetching them away."

"What are we looking for, Mr. McCree?"

"Epiphytes, Little Hawk."

"What is that?"

"That is a plant that gets its nourishment from air, rain, dust. Air plants, flower sellers call them."

The mid-morning still was broken only by water dripping from McCree's pole when it was lifted, poised, the boat riding on momentum.

"Bobcat, Mr. McCree."

"Where?" whispered.

Terry pointed. The tawny cat was statue-still, yellow eyes alert, tufted ears erect. Its front paws submerged, water dribbled from the cat's chin. Then, with a silent bound, the feline disappeared into the underbrush.

"You have sharp eyes, Little Hawk."

But it was the old man who first spied a fox bitch and her cubs playing in a hammock and the nesting mound of a female alligator.

"Where do we look for air plants?" Terry asked.

"Trees with rough bark," McCree said. "Water oaks, mostly. On limbs you'll see them. We're after a particular kind. It's called a butterfly orchid."

When they found the plants, McCree poled his boat under the tree, from where he and Terry climbed up to get them.

"We're going to be covered with chiggers, Mr. McCree."

"I brought some axle-grease salve, Little Hawk."

They worked the afternoon away. The sun was a huge globe settling toward the horizon when McCree called up to Terry. "Best make camp, Little Hawk. Be night before long."

They located high ground and stomped down surrounding grasses to drive away insects. McCree sent Terry to gather firewood. The old man fashioned a lean-to with fronds of palmettos laid like overlapping shingles atop poles tied tepee fashion. So they wouldn't be on the ground, McCree built a hammock in the structure, using bamboo and saplings trimmed of leaves.

"Seminoles call this a chickee," McCree stated, referring to the shelter he'd erected.

To smother the chiggers which were surely on them, they took turns smearing black grease over one another from neck to ankle. The grease had been mixed with a residue rendered from boiled camphor leaves.

From the shallow lake around which they'd been working, McCree dipped water, strained it through cloth to remove algae, then boiled it for purification.

"It's going to be a one-pot meal, Little Hawk."

"Okay."

"Wild potatoes, swamp cabbage and a chunk of pork for seasoning."

"Sounds good."

"Chicory coffee, or tea?"

"Coffee."

"So be it."

With nightfall came a chilled north wind that swept the lake, bending grasses and bringing a chatter to Terry's teeth. McCree gave the boy a dank woolen blanket and put him to bed. Terry felt warmth returning to his extremities as McCree put hot coals in the chickee, covering these with moss to make just enough smoke to drive off nocturnal pests.

"How do you feel, Little Hawk?"

Terry mumbled a satisfied reply, sighed heavily and went to sleep. His last thought before slumber was a vague concern for Mama. He wondered if she was worrying.

"Do you know anybody named Mack something-or-other?" Gerald questioned.

"No," Mickey said. She had been crying.

"An old man."

"No," Mickey repeated.

"The Dallas boy says that the old man taught Terry how to take care of himself in the swamps."

"Gerald, we must go to someone about this. Three nights now. He wouldn't stay gone three nights unless something had happened."

"Mickey, I think we should try to find him ourselves, first."

"But you didn't find him!"

"No, not today."

"Gerald, I called Terrell's teacher, Nancy Wright."

"Very well," Gerald said, noncommittally.

"I asked who Terrell's friends are."

"What did she say?"

"She said Terrell didn't seem to have any friends." Mickey began crying again.

"Did you tell her Terrell was missing?"

"No."

"She must suspect something, you asking about his friends like that."

"Gerald, we need help!"

"Do you have any suggestions, Mickey?"

"Yes! Go to the sheriff."

Gerald took a deep breath, exhaled slowly. "I want to try another day or two, first. I believe we can find him without bringing all this to the attention of the authorities."

"What if he isn't in Belle Glade?"

"Then, of course, we have to tell the sheriff."

"It's getting colder," Mickey said.

"I'll close the windows."

"I wasn't thinking about the windows."

"Mickey," Gerald knelt before her chair, "if Terrell gets cold, or hungry, the sooner he'll come home."

"He must not love us."

"That isn't true, Mickey. Little boys don't think."

"He goes swimming in those filthy canals."

"He can swim very well, though."

"Gerald, I can't stand much more of this. I'm going crazy with worry."

He stood, pulling her head to him, holding her. Her sobs were silent, pulsing movements.

"There has to be somebody who has seen him," Gerald reasoned. "With that little red head, surely they would've noticed. Mickey?"

"What?"

"I think I'll run over to the packing houses."

"At this hour?"

"They're running full shifts. There'll be plenty of people over there."

"I'll go with you."

Gerald approached one person after another, walking the platform of each packing house. Mickey had given him a recent snapshot of Terrell, and this he showed to anyone who would take time to look.

"Have you seen this child recently?"

"Afraid not."

"He has red hair."

"A hundred kids hang around here, mister."

"He's small for his age. Looks four or five."

"No sir, I don't know him."

They drove to the icehouse and Gerald found Bucky. The boy wrangled another package of cigarettes and said he still hadn't seen Terrell.

"Ask other boys and girls, will you, Bucky?" Mickey pleaded.

"Yeah, sure, Missus Calder. I'll do that."

"Thanks, Bucky." Gerald returned to the driver's side of his vehicle.

There were five major packing houses. At each, the response was the same: nobody had seen a small red-haired boy during the late shift.

"He talks about the packing houses constantly," Mickey declared. "Surely somebody would have noticed him!"

"He spends a lot of time here," Gerald conceded. "But not this late at night. I'll come back in the morning. Catch each shift in turn. We'll find someone who's seen him."

It was another night of sleepless tossing, frantic involuntary jerks of the muscles as Gerald or Mickey dozed, only to awake with a start as bad dreams assailed them.

The next morning Gerald began to locate people who knew Terrell.

"Yeah, I know him. Comes through here bumming cigarettes. You know the kid smokes, don't you?"

"I've caught him now and then," Gerald acknowledged.

Laughter. "That's what he said, all right."

"Have any of you seen this boy in the last few days?"

"Not since Tuesday or Wednesday," the consistent reply.

Mickey waited in the car, soaked with perspiration despite the cooler daytime temperature. The flesh of her abdomen felt stretched as though the skin would rip at any moment. She couldn't find a comfortable position, no matter how she twisted and turned.

"Any luck?" she asked. She knew by Gerald's expression even before he replied.

"Nobody's seen him for several days. Let's go to the next packing house."

By midday, they could almost trace Terrell's path to school. He never went through the International Vegetable Growers packing house. He seldom passed through Glades Seed, Feed and Equipment storage areas. But throughout the morning at the Blue Goose Packing Company; one after another of the workers knew Terrell well, by sight.

"Redheaded boy?" the guard said. "Sure I know that boy! Your son, you say? You know, you're going to lose that child someday, mister. He comes over here riding packing crates from the third floor down through the washing machines—mother of God, it's a miracle those youngsters haven't been hurt before now. And say, who's that old man with him the last time?"

"Old man?" Gerald's heart skipped a beat.

"Is it the boy's grandfather?"

"No."

"That old codger ought to know better, mister. Riding the same crates. You see that chute?"

Gerald looked up a corkscrew spiral winding two floors above.

"They come out of that chute in a free-fall. Hit the ramp here, riding these rollers to that washing machine. I've seen boxes with nothing in them jump the track and shatter. Imagine what would happen with a child in it. And that old man! Godamighty! When I saw him doing it, I couldn't believe my eyes!"

"You wouldn't know the old man's name?" Gerald asked.

"No. I see him around now and then. Usually picking up broken crates and boxes out in the dump area. Drives a beat-up '34 Ford pickup. No tag on it."

"No license tag?"

"No. That's pretty common with transients, of course."

"Well," Gerald shook the guard's hand, "thanks for your help."

"If I see him, what?"

Gerald scribbled his phone number on a card and gave it to the guard. "Call me, if you do, will you? Call if you see the old man, too."

"I'll do that. Listen, mister, I hope I didn't make you mad, talking about your boy that way."

"No. I appreciate it. I think his mother and I had better provide more supervision hereafter."

"Yeah, really. A child could get killed over here."

"Again, thanks."

Gerald returned to find Mickey soaking wet.

"I'm taking you home, Mickey."

"No. I want to go with you."

"This is too hard on you."

"Gerald," fiercely, "I'm going with you!"

Gerald drove downtown. He halted before a small, white stucco building. Inside he gained quick admittance to the office of Buddy Willis, in charge of the Social Security Administration.

"Buddy, do you know an elderly man named Mack something?"

"Not right offhand. How old is he?"

"I don't know."

"Could be a nickname, not a given name."

"You're right."

"Know anything else about him?"

"No."

"I'm sorry, Gerald. I have no idea who he could be."

From there to the sheriff's office. Ed Lambert, the sheriff, wasn't in. Gerald questioned a deputy. "I wouldn't know, Mr. Calder. There are so many migrant workers coming and going around here, we don't know folks like we once did."

Gerald went to the health department. He ran into Dr. Phillip Norman on his way to lunch.

"I have no idea how old the man might be," Gerald confessed. "I only know he's called Mack something or another."

"Mack?" Dr. Norman said. "That could be anybody, Gerald."

They walked toward the parking lot. "Is he one of the camp people?" Dr. Norman questioned.

"I'm not sure. I doubt it."

"Mack?" the doctor repeated. Then, glancing up, he saw Mickey. "Good God, Mickey, you look like you don't feel well!"

"I'm all right."

"Gerald, help me get her into the clinic."

"I'm all right, I said."

"Like hell you are! You're within a few degrees of a heat stroke. Come on Gerald!"

Her face was beet-red, hair plastered to her head by perspiration. Her dress clung in a wet sheet of cotton, adhered to her back, breasts and thighs.

"Damn it, Gerald!" Dr. Norman fumed. "What are you thinking about these days? Are you trying to kill this baby?"

"I—I didn't realize."

"I told you, I'm all right," Mickey protested.

"Come on, Mickey." Dr. Norman took one arm, Gerald the other.

"Phillip Norman, will you stop this?" Mickey said, sharply. "I'm all right."

"Hold her arm, Gerald."

Gerald was stunned to find himself supporting her weight as Mickey's legs buckled, head dropping to her chest.

"We'll have to let her down while I get a stretcher," Dr. Norman said, all evidence of disapproval gone as his professional manner assumed control.

"What happened?" Gerald asked.

"The heat," Dr. Norman said, easing Mickey to the

grass. "I told her to stay off her feet, Gerald. You're going to have to see that she follows my instructions."

Gerald cupped Mickey's head. She groaned, eyes fluttering, trying to turn.

"Easy, baby," Gerald soothed. People were running toward them. "Easy, Mickey."

13

~ ~~~ ~

Terry itched from applications of mud and grease. He followed McCree through towering leather ferns, carefully avoiding the thick leaves and hairy stalks where hordes of ticks lived. The old man was working his way toward a grove of wild tamarind, stunted water oaks and twisted Caribbean pines. From somewhere afar, the bellow of a bull 'gator rose, echoed, rippled away to silence.

"Watch your step, Little Hawk." McCree pointed at a seemingly firm area. "Quicksand."

They waded a shallow sedimentary pool of stagnant water filled with frogs and the hundreds of water snakes that came to feed upon them.

"Snakes, Mr. McCree."

"They'll move aside, Little Hawk. Stay nearby me."

When they gained solid footing again, Terry's bare legs were coated with a film of greenish, smelly scum and globules of oil forming from the axle grease.

"Are you doing all right?" McCree questioned.

"Yessir."

"We're almost there."

Terry gazed up at the rumpled blanket of low scudding clouds. Observing this, McCree said, "We could use some rain."

When they reached the trees, McCree nodded, satisfied. Hundreds of butterfly orchids dotted the limbs. The old man suggested they both climb, break off plants and drop them at random.

"We can gather them up later, Little Hawk."

With an agility that rivaled Terry's, McCree selected a particularly tall tree and climbed, stretching out along the limbs to reach the furthermost plants.

"We'll be finished before long," McCree called. "This is about all we'll need, Little Hawk."

"Want me to climb that big tree?" Terry asked, when they both met below.

"I'll take that one," McCree said. "You get the smaller tree over there. Those skinny limbs won't support my weight."

Terry was out as far as he dared go, trying to pull loose a plant with a tenacious root system woven to the bark. He heard McCree yell—

Thump. A leaden, dull sound. Terry parted foliage around him, peering toward the tree he knew McCree had taken.

"Mr. McCree?"

His voice came back to him, "Cree . . . ree . . . ee . . ."

"Mr. McCree? Are you all right?"

Terry's heart quickened. He scooted backward along the bough, feeling behind himself until he touched the trunk. He swung down.

Under McCree's tree, Terry squinted up, trying to see among the limbs. Backlighted by filtered sun through the clouds, Terry couldn't make out a form. He watched for telltale movements.

"Mr. McCree!" Louder, echoing, gone.

Waist-deep in grass, Terry circled the tree. He found the old man lying face down. Heart hammering, Terry knelt at McCree's head.

The old man's eyes were half-closed. His right arm was oddly twisted. Terry tried to turn him, but halted when he saw blood seeping through McCree's shirt-sleeve. Terry leaned across McCree, looking, and his stomach twisted. A jagged sliver of bone pierced the fabric just above McCree's elbow.

"Oh, Mr. McCree!"

He put a hand on the old man's sweat-soaked back. McCree wasn't breathing. He bent low, his ear close to McCree's face. He shook the old man's shoulder. Nothing. Terry pounded McCree's back, his hands thumping as though drumming a ripened watermelon.

"Mr. McCree—please—" Terry stood, looking this way and that. The glades stretched as far as he could see. Should he go for help? Where? How could he get out, much less back again to find this place?

From the old man came a sudden rush of air, sucking in, then exhaled with a blubbery sound between his lips. Terry knelt, a hand on McCree's shoulder. Another liquid inhalation and long, wheezing exhale.

The eyes opened, winced. McCree gasped. He tried to turn over and cried out.

"Mr. McCree, your arm is broken."

McCree eased himself down again, turning this time in the opposite direction, away from the injured arm. He sat up, taking the injured appendage with his good hand, pulling it around so he could see. McCree groaned, eyes turned up into his skull and he fell back, unconscious.

"Gerald, this is Burrell Mason. Just what the hell is going on?"

"In regard to what, Burrell?" Gerald pulled a cigarette from a pack on a bedside table.

"You know what, damn you," Burrell growled. "The *Miami Herald* has a story about you taking the management of the new camp."

"Wait a minute, Burrell. I didn't actually accept that."

"Bullshit, damn it! I called Washington and they confirmed it!"

"Burrell, I didn't deliberately keep this from you. I've had a lot of problems this past week and—"

"If other papers got a release on it, why didn't we?"

"I didn't authorize a news release. Washington did that without my—"

"Let me tell you my position, Gerald. So there'll be no misunderstanding. I am flatly opposed to a black camp designed to house cheap imported Bahamian labor. In deference to you, I haven't taken an editorial stand. But I will now. American farm workers need to to be warned what's going to happen to them."

"Burrell, be reasonable. Let's sit down and discuss this matter."

"I had hoped you'd convince Washington to make that camp white, Gerald. I had hoped you were working for farm labor, not against it."

"Burrell, damn it, I've been up to my eyeballs in problems the past few days! I haven't had a chance to tell Washington anything."

"Is the camp going to be black?"

"Yes, black."

"For Bahamian labor."

"For *black* laborers, Burrell. We need that camp."

"You mean the growers need it! You're condemning American laborers to an indecent wage scale for years to come. For a guy who claims to be for the common man, you do odd things, Gerald. If you manage that camp, it lends a certain respectability that Washington couldn't get from anybody else and you know it! Whose side are you on, anyway? That's a stupid question. You're on Washington's side!"

"Burrell—"

"I'm writing that editorial today, Gerald." The line went dead.

Mickey was lying on her side, looking at him. "What on earth was that about?"

"Burrell. Angry about the new camp."

"That's nothing new. What has him so mad with you?"

Gerald stubbed out the cigarette. "Bert Arthur called me this past week."

Mickey was sitting now, face pale.

"He told me Mrs. Roosevelt had recommended me to manage the black camp and—"

"You accepted." Accusingly.

"No, I said I needed time to talk it over with you."

"You didn't refuse it, though."

"I didn't accept or refuse, Mickey."

"Damn it, Gerald!"

"Damn it is right!" Gerald exploded. "Burrell is angry because it's in the Miami paper. Washington sent out a news release on it and they did it to put pressure on me. I'm getting pressure from Burrell, from Washington, from you, damn it! Damn you all!"

"Gerald!"

Mickey eased off the bed, going after him. She heard the front door slam.

"Gerald!"

Terry tried to help the old man rise, his muscles quivering with the effort. McCree cried out again, grabbing the fractured arm. The sleeve was now drenched in blood. Gnats had begun to dart around them.

"Wait, Little Hawk. Wait!"

McCree was on his knees, face starkly white beneath the stains of mud and grease. "Let me get my wind," he whispered.

Together, somehow, they got McCree to his feet. The old man's hand bore down hard on Terry's frail shoulder, pain causing McCree to halt often.

"Go back the way we came?" Terry questioned.

"Only way to go, Little Hawk. Watch for—"

"I will."

They sloshed through the shallow pond, McCree leaning against a tree now and then. He avoided looking at the ugly bone protruding through his sleeve.

Lightning streaked unexpectedly and a deafening clap of thunder followed.

"We could use some rain," McCree murmured. Instantly it began to fall. Driving sheets of it, drops that stung like wind-thrown sand against the cheeks and arms.

"Notice any mistletoe about, Little Hawk?"

"No sir. Why?"

"Chew the leaves—kills pain."

Terry cupped his eyes against the torrent of rain, shaking with a chill wrought by the water and exhaustion.

"I don't see any, Mr. McCree."

"Not here," McCree said, too severely. "Only grows on high-ground trees. Seen any—anywhere?"

Terry tried to remember, and shook his head. "I don't recall any."

In the way of the Everglades, parched soil suddenly grew boggy, shallow water stirred restlessly, invisible currents quickened and became ominous swirls of black motion sweeping twigs, loose plants and other debris seaward. A raft of uprooted shrubs drifted by, crawling with tens of thousands of ants.

"Chickee," McCree whispered, seeing the camp. "Got to get in the chickee."

Alarmed, Terry felt McCree's legs wobble, buckle, then straighten. The old man turned aside and vomited, leaning heavily against the boy for support.

"Not much further, Mr. McCree!" He had to shout to be heard over the rumble of water, crashing thunder, jagged, ripping flashes of lightning. Terry heard an electrical sizzle and from the corner of his eye caught the blue tongue of flame as lightning struck a pine nearby.

McCree had chosen the site for the chickee with care. The thatched roof was holding well in the gusts of wind, shielded by a stand of trees. Terry followed McCree's instructions and dug below the hammock until he found a few glowing coals left from last night. He gathered palmetto fronds and put these over the embers. A short time later the chickee filled with smoke.

"Blow on it, Little Hawk."

A tiny poof! The palmetto fronds caught fire. On this, Terry put successively larger twigs, which slowly dried and finally burned. He put chicory into a pan and caught water from the thatched roof. The smell of coffee seemed to revive the old man.

"We got something bad to do, sooner or later, Little Hawk."

"What, Mr. McCree?"

"Reckon you could pull this arm hard enough to get the bone back inside where it belongs?"

Terry fought a rising taste of bile. "I could try."

"What, Little Hawk?"

Louder, "I could try."

"I might holler a little. But it has to be done."

"Yessir."

"Want to wait until we have some coffee?"

"Yessir."

McCree fell back on the hammock, breathing heavily. His eyes closed. Terry squatted by the fire, shivering despite the heat on his face, chest and legs. McCree groaned, trying to find a more comfortable position.

Terry wished he were home, bathed, dry and in bed.

Rain inundated the streets as water left the canals and spread. Gerald peered through the windshield, using the back of his hand to clear away moisture. The wipers paused after each stroke as the suction hose reasserted itself to draw them up again. He wished he had the old-fashioned Model-A kind that worked manually.

He turned back toward home, knowing Mickey would be thinking the same haunting thoughts Gerald was now having. Was Terrell out in this? In the flat terrain of the glades, a heavy rainfall could cause sudden and unexpected flooding, sweeping snakes, stumps and other snagging obstacles in a rush of water. Gerald crossed the main-entrance bridge, and dark currents below intensified his worry.

Mickey was standing in the front door when Gerald reached the screened porch. Soaked, he took her in his arms and they held one another close for a long time.

"You need dry clothes," Mickey said, as though to a child.

"Tomorrow is Monday," Gerald noted. "Tomorrow we should go to the sheriff."

"No," Mickey said. "I've been thinking about it. I think we should go see Ike Franklin. He'll call the sheriff. He'll get more action than we will. He'll also be sympathetic to our problem, Gerald."

Numbed mentally and physically, Gerald nodded.

"We should have done that several days ago," Mickey commented.

"Yes," Gerald sighed, "we should have."

The rain fell incessantly through the afternoon and into the night. The fire fizzled and died, with Terry struggling to keep it alive. The roof of the chickee had begun leaking, as water found every crack and crevice, trickling down on Terry's wool blanket.

Through the dark hours, McCree moaned, mumbled, his words incoherent. The roar of water seemed so near, Terry reached down from the hammock to see if they were being flooded. Finally, before dawn, the wind died, the rain eased to a steady downpour.

Terry awoke as McCree cried aloud. He sat up, disoriented, frightened, cold and wet.

"Mr. McCree!"

"Oh! God have mercy. Oh!" McCree spoke between teeth tightly clenched, muscles in his face corded.

"Can I help, Mr. McCree?"

"Is the fire out?"

"Yessir."

"Get—oh! Get another one—oh, *damn!*"

Terry threw off the smelly wool blanket and went out in the half-light of daybreak. Fronds of palmettos hung limp, every fiber drenched. He dug around beneath the plants, seeking dry tinder. He returned to the chickee with what he could find.

"Shouldn't have let it die, Little Hawk."

"I'm sorry, Mr. McCree."

"Not you," McCree amended softly. "Me."

"It was my fault."

"No, Little Hawk. You did good. I—I'm proud of you. Reckon you can get a fire started with all that wet stuff?"

"I don't think so."

"Okay. Don't waste matches. Let's get out of here and go home."

"There's some cold coffee left from last night."

"No," McCree said. He worked himself to a sitting position, bent beneath the low roof. He closed his eyes, cracked lips taut against his teeth.

"Can I help?"

"We got to—pull this arm."

"Now?"

"Now."

Terry's hands were shaking so hard just holding McCree's wrist made the old man cry out.

"Hang on it, Little Hawk."

But when Terry tried to do this, McCree screamed and thrashed at him with the other hand. "Wait! Wait! Oh, God!"

"I'm sorry, Mr. McCree!"

McCree fell back, unconscious.

He tried to lift the old man's booted feet onto the hammock and couldn't. He could only stand there, waiting for McCree to regain his senses.

"Do you want breakfast, Gerald?" Mickey wore a flowered maternity dress she'd been saving for the drive to the hospital.

"Coffee," Gerald said, adjusting his tie. "Did you call Ike?"

"He says he can see us around ten at his office."

Gerald sat at the kitchen table, sipping coffee. "You look beautiful," he said.

"I walk like a duck, waddling through doors touching both jambs, I have been bitchy, irritable and unresponsive. So I assume you must love me."

Gerald nodded soberly. "I do."

They drove to town in a steady drizzle. The streets were littered with refuse deposited from overflowing gutters and canals. They were thirty minutes early but waited outside the opaque glass doors of Judge Ike Franklin's chambers.

"Good morning, Mickey, Gerald."

"Ike," Gerald said by way of greeting.

"Come in. Have you two had coffee?"

"I could use another cup," Gerald confessed. He watched the thin, intense judge pour three cups from a pot on a one-eyed hot plate. They sat at a conference table, passing cream and sugar before anyone spoke.

"Ike, we have a problem," Gerald began.

"Okay, let's talk about it."

"It's our son, Terrell."

Ike chuckled. "That boy is a real boy, Mickey."

Mickey nodded, uncertainly. "He's run away, Ike." She began to cry and Ike reached across the table, patting Mickey's forearm.

"We're worried to death, Ike," Mickey said.

"I know you must be. Gerald, why don't you tell me about it?"

Gerald spoke in flat, unemotional tones. He told Ike what a carefree and pleasant child Terrell had always been. He noted the problems of playmates out at the camp, influences that perhaps led Terrell to start smoking and going to the packing houses. Until school started, however, neither he nor Mickey had ever seriously considered Terrell a problem child.

"When Miss Ramsey came to us," Gerald admitted, "we tried reasoning with Terrell. We tried spanking

174

him. We delivered him directly to school and watched him enter the building. Still he ran."

"Do you have any idea what lies at the root of the problem?" Ike asked, deep voice gentle.

"No."

"No problems at home to speak of?" Ike questioned.

"No, Ike. Not that we know of. Terrell is well mannered, usually obedient. He expresses himself physically, kissing and hugging both his mother and me. We are a close family, I would say. At first, I really assumed he was just a freedom-loving child who didn't want to be confined to a classroom."

Ike stood. "That may be all there is to it."

"Yes," Gerald said, "but now he's carried it to such an extreme, running away like this."

"All right," Ike said, "the first thing to do is find him. I'll call Sheriff Lambert. We'll notify Miss Ramsey. She's a very sharp young lady, Gerald. She knows where children go to hide. You tell your camp personnel to watch for Terrell. I suspect we'll find him staying with a friend somewhere, safe and sound, dry as gunpowder and well fed."

"I hope so," Mickey said.

Ike extended his hand in a firm, pleasant shake. "When we get him back home, then we can go to work on changing his attitude about school. Right, Gerald?"

For the first time in several days, Gerald smiled. "Thanks, Ike."

"That's what we're here for," Ike said. "Try not to worry."

As they stepped outside, Mickey took Gerald's arm. "Maybe that's a good sign," she said.

"What?"

"It just quit raining."

14

Terry's stomach cramped. He bent over one arm, trying to ease knotting muscles. They had eaten nothing since breakfast yesterday. Thirst and hunger were sapping his strength. Now in McCree's boat, Terry struggled to move the craft, every push on the long staff taking greater effort.

McCree sat forward, head hung, the fractured arm cradled in his lap. Terry's clothing had become stiff from water and abrasive with salt left when sweat evaporated. His flesh burned from exposure, chafing against his clothing. Gnats swam before Terry's face, hummed in his ears.

He put his weight first against the pole to propel the boat forward, then, using the stern as a fulcrum, he swung down on the pole to wrench it free from sucking mud.

The rain had stopped in mid-morning, replaced now by a sweltering humidity that intensified the heat. Not a breath of air stirred. They crossed a glasslike surface of water, oddly out of place among cattle egrets and blue herons roosting in mangroves, watching, unafraid. Alligators sunned themselves on the banks.

"You know east, Little Hawk?"

"Sir?"

"You know which is east?"

"No sir."

McCree's head lifted, folds of skin in his neck pulled tight. He looked at Terry with an expression which suggested the old man didn't truly see him.

"Sun rises in the east."

Terry shoved against the pole, arm muscles trembling. When he turned and looked at McCree, the man's head was down again, chin on chest, breathing with a gurgle in his throat.

"Mr. McCree."

McCree grunted.

"I don't know which way to go."

"North."

The boat turned slowly, gliding to a halt, but yielding to an imperceptible current.

"Which way is that, Mr. McCree?"

"You know east?"

"Where the sun comes up."

"North is left, left of east."

The sun was on the afternoon side of overhead.

"Mr. McCree. I'm lost."

McCree drew a deep breath, let it escape with an abrupt exhalation. He lifted his head, wobbling. "We got some troubles, Little Hawk."

"Yessir."

McCree's head slowly sank back to his chest. Terry moved forward on his knees, dragging the pole after him. He touched the old man's knee.

"Which way?"

"Which way what?"

"Which way to go?"

McCree straightened, looking around. He squinted his eyes, seeking landmarks.

"Little Hawk, if something happens. I get down and don't get up, maybe. Go north. Always north."

"Which way is north?"

McCree's face was blanched with shock and pain. He breathed through an open mouth, eyes tortured. "Listen to me," he commanded hoarsely. "East is where the sun comes up. Say it!"

"East is where the sun comes up."

"West is where the sun sets."

"Yessir."

"Say it!"

"West is where the sun goes down."

"Face east, then."

Terry remembered the shadow fall. He turned slightly.

"That's east," McCree whispered. "Where's north?"

"I don't know."

McCree hissed, face twisted, "Listen to me! You want to die out here, Little Hawk?"

"No sir." A small voice.

"Face east . . . north is left of east."

"That way?"

McCree nodded. "Go north."

Terry returned to the rear of the boat, pushing down on the pole. *Sunrise east . . . sunset west . . . north is left of east . . .*

"Tell me, Little Hawk."

Terry repeated the directions and McCree groaned to himself, shoulders stooped, head down.

They reached the truck as the sun was sinking. Terry had to get into the warm, murky water and shove the boat toward shore. This done, he urged the old man to get out. He had to repeat himself many times before McCree responded.

"Think you could get home?" McCree asked. "From here?"

"No sir."

"You might have to do it, Little Hawk."

"I won't go without you."

"Might have to."

"No."

Every move an agony, crying out or halting to suck gulps of air, McCree finally made it to the pickup. Inside, he sat staring at the dashboard a moment, then closed his eyes and moaned.

"We can make it now, Mr. McCree."

"Can't drive, boy. God. God. Don't know when

179

something hurt so much. *Crotalus* bit, catfish finned, thistle stuck—nothing like this. Oh, God."

With his own heart the loudest thing he heard, Terry sat watching the old man.

"Did we get the tea?" McCree asked.

"No sir. Left everything. Remember?"

"Thirsty."

Terry looked behind the seat where McCree carried his sassafras tea. Nothing there. He looked through the dash pocket, out the rear window into the truck bed.

"We don't have anything, Mr. McCree."

"We got us trouble."

It was getting dark. Mosquitoes buzzed through the open windows.

"Mr. McCree, we have to go now."

"Can't drive!"

"Reckon I could do it?"

McCree's head was lolling again. Terry touched the old man's leg. "Let me drive, Mr. McCree. Do it just like we did it before."

"Won't work."

"Why?"

"Can't reach gears."

"Can I do it?"

"You know east?"

Terry said, quickly, "Show me the gear."

To Terry it seemed hours before McCree agreed and allowed the boy to stand between his legs. The ground was marshy from rain, the sun down, dark. McCree's cries of pain, mumbled instructions, mosquitoes seeking blood, and Terry's own empty stomach had tears running down his cheeks.

"How do we start the motor, Mr. McCree?" A whir of insects, McCree's breathing his only response, Terry examined the dashboard, pulling one knob, then another. He found the lights.

"What do I do first, Mr. McCree?"

Aroused, the old man instructed: shift to neutral,

turn the key, pull out choke, push starter button. The motor turned, turned, caught, sputtered. Terry tried again. The engine raced and McCree told him how to ease in the choke, adjust the throttle.

"Have to go fast, else—stuck."

"Yessir."

Somehow, lurching, headlights dipping, slashing the night sky, they began to move, shifted to second, then third, and with the wind in their faces, crossed the glade. Every jolt made McCree cry aloud; once Terry felt the old man's head fall against his back, but Mc-Cree soon straightened.

"Woods ahead!"

"Good," McCree's only reply. Terry pushed in the throttle and the vehicle slowed. His legs were trembling from tension and exhaustion. He heard McCree murmuring, words jumbled, head bouncing on Terry's shoulder.

Terry approached the polished counter and a nurse in crisp white clothing. Somewhere in the hospital, a soft bell made dinging sounds calling a signal only the staff would understand.

"Please ma'am."

"Yes?"

"Mr. McCree is outside. He broke his arm."

"I can't hear you, son."

"Please come help Mr. McCree!"

"Where is he?"

"Outside."

The nurse dialed a telephone, her eyes touching on Terry's face, clothing, legs. "I need an aide, please. Emergency ward."

They carried McCree inside on a stretcher. Somebody cut off the motor in the truck.

"What's your name, sonny?"

"Terry."

"What's your last name?"

"McCree."

The nurse was on the telephone, talking. "Dr. Norman, this is the clinic. We have a compound fracture several days old. The man is in his late seventies or early eighties. A child brought him in. Could you come out?"

"Did you drive that truck?" the orderly persisted.

"Yes."

"Is this man your grandfather?"

"I'm hungry," Terry said. "Could I have something to eat?"

"The kitchen is closed. How about some candy?"

Terry was asleep when Dr. Phillip Norman passed in the hall. The boy, covered with mud and grease, was curled on a bench. Somebody had put a pillow under his head.

"Camp people?" Dr. Norman asked the nurse.

"I would think so. The child is filthy."

"Better find out who to call. This old man isn't going anywhere for a while. I'll need glucose."

Terry awoke, a hand on his shoulder. The nurse's face was close to him. "Who can we call to come get you?"

"Is Mr. McCree dead?"

"No, he's not dead."

"I'll wait for him."

"He has to stay awhile. Is there somebody who can come to take you home?"

Terry sat up, rubbing his eyes. His ears were ringing. He glanced down the hall and saw Dr. Norman talking to an orderly.

"I have to go," Terry said.

"Let me get someone to take you home," the nurse insisted. She was holding Terry's arm, her eyes troubled. Terry suddenly snatched loose and began running.

"What's going on?" Dr. Norman demanded as she returned to her desk.

"I don't know," the nurse confessed. "The child wouldn't tell me where he lived, and when I pushed him on it, he ran."

"My God, these people!" Dr. Norman took off his white smock. "I'm going home. Put the man in the ward until I check on him tomorrow. He may lose that arm. He needs to be bathed."

"Yes, doctor."

Dr. Norman was getting into his automobile when he noticed McCree's pickup truck. The windows were open. He hesitated. If it rained, the interior would be ruined. The old man wasn't coming out for several days. He walked over to close the windows and glanced inside. A small form lay curled on the front seat, bare legs dotted with mosquitoes.

Dr. Norman turned on his heel, returned to the hospital and called Sheriff Lambert.

"He's in a battered pickup truck," Dr. Norman related. "He can't stay here. Come get him and keep him there, if you have to. Better that than sleeping outside overnight. He'll be eaten alive by mosquitoes."

Terry was vaguely aware of strong arms lifting him. He sighed deeply, drugged by exhaustion, and closed his eyes again. The deputy put him on the front seat, rounded the patrol car and drove to the city jail.

Bert Arthur's words crackled on the long-distance wires. "That editorial will incite the community needlessly," Arthur said. "It will be detrimental to the Farm Security Administration, to you personally, Calder."

"What do you suggest, Mr. Arthur?"

"Go talk to the man! He wouldn't have called to read the thing if he seriously wanted to publish it."

"I'm afraid he would, Mr. Arthur. Burrell Mason is the kind of newspaperman who likes to create a response."

"Get that editorial killed, Calder."

"How do you propose I do that?" Gerald asked,

mildly. "I don't think we've reached a point where government employees can issue orders to the fourth estate."

"Reason with the man, Calder. That camp in time of war will become a vital manpower link in the chain of supply and demand. The very thing he's complaining about, Bahamian labor, could be our salvation."

"If we have a war, he might understand that," Gerald said. "There is no war. Burrell thinks we're hurting American laborers."

"We're running into this everywhere in the nation," Bert Arthur said angrily. "The Supreme Court is supposed to rule today on the constitutionality of the California antimigrant law, which was enacted to keep Okies out of that state. The state of California is giving the same argument as this fellow Mason. Everybody claims everything is hurting their special interests. Well, damn it, Calder, the national interest must be considered, too. Tell Mason that camp may be vital to national security."

"I'll go see him this afternoon, Mr. Arthur."

"Do it, Calder. Appeal to his patriotic pride."

"I'll try, Mr. Arthur. Nobody is more patriotic than Burrell Mason. He just happens to disagree with you on what makes a patriot."

"Do what you can, Calder. Get back to me. We're counting on you down there."

Gerald hooked the receiver and pushed the telephone back on his desk.

"Mr. Calder, Burrell Mason on the phone."

Gerald hesitated, lifted the receiver. "Good afternoon, Burrell."

"Did they call you?"

"They called."

Burrell chuckled. Gerald quelled his irritation. "They want me to try and dissuade you, Burrell. They said I should appeal to your patriotism."

"Pinko bastards."

Gerald sighed into the receiver. "Well, at least it gives us an excuse to have coffee. Want to meet me at the drugstore?"

"Why not? Come on, I need a break."

Gerald grabbed his suit coat in passing, going toward the door.

"Mr. Calder!"

"I'm going out, Marilyn."

"Miss Ramsey calling you."

"Ask her to call my wife."

Gerald let the door slam shut, felt the suffocating heat radiating from the building wall and paved parking lot. Damn! He'd forgotton to leave his car windows rolled down it. It would be hot enough in there to bake bread.

Mickey reached for the ringing telephone. The bed was moist where her back had been.

"Mrs. Calder, this is Miss Ramsey."

"Hello, Miss Ramsey."

"I'm out at Chosen. I located the girl named LuBelle. Did you know she's black?"

"No. I didn't."

"The child lives with her grandmother. She's illegitimate."

Mickey disliked the nuances of the truant officer's words. She asked, "Who is illegitimate, Miss Ramsey, the child or the grandmother?"

"The child. They live in deplorable conditions. As I was saying, I found them and they say Terrell spent a couple of nights there."

"He did?"

"The black woman is quite worried about any repercussions because she gave Terrell shelter. Evidently Terrell told them he was an orphan."

A stab in Mickey's chest. She felt tears welling in her eyes.

"Many children do that, of course, seeking sympathy."

"I don't truly care about other children, Miss Ramsey. Only about Terrell—"

"Yes. Well, the black woman seems to think Terrell might have gone to see an elderly man who lives out here somewhere. His name is Cree, I think. They didn't know how to spell it. I doubt they can spell."

"I don't know the name," Mickey said.

"That's what I was calling about. I had hoped you might know where he lives."

"No."

"All right," Miss Ramsey bumped the receiver noisily. "I'll ask around about this man. I tried to call your husband. He was out. I hope I haven't disturbed you."

"No, I—thanks for calling, Miss Ramsey."

A deputy awoke Terry the next morning. He had been sleeping on a hard cotton mattress in an unlocked cell.

"Slip right in there and scrub good, lad."

The deputy gave Terry a stiff washcloth, a bar of Octagon soap and a thin towel.

"After you bathe, we'll get some vittles."

"Okay." Terry eased into the shower which the deputy had already started.

"I'll throw these dirty duds in the washing machine," the deputy said. "When you get out, wrap the towel around yourself until the clothes are dry."

"Yessir."

The hot water felt good. Terry put the bar of soap to his tangled hair and rubbed vigorously. He discovered a tick on his scalp and pulled it off.

His bath complete, Terry ate two heaping plates of scrambled eggs and several slices of limp bacon prepared by a black inmate who fussed constantly about "having a second breakfast to cook for a lazy young 'un."

186

"What did Ike say?" Terry could hear Sheriff Lambert speaking.

"He said call Elizabeth Ramsey."

"Did you do it?"

"She's out chasing hooky players. I left word at her office and at the high school. They said it would most likely be late afternoon before she comes back."

Terry's mouth went dry. He chewed the now-tasteless egg and forced it down.

"Whatcha want to drink?" the cook asked, brusquely.

"Coffee."

"Coffee! You too young for coffee. How about milk?"

"You asked me," Terry replied. "I want coffee."

The cook gave him milk anyway, pouring the liquid into a metal cup. He set it on the tray with Terry's food.

"Where're my clothes?"

"On the line. They ain't dry yet."

Terry downed as much of the food as he could, each mouthful gagging him when a door rattled, a female voice rose in the office outside or a car door slammed. He drank most of the milk and set the tray aside.

"I want my clothes, please."

"Get them in a second," the cook said, washing a frying pan.

"Can I get them?"

"If they's dry."

Terry dropped the towel in the yard, slipping into his clothes where he stood. With a furtive glance back toward the cell compound as he skirted the outside of the building, he climbed a chain-link fence and dropped quietly on the other side. He ran through a back alley along a row of tenement houses, heading for the hospital.

He avoided the main streets, darting between buildings or behind trees when he heard automobiles. At last, the red brick hospital appeared and Terry cut across a side yard to enter from the parking lot. Mc-Cree's truck was gone!

He approached the nurse on duty in the emergency clinic. "Is Mr. McCree still here?"

"No children allowed in the wards, son."

"Is he still here?"

"What's his name?"

"McCree."

"Spelled how?"

"I don't know."

She telephoned someone, asking. She hung up and leaned over the counter. "Are you related to this man?"

"Yes."

"Your grandfather?"

"Yes."

"He's still here. He's doing fine. But he can't have you in to visit. I'm sorry. It's against the rules for children to go into the wards."

The expression on Terry's face made the nurse bend. "Would you like to see him through a window?"

"Yes ma'am."

"Okay, we can do that. Come with me."

They walked a long hall, Terry holding her hand, her skirt whisking, white stockings and low-heeled shoes setting a brisk pace. She pulled a small stepladder to one of the two swinging doors. She put her head inside and called, "Mr. McCree! Your grandson is at the window."

Terry saw McCree's bare shoulder, the other wrapped in a rigid white cast that extended to the tips of his fingers. He was shaved! Terry waved, grinning. McCree waved in long swoops of the hand, smiling.

"See," the nurse said, "he's doing fine. You run along home now."

"Thanks!"

"You're welcome," she said, cheerily. Terry ran ahead, going out the doors with the smile still on his face.

15

Terry found Dog hungry. Following McCree's example, he prepared food for the snake-bitten animal, and as Dog ate his fill, Terry removed the poultice bandana and daubed camphor water onto the pup's inflamed neck.

He looked in on the rattlesnakes, debated giving them water, then remembered McCree's firm command never to reach into the cage when there alone. Terry replaced the lid of the washing machine used to confine the snakes, anchoring it with a heavy rock.

He wandered around McCree's shack, examining jars of dried foodstuffs, considered cooking something, then realized he had no matches. He went to LuBelle's.

Eunice was gone. LuBelle sat on the steps drawing taut a string tied to her index fingers. On the string the whirring blur of a button "buzz saw" droned like an angry wasp.

"They been here looking for you," LuBelle said.

"Who has?"

"Some white woman. She ask Mawmaw where you went."

"What did Eunice say?"

"You went to see Cree."

Terry stared at the buzzing button as though hypnotized.

"Mawmaw says you can't stay here with us again."

"Is she mad with me?"

"I reckon."

"If you get your hair caught in that, it'll snatch it out, LuBelle." Terry referred to the button buzz saw.

"I done it already. Snatched out a handful, too."

"Where's Eunice now?"

"To town."

"Is there anything to eat, LuBelle? I'm awful hungry."

The string broke and curled around one of LuBelle's fingers. She retrieved the large two-hole button for another time.

"Beans maybe," she said. "But they's cold."

"It's okay. I'm awful hungry."

"Corn bread."

"Sounds good."

LuBelle led the way and Terry ate directly from a pot on the wood stove. He broke chunks of pone and ate them dry. LuBelle took alternate bites from the same spoon, both of them standing.

"How come you lie about your folks?" LuBelle asked.

"I didn't lie."

"That white woman says you got a mama and a daddy."

"She did?" Terry now realized it must have been Miss Ramsey.

"She say there's going to be lots of troubles for anybody what keeps you with them."

"I won't stay the night."

"I don't mind."

"You said Eunice wouldn't let me."

"She won't."

Terry got a dipper of water from a bucket and drank some to ease down the dry corn bread.

"How come you lie about your folks?" LuBelle persisted.

"I don't know."

LuBelle suggested they play hopscotch. But Terry, afraid to face Eunice, said he was going home. He then left in a direction that might lead LuBelle to believe him. Instead, he went to McCree's shack again.

He picked rabbit tobacco as he walked. Carefully selecting only curled, dried leaves, he sat on McCree's stoop crumbling the leaves into a pan McCree sometimes used to water Dog. He then found a piece of paper and rolled a cigarette. He was searching for matches when he heard an automobile drive up and stop.

Terry ran to a dark corner of a back room where he could crouch behind a mound of burlap sacks. Peering through holes in the siding, he saw Miss Ramsey get out of her car. The sun was so low she would have difficulty seeing him. Like a wild animal frozen in the hope of eluding a predator, Terry was motionless, every muscle tensed.

"Terrell!"

His own breathing sounded extraordinarily loud. Terry held his breath.

"Terrell!" Miss Ramsey was walking around the outside, her steps indicating a wariness for snakes in the knee-high grasses. He lost sight of her as she rounded a corner.

"Terrell, are you here, son?"

He exhaled with great control, inhaled with equal care.

"Your mother is very worried about you, Terrell. Don't you think it's about time to go home? Your parents would be so happy to see you."

Did she know he was here? Or was she bluffing? Games of hide-and-seek had taught Terry never to fall for a bluff.

"Day after tomorrow is Thanksgiving, Terrell. It would be a very sad Thanksgiving without you."

In the twilight, he saw the truant officer come full circle around the house.

"Hey, doggie. Do you bite?" He heard Miss Ramsey

191

speak in a more conversational tone. "Are you a nice doggie?"

Her footstep sounded as she entered the dark building. "Terrell, please let me take you home. I know you're here. Let's go see your mother. She would be greatly relieved if you came home."

Terry held his breath until his chest ached. Slowly, quietly, he exhaled, then, with tremendous control, inhaled.

Miss Ramsey bumped something. Terry saw a dim flicker through the door of his hiding place. A match flame pushed futilely at the dark, then died. He knew by the sound of her steps about where she was. Looking behind things, striking matches. She was at the door now. A sputtering sizzle and a phosphorous smell as another match flared. Terry eased down onto his knees.

"Terrell, wouldn't you like something to eat? A hot bath? Your parents aren't angry with you. Nobody is angry. We only want you to come home. We can work out any problems, you know. I'll help you."

She was in the same room now; the match died. Terry heard her scrape another, more light.

"Terrell."

He knew by her tone she had seen him. He uncovered his head and looked up. Miss Ramsey stared at him unsmiling. She held out her hand. "Come on, Terrell. Let's go home."

They got into her automobile and Terry sat, back straight, the rabbit-tobacco cigarette still in his hand. He reached out the window and dropped it.

"I'm glad we found you, Terrell," Miss Ramsey said as they drove. "Your mother and father have been very worried about you."

She reached the paved road and turned toward Camp Osceola. "I know they will be happy to have you home for Thanksgiving."

The smell of oleander came and went as Miss Ramsey drove slowly toward town. Terry's mind raced with desperate thoughts: jump, run, get away!

"Nobody is unhappy with you, you know," Miss Ramsey said. Her face was a pale reflection illuminated by a glow from the dashboard.

Lights from the packing houses came into view.

"Can you stop a minute?" Terry asked.

"Why?"

"I have to go to the bathroom."

"We'll be home in a second."

"I have to go now!"

"Terrell, your house is just—"

"You better stop."

"You can't wait until we get home?" Miss Ramsey asked, but she was already slowing the vehicle. Terry tried to open the door and only then realized there was no handle on the inside.

"Hurry," he said, "please."

Miss Ramsey rounded the vehicle and opened his door. Terry stepped out. A chorus of crickets and the burp of frogs rose from a familiar pond nearby.

"Watch for snakes, son."

"Yes ma'am."

"Stay on the pavement."

"Are you going to watch?"

"Oh. I'm sorry. Stay on the pavement out of the grass. I wouldn't want to rush you to the hospital with snakebite."

In the scant few seconds her back was turned, on bare feet, Terry slipped out of the red glow of the tail-lights and was gone.

"Are you about through?"

She knew children. She knew before she looked. She put a hand to her forehead and permitted herself a rare obscenity.

*   *   *

"At least you can take comfort from the fact that he is apparently hale and hearty," Miss Ramsey reported. Gerald and Mickey listened in stunned silence.

"That rascal conned me as sweetly as you please," Miss Ramsey said, managing a smile. "I wasn't three hundred yards from the entrance to the camp."

"He couldn't have gone far," Gerald said, angrily.

"No," Miss Ramsey agreed. "But you might look right over him in the dark. I suggest we wait until morning. I have a good idea where to find him now."

"Where?" Mickey demanded.

"At the old man's place. McCree. He's in the hospital with a broken arm. He fell out of a tree. Eighty-three years old and fell out of a tree, mind you. He says Terrell brought him in from the glades. I'll have another talk with him in the morning. Judge Franklin wants me to ascertain exactly where Terrell went, with whom he stayed, what he did and so forth."

"Why?" Gerald asked cautiously.

"It's standard procedure, Mr. Calder. Most runaways commit a minor crime or two during their days away from home. Usually stealing food, candy, that sort of thing."

"Dear Lord," Mickey groaned.

"We submit reports to the police routinely so they can consider the matter resolved. However, I doubt that Terrell has done any of that."

"What makes you say that?" Mickey questioned.

"Because, apparently, he's spent his entire time with the black washerwoman and this elderly man. They fed and clothed him. He had no need to steal anything."

"What kind of people would take in a six-year-old child?" Mickey fumed. "Don't they question whether he had a home? They surely didn't believe he was truly orphaned."

"Orphaned!" Gerald's face reddened.

"Terrell told them he had no parents, Gerald."

"That—that boy!"

194

Miss Ramsey stood and smiled tightly. "To answer your question, Mrs. Calder, the kind of people who would do that are either ignorant, such as the black woman and her illegitimate grandchild, or an old man who is senile and incapable of functioning as a member of a responsible society. I will report to Judge Franklin on both cases."

Then to both of them, Miss Ramsey said, "If I catch that youngster again, I won't let him get away, I promise you."

When Gerald returned from seeing Miss Ramsey to her car, he took Mickey in his arms. He held her, saying nothing, tears of disappointment and humiliation in his eyes.

"He must not love us, Gerald."

This time there was no denial.

Terry made a bed of burlap sacks. Below, from the second floor of the packing house, vibrant sounds of humming machinery lulled him. To keep off the chill of night and the mosquitoes, Terry covered himself with sacks. He drifted off to sleep thinking about lights he'd seen burning at home, Miss Ramsey's automobile in the driveway.

He awoke before the midnight shift changed to day workers. He walked down from person to person asking for cigarettes, and after an hour only had four. He smoked one of these, waiting for the regular day staff to arrive.

"Can I have a cigarette?"

"Have you been home, redhead?"

"I just came from there."

"Like hell. You're filthy dirty."

"May I please have a cigarette?"

"Give the little twerp a fag, for God's sake!"

He accumulated six more in half an hour. He was waiting in the cane stand near school when several older boys arrived. He started to barter.

"Want to buy a cigarette?"

"I don't have any money."

"What kind of sandwiches do you have in your lunch?"

"Pimento cheese. One's bologna."

"I'll give you two cigarettes for your lunch, then."

"Make it four."

"Three."

A deal was made. Satisfied, Terry started toward the packing house. Bucky Dallas spied him and ran out, grinning.

"Where'd you go?" Bucky whispered.

"New York."

"New York! Godamighty! How'd you get back?"

"Walked."

Skepticism crept into Bucky's eyes and Terry amended, "Part of the way. Partway I rode boxcars. Listen, Bucky, you want to buy a cigarette?"

"I don't have any money. Besides, I have cigarettes."

Terry reached the steps of the Blue Goose Packing Company and lingered close to Bucky, watching a boy he'd caused to be whipped. The eighth grader passed without speaking, aware of Bucky's reputation for a knee in the groin and other dirty fighting.

"Your ma and pa come by to see me two or three times."

"What for?" Terry asked, eyes narrowing.

"To ask questions. I didn't tell them nothing!"

"You sure?"

"Hell yeah! I bummed a few smokes from your pa is all. He asked about that old man."

"What'd you tell him?"

"I told you, nothing!"

Terry offered a cigarette and Bucky accepted. They shared the smoke.

"Where you going, Terry?"

"I don't know."

"Want to stay at my house?"

"No."

"Looks like you got the start of some muck sores on your legs," Bucky observed.

"Mosquito bites."

"That's how muck sores get started sometimes. Gimme another drag, will you?"

"Bucky, you been out to the hobo jungle lately?"

"Yeah. Nobody there. Getting too cold nights. Besides, the johns've been chasing those guys off."

"How come?"

"Looking for kids like us, mostly."

"I got to see if I can sell this lunch," Terry said.

"Okay if I go with you?"

"Stay back is all. They don't trade so good when they see older boys around."

It took six approaches before a sale was made. The lunch went for twenty cents. This was spent on one hot dog all the way and a bottled NuGrape. Bucky sat at the snack table with Terry as the younger boy ate.

"You know they're going to put you in the hoosegow," Bucky said in a low voice.

"They got to catch me first."

"Yeah, but they will. Unless your folks send you out of state someplace. Reckon they'd do that to keep you out of the hoosegow?"

"I don't know."

"Your pa said he didn't want anybody to know you ran away. Makes me think he's trying to keep it a secret."

"Everybody knows it now," Terry deduced. He sucked mustard off a dirty finger, then poured salt into an open palm and licked it. He'd had a craving for salt lately.

"Uh-oh," Bucky warned. It was all the alarm needed. Terry dashed one way and Bucky the other. Terry heard the packing-house guard shouting, "Catch him! Catch the redheaded one! Catch him!"

Terry ducked reaching hands, skirted a man with

arms outstretched, raced across the building and disappeared through a maze of boxcars, shuttle engines and workmen repairing the cinder bed and tracks. He slid down an embankment, legs cutting on rough shale, hit the bottom next to a canal and raced along a well-worn path back toward camp. He went directly to a favorite place in a cane field and only then permitted himself to collapse, panting. He carefully removed his cigarettes and noted that two had been moistened by his perspiration. Then, with disgust, Terry realized he had left half of his NuGrape sitting on the snack table.

Gerald entered the newspaper office. Printing stock, liquid ink and a metallic smell of typesetting equipment were a pleasant aroma. There'd been a time when he wanted to pursue a writing career—

"Morning, Gerald!" Burrell somehow managed to remain immaculate in his perpetual white suits. He had a huge cigar clamped between his teeth, lips smiling around it.

"Burrell, may I see you privately?"

The newspaper publisher gestured grandly toward his glassed-in office and followed Gerald inside.

"Burrell, this editorial is unforgivable."

"Syntax, content, what?" Burrell said, eyes sparkling.

"Burrell, this is going to turn every white laborer into a raging racist! It could cause violence. You surprise me, Burrell. Really, this is irresponsible journalism."

"Let me tell you about that irresponsible journalism, Gerald. It has been picked up by the wire services and tomorrow morning it will run nationally. Not everyone has the same view."

"Burrell, this kind of thing is inflammatory. It's blatantly racial in tone."

"I resent that, Gerald."

"I resent it too, Burrell!"

"All right," Burrell said, evenly, "how about a rebuttal? You may have an equal number of column inches to make a reply. What you write on the subject, I'll print. Fair enough?"

"I can't do that and you know it."

"Why not? You're an old journalism major, aren't you? Sit down and attack the attacker."

"I'd have to get it approved in Washington before I could submit it, Burrell. This is too delicate to be casually batted back and forth."

"You're the manager of the new camp; who is better qualified to defend it?"

"Burrell, damn you—"

"Your Washington people give me a pain in the backside, Gerald! I think people are fed up with petty bureaucrats. They want some intelligent and honest responses to questions of the day. Now, by God, I have stated my opinion. You have the wherewithal to make a meaningful reply. If you want a committee action, that's all right by me. Call Washington and ask them what you should say!"

Gerald slammed the door on his way out.

"Tomorrow is Thanksgiving, Gerald."

"I know that, Mickey."

"What kind of Thanksgiving is this going to be?" She was crying again.

Gerald wearily put aside his newspaper. He pushed his head back against the chair and closed his eyes.

"Don't worry about cooking, Mickey. Let's play it as it comes."

"Somewhere along the way, we've made a terrible mistake with Terrell, Gerald."

"Why must it be our fault, Mickey? Why can't he be what he is, without blaming us?"

He kept his eyes closed. Mickey's sniffling terminated with a crude sound of blowing her nose. "I feel like he's a stranger, Gerald."

"I don't see how we can love that boy as much as

199

we do," Gerald said, softly, "and then he does the things he does. It makes you want to kill the little bastard."

Mickey nodded. "Then I hate myself for feeling so angry toward him. He's just a child! I keep telling myself that."

Gerald stared at her a long minute, then came to her, kneeling, taking her hands. "Baby, I know you're uncomfortable. I know things have been going badly, and this is your last week of pregnancy. I know you are worried about Terrell. I've been so upset and worried myself—about the world situation, about the camps— it must appear to you that I don't worry a whit about you. But I do. I have been."

"It's so unfair of Terrell to do this, especially now," Mickey said, brusquely.

"Very unfair," Gerald said. "Very thoughtless."

"I keep telling myself," Mickey whispered, "he's just a child."

Terry saw Mr. McCree's pickup truck parked inside a locked fence behind the sheriff's office. He stood, fingers hooked through the links of the fence, staring at it. How could Mr. McCree get from the hospital to home? Why had they moved it?

He walked slowly, shuffling his bare toes in dust bowls, kicking up puffs of arid sediment in passing. He needed to talk to Mr. McCree. When was he getting out of the hospital? What should he do about Dog? Watering the snakes?

He stopped under the marquee of the theater, looking at photographs of Tom Mix, Gene Autry, posters advertising the next feature. He wondered what had happened to Captain Midnight since the last episode, and whether the girl who fell into a volcano was saved before sinking in hot lava.

A reflection in the glass covering the posters was Terry's only warning. With an intuitive jump, he was off and running. A deputy grabbed for Terry but he slithered free, spinning, racing for a corner where he could dart down an alley.

"You little punk!" The deputy overtook Terry, grabbing the waist of his trousers and back of his shirt, snatching his feet from the ground.

"I ought to paddle your ass right here and now," the deputy fumed. He put Terry in the rear of the patrol car and slammed the door. Terry scooted all the way across the seat, scrambling for a door handle. There was none. He was locked in. The odor of human perspiration made him slightly ill.

The car lunged forward, tires squealing briefly. They turned a corner, another corner. Terry saw the jail. The black cook was out back, scrubbing out two garbage cans with a brush and a garden hose. There was no gentleness in the deputy's manner now as he hauled Terry into the sheriff's office.

"I found him, Sheriff."

"Put him in the women's cell. And lock the door."

Terry was pushed into the same cell he'd slept in the night before last. The door shut with a clang, echoing through the building. Down the cement walkway, unseen, a drunken voice came hollow and harsh, "You can't keep me in here, damn ya'll!"

Terry heard footsteps and Sheriff Lambert loomed over him. "We called your folks, boy. We called Judge Franklin and Miss Ramsey, too. Take a good look at that cell. That's where you're going to be someday for a very long time. Locked up so you can't go out and play. It gets smaller and smaller with every day that passes, and time crawls."

Terry was staring at the huge, drawling man.

"Runaways and boys who play hooky all end up right here, son. Sooner or later, for stealing or hurting somebody. If you don't follow the rules, you go to jail. That's how simple it is. The rules say a boy your age must go to school and do what his mommy and daddy

201

say he should do. You sit there and think about it. See how you like those iron bars and that hard bed. Think how you'd like to stay there for weeks, or months, or even years."

The sheriff walked away. He said something to the drunk and the inmate fell silent. A far door banged shut. Terry stood in the center of the cell, surrounded by gray walls, bars, a narrow shaft of light coming from a latticed window high overhead. Tears poured down his cheeks, his sobs muffled.

16

Mickey massaged her abdomen with hand lotion. She was fighting the onslaught of morning sickness, determined by will alone to stave it off.

"That was some Thanksgiving yesterday," she said flatly.

"It was all right," Gerald commented. "Have you seen my burgundy tie?"

"No. Gerald?"

"What?"

"What do you suppose Ike is going to say tomorrow?"

"He said he would like to talk to Terrell. I suspect he wants to see for himself what kind of child Terrell is."

"Do judges work on Saturday, usually?"

"He agreed to Saturday because of my schedule," Gerald said. "I have to meet with the contractors today."

Mickey capped the lotion, completed dressing. "Terrell isn't the same child he was, Gerald. He sits and stares into space. He answers questions with yes and no, nothing more. He acts so—lonely."

"He'll get over that."

"I can't draw him out. The only thing he's interested in seems to be some animals that old man owns. He said they need food and water."

"That's certainly a sense of responsibility, Mickey. That encourages me. What did you tell him?"

"He wanted to go out there by himself and I told him I'd take him this morning."

"That was wise."

"At least then I'll know where this McCree lives. Miss Ramsey says it's very difficult to find. Down in a hollow somewhere, I believe."

"I'm going." He kissed her lightly on the forehead. "I'll be at the new camp all day. If you need me, you'll have to send for me. I won't be near a telephone."

"I won't need you—I hope."

Gerald stepped out of the bedroom, pausing in the hall to look at Terrell. The boy was sitting, both hands in his lap, dressed and ready to go. He was barefoot, hair tousled. He was gazing out the living-room window.

"Going out to feed McCree's animals, son?"

Terrell nodded.

"That's good. Is there plenty of food there?"

Another nod.

Gerald spoke in a low voice, "I love you, Terrell."

"Love you." Automatic response.

"Want to give Daddy a kiss and hug good-bye? I have to go to work now."

A long hesitation, then Terrell came and stood before Gerald, arms limp at his sides. Gerald hugged and kissed him.

"Have fun today, son."

"Terrell!"

"Ma'am?"

"Did you brush your teeth?"

Terry went into the bathroom and wet the brush, replaced it.

"Comb your hair," Mama called from the bedroom. He did this.

"Shoes on?"

"Do I have to wear shoes?"

A pause. "No, I suppose not."

Terry returned to the living room and sat on the edge of the divan. Yesterday he had asked Mama and

Daddy to take him to the hospital to visit Mr. McCree. Their eyes had met across the Thanksgiving table and Mama said, "I don't think that would be wise, Terrell. Let's wait awhile. Judge Franklin might not understand that."

"Are you ready, Terrell?"

He ran to the automobile and sat waiting. Mama slid behind the wheel, pausing to catch her breath. "Let the seat back," she commanded. At last, they were on their way.

"Where does LuBelle live, Terrell?"

"We aren't going there." Mickey wasn't sure whether that was a statement or a frightened question.

"I only wanted to know where she lives, Terrell."

He sat without response for several minutes. Mickey had decided to drop the question when he pointed a small finger.

"LuBelle lives down there."

"I don't see any houses."

"It's back through the woods, across the canal."

They were almost to the Chosen bridge when Terry pointed again. "Left here."

Mickey smiled. "You know left and right?"

"Yes ma'am."

The road was rutted, ill-defined. "Are you sure we can get through here, Terrell?"

"Mr. McCree does it." Terrell was sitting forward on the seat now, hands on the dashboard. Weeds scraped both sides of the car as they pushed through, winding along a marshy path.

"There it is, Mama."

Whatever Mickey had expected, the shack was a shock. The siding was nailed haphazardly to the walls, with cracks between, knotholes missing. The windows were simple shutters without screens. The front door stood wide open. The sheet-metal roof was rusted.

With obvious familiarity, Terrell bounded from the

car and walked directly inside. Mickey trailed behind, taking steps through the high grass with trepidation.

"Dog!" Terrell called.

From under the shack came the mongrel, tail slowly wagging.

"I think that dog has mange, Terrell."

"No ma'am. He got snake-bit."

"What are you doing to it?"

"Putting on camphor water. It holds down pain and soreness."

"Be sure you wash your hands afterward."

Terrell looked at her with an oddly discomforting expression, then continued daubing water onto the pup's neck.

"Good Lord," Mickey said, looking at the walls of McCree's dwelling. "What a mess, Terrell. How could you enjoy staying out here?"

Terry worked, head down, holding Dog's front feet with one hand, pushing the animal against his leg to expose the bite.

"What does he do with all this junk?"

"He sells it."

"Who on earth would want it?"

"Some of it florists want. Some he sells to other people."

Mickey gingerly lifted a burlap sack covering several boxes.

"Those are cocoons," Terry said, quietly.

Mickey dropped the sack, dusted her fingertips. She scanned the dried snakeskins, turtle shells, wasp nests, and her eyes came to rest on Terrell. The boy was staring at her with an expression that was disturbing.

"What is it?" she asked, her tone more biting than she'd intended.

"Nothing." The boy went to a bucket and carried it to a drum out back. He lifted a screen from the reservoir and scooped rainwater funneled from the eaves of the roof.

"Dog!" Terrell put the bucket where the mongrel could drink. He left her standing in the yard, went inside and got a saucepan, then returned to scoop more water. He carefully replaced the screen cover over the water tank.

"Do you need some help with that?" Mickey asked, watching Terrell wrestle a large rock from the top of an abandoned washing machine.

"I got it," he said, dropping the stone to the ground. He reached for a knob which served as a handle in the center of the lid and lifted it, drawing it toward him, holding the cover almost like a shield as he stood on tiptoes and peered inside. Then he quickly replaced the lid and looked around.

"What is it?" Mickey asked.

"I need a stick." Terry picked up a bamboo rod.

He removed the lid again and, with the stick, poked at something inside the washing machine.

"Terrell, what's in there?" Mickey walked toward him.

The sudden whir of a disturbed rattler froze her where she stood. Her heart slamming, stomach drawing tight, a pain shot from her lower back.

"Terrell!"

He was pouring the saucepan of water into the washing machine.

"Get away from there!"

"Just a minute."

"Now! Get back!" She ran to him and yanked him violently, the saucepan spilling on both of them.

"Mama!"

"Are you trying to get killed?" She hauled him around the house.

"Mama, wait! I have to put the lid back on!"

"No!"

"Mama!" Terrell twisted suddenly, pulling free. His defiance stunned Mickey.

"I have to put the lid on," Terrell said, voice low.

"Terrell, you might get bitten!"

"No, I won't."

Terrell sidestepped around her, then ran toward the rear of the building as she followed.

"Oh, God, Terrell, no!"

The lolling black tongue from a triangular head licked the air. The rattling had halted, but now two diamond-scaled reptiles were attempting to slither free. Terrell grabbed a piece of bamboo and put it under the body of one snake, trying to lift him back before the serpent fell to the ground.

"Dear God!" Mickey screamed.

The rattler slid down the pole toward Terrell's quivering arms. "Terrell, let him alone!"

The other snake plopped, lay motionless a second, then began moving away.

"Terrell! Let him go!"

He now held the lid of the washing machine, peering over it as he somehow shoved the first large snake back inside. He pushed the cap into place.

"Terrell! For God's sake! Let him go!"

The boy ran inside, seized a burlap sack and came out again. Mickey grabbed for him and he yanked away, turning to glare at her an instant, then running toward the escaping serpent. Mickey saw the washing machine lid jiggle as a captive tried to push it aside. She picked up a broken hoe handle and whammed the lid hard. She heard the electrifying whir of rattles inside, now several.

She clutched her stomach with both hands, gasping. Terrell stood before the rattlesnake now, legs spread, the reptile drawing into a defensive coil, head lifted.

"Terrell! Terrell!"

He stood as though trying to stare the creature into submission. The snake's undulating body forming a heap, tail buzzing, the angry reptile was almost as high as Terrell's waist.

"Let that damned snake alone!"

He tossed the burlap sack toward the reptile, and in that instant, the snake struck! A blur, stabbing, snapping back to a coil so fast it left Mickey with mouth open, lungs locked, heart pounding. Terrell used his stick to fish the burlap sack over the snake.

"Terrell," Mickey tried to hold her tone to a calm, forceful, more insistent—

"Stay back," Terrell ordered. "He can feel you walking."

"Terrell, please—let him alone."

"He doesn't have ears. He feels things move."

"Terrell! Get away from there."

"Don't move, Mama. See, he's stopped rattling. He doesn't feel us and he doesn't see us, so he stopped rattling. He can't hear us talking because—"

"Terrell! What are you going to do?"

"Put him back in the tub."

"No you're not, young man!"

"Mama! Don't walk!"

The sack moved and the snake's head appeared, tongue flicking.

"Oh, God, Terrell! Please. This is killing me. Please! Let him go. I'll pay for the snake. Let him go!"

Terrell looked at her steadily. "He'd sell for a dollar."

"I'll pay the dollar. Let him go, son."

"You promise?"

Mickey was gasping, shaking, voice quaking. "I promise. I'll pay the dollar. Come away. Please."

Terrell dropped the stick and walked toward her. Mickey seized his hand and together they rounded the house, moving as fast as her cramping would allow. Inside the automobile, she sat, soaked with perspiration, shivering violently.

"I have to go back."

She lunged for him and Terrell eluded her, scampering out the door, leaving it open.

Mickey was crying now, groaning. She tried to open

her door and her hands slid, made slippery by her own perspiration. She was almost out of the vehicle when Terrell came running to the car.

"I had to put the rock on the lid," he said.

"Oh—" Mickey eased her head back on the seat. "Oh, dear God—oh—"

"Are you all right, Mama?"

Mickey was sobbing, her body wrenching with convulsions. She felt Terrell's hand on her arm, patting. "Are you all right, Mama?"

Mickey cried, without answering, the tiny hand patting, patting, whispering, "Are you all right, Mama?"

Ike Franklin offered coffee to everyone. He had a deputy go downstairs and get a soft drink from a machine for Terry. Miss Ramsey, the deputy, Sheriff Lambert; Mr. Hammond, the principal, and Mrs. Wright, Terry's teacher, were there. Mickey and Gerald sat stiffly, trying to make casual conversation seem natural, but to Terry, it sounded strained and out of place.

After everyone had prepared their coffees, Judge Franklin said, "I have considered everything carefully. I want everybody to know that. One thing we must all recognize is that everyone here has the interest of this little fellow at heart. We want what is best for him. You understand that, don't you, Terrell?"

Terry nodded.

"I have some good news, actually." Ike Franklin smiled, shuffling several manila folders into a pile. "I think I know what's been happening to our adventurer. I think I've found the root to his problem."

Terry looked from one adult to another. Mama was pale, face drawn.

"Terrell has been under the influence of an interesting, exciting man. He has been doing what any lad of comparable age would do, I think. He's been going where it's most fun to be. Isn't that right, Terrell?"

Not fully understanding, Terry nodded anyway.

"I want to say this, Gerald. We will be holding hearings this coming Thursday and possibly Friday. It will be that long before the elderly gentleman can be released from the hospital. He was slightly anemic, dehydrated, suffering a neglected compound fracture and there was some question as to whether they could save his arm. But now Dr. Norman says it appears McCree will be all right. He seems to have remarkable stamina.

"Sheriff Lambert has issued a summons. Ostensibly it is for contributing to the delinquency of a minor, but in fact it is a prelude to legal action aimed at having the man committed. I'm convinced from our investigation that he is not capable of functioning as a responsible member of society. Due process demands a formal hearing, then rigorous testing. Hopefully we can convince him to voluntarily have himself placed where somebody can look after him."

"What if he leaves town?" Mickey asked.

"He won't, Mickey," Judge Franklin said. "His truck is impounded for operating without a license. He couldn't go far with a broken arm. Besides, I don't think he'd do that. I've spoken to him and he's an agreeable fellow, actually."

"What about—Terrell?" Mickey's voice was small.

"He'll have to go to school," Judge Franklin said, suddenly stern. He was looking at Terrell. "If you don't go, son, they're going to find you and put you in a place where the doors are locked and you are watched every minute. Do you understand that?"

"Yessir."

"I want you to give your word to everybody here that you are going to school."

"Yessir."

"Let me hear you say that, son."

"I'm going to school."

Judge Franklin glanced at the parents. "You are

going to do what your mommy and daddy tell you. Let me hear you say that."

"I'm going to do what Mama and Daddy tell me."

"Yes," Judge Franklin said. He took a deep breath and looked at the assembly. "It will be necessary to have everyone in court Thursday morning, ten o'clock, Ed."

Sheriff Lambert nodded. Judge Franklin pushed several folded pieces of paper at the sheriff.

"Serve those subpoenas first thing Monday morning."

The sheriff passed the papers to the deputy.

"Need I issue formal summonses to the rest of you?" Judge Franklin inquired. All of them shook their heads.

"Terrell," Judge Franklin's tone softened.

"Look at Judge Franklin, Terrell," Daddy commanded.

"Terrell," Judge Franklin said, "I know you don't think so this minute, but all these people are your friends. Someday, when you look back, you will be thankful all this happened. Otherwise, son, your life would be a dark, unhappy road. Without education, doomed to a laborer's job, you would become one of the millions of people who can never become something special. Your father, with a college education, wants his son to have the best possible education, too. He and your mother want you to grow up and become President of the United States. Who knows, that might happen. We think you are a very smart little boy. We think you will make a superb student and someday a fine member of society. All that makes little sense to you now. It will someday."

Judge Franklin stood. "I'll see you all Thursday, December fourth, at ten o'clock, if I don't see you before."

"Thank you, Judge."

"I think everything is going to work out just fine." Judge Franklin smiled, putting a hand on Terrell's shoulder.

"Thank you, Ike," Mickey said. Judge Franklin hugged her gently as Mama blinked back tears.

Their footsteps echoed as they went down the flight of marble steps. Terry heard the sheriff and Miss Ramsey laughing somewhere back upstairs.

"Anybody want a banana split?" Gerald asked.

"I shouldn't," Mickey said, "but I do."

They crossed the street, going toward the drugstore. "How about you, Terrell?"

Terry nodded. He caught his parents looking at one another across his head.

The drugstore had double doors which folded back, forming an open corner of the building. Seated at a round table, Terry could gaze out at pedestrians who had come to town for their weekly shopping. Across the street, queued before the theater, children awaited the first of a double feature, cartoons and another installment of Captain Midnight.

"Ike is a thoughtful man," Gerald said.

"Yes. He handles children well."

Gerald nodded, spooning ice cream in such a way that he also got a piece of banana.

"He's very thorough, too," Gerald said. "Going to see McCree, talking to the washerwoman and the packing-house guard. I don't think he missed a trick."

"Really, Gerald, Ike is right. That old man needs to be committed. The idea of allowing a six-year-old to handle rattlesnakes!"

"I didn't get bit," Terry said, firmly.

"Through no fault of your own!" Mickey snapped.

"I know how to do it."

"Eat your split," Gerald ordered Terry. Then to Mickey, "Relax, baby. Enjoy your calories."

"Oh, you!" Mama laughed shortly.

Two black children on roller skates whizzed past, metal wheels zinging. They wheeled, returned and stood watching Terry eat his ice cream. Terry took a bite, returning their gaze.

"Where are you going, Terrell?"

He carried the remainder of his ice cream to the two children and held it out. They studied him soberly, glanced at his parents, then dashed off down the street.

"That's some boy, Mickey," Gerald said gently. "Some boy."

Mickey stood abruptly. She took the ice cream from Terry's hands, the fingers of her other hand digging into his shoulder.

"Come sit down," she said. "Eat, or don't eat, as you choose. But don't get up from the table again."

Terry winced as she pushed him back to his seat.

"You don't want that?" Daddy asked.

"No."

"Mind if I eat it?"

Terry pushed it toward Gerald. He sat, head hung, blinking fast.

"Terrell?"

"Ma'am."

"I'm sorry," Mama said, her voice low. "I was wrong to do that. You were being very generous. I'm sorry."

Terry nodded, head still down.

17

~ ~ ~

Terry got out of the automobile, his lunch sack in hand, and walked toward Mrs. Wright. He stood before the teacher as she smiled and waved at Mama. Mrs. Wright took Terry's wrist and led him to the classroom. He was the only student there. She busied herself at her desk as he sat looking at students playing before school started.

"If I give you work to do at home, do you think you could get caught up?" Mrs. Wright asked. Her voice sounded hollow in the empty room.

"Yes ma'am."

"Your mother isn't feeling too well these days, Terrell. I expect you to be a big boy about this and do the work as much as you can by yourself."

"Yes ma'am."

The bell rang and Mrs. Wright went to the classroom door, watching students line up outside for an orderly entrance. Terry kept his face averted as the boys and girls came in, panting from play, taking their seats, faces glistening with perspiration.

"Hands on the desks," Mrs. Wright instructed. "No talking, please."

A lump in Terry's stomach grew ever larger, a bad taste in his mouth. Cooty whispered in his ear.

"Did you really go to New York?"

Terry nodded.

"No talking, students," Mrs. Wright stated, her back to the class.

"They put you in jail?" Cooty marveled.

Another nod.

"There're some eighth graders who say they're going to give you a whipping," Cooty related. Terry's heart jumped.

"They've been waiting for you every day. They say they'll get you after school."

"What did I say?" Mrs. Wright snapped, turning.

"No talking," Eddy Kent said.

"That's right, no talking!"

Terry was sitting alone, eating his lunch, the nickel in his pocket for better uses than milk. He had to make frequent trips to the water fountain to choke down the thick peanut butter Mama had prepared. The eighth grader caught him on his way back from the fountain.

Terry sprawled headlong, lunch scattering from the blow to the back of his head. His knee scraped on concrete. He sat up and for a moment watched blood rise in the abrasion. Then, eyes narrowed, lips pursed, he got to his feet.

"You lying puke!" the eighth grader said. "I'm going to knock your head off. Little punk!"

Terry remembered Bucky's sage advice, "Don't put your thumb inside your fist; when they're bigger than you, anything's fair."

The eighth grader lunged at Terry. The smaller boy twisted and with a vicious jab drove a thumb into the right eye of the attacker.

"Ow! Dirty!"

Terry's foot came up as hard as he could kick, and he heard a satisfying groan before the assailant shrieked and fell to his knees. Again, recalling Bucky's counsel, "Whip 'em good, or you got to whip 'em twice," he grabbed the eighth grader's head with both hands and clamped his teeth into an ear. The breathless, beaten boy first moaned, then screamed as Terry's mouth filled with the salty taste of blood.

"Terrell!"

Terry held the head and worked his teeth back and forth, grinding into the ear.

"Terrell! Let go! Good God! Terrell!" Somebody slapped Terry's head and his ears rang, still he rasped teeth into flesh. "Terrell! My God he's going to bite it off! Somebody help me with these students! Somebody! Terrell!"

Mr. Hammond led Terry past his mother into the living room. Mama's hands were shaking as she gestured toward a chair for the principal.

"Mrs. Calder, I hate to do this. I have never actually expelled a first-grade student before. But really, we can't have this sort of thing. Terrell is disrupting the entire school. I'm truly sorry, but you'd better keep him here at home. He has to be in court Thursday anyway, so let's wait until everything has been settled before trying to put him back in class again."

Mama said something, too whispered for Terry to catch it.

"I know, Mrs. Calder," Mr. Hammond said. He appeared nervous, face worried.

"I don't know what to do, Mr. Hammond."

"I know, Mrs. Calder."

"I've tried everything."

Mr. Hammond nodded, brow furrowed.

"I just don't know what to do anymore."

Mama dabbed her eyes and nose, Terry and the principal sitting silent, uncomfortable.

"How's the boy's ear?" Mama asked.

"They think they can sew it up."

"Gerald and I will pay—"

"No, that isn't necessary. The school pays for damages up to a point. In defense of your son, I think you should know the other boy outweighed Terrell by forty pounds. He also attacked Terrell. Mrs. Wright saw the entire incident. That boy has been a bully for years, in and out of trouble since the first grade. He really deserved the trouncing he got, Mrs. Calder."

"I don't know what Judge Franklin is going to say about this," Mama wept.

"I think he'd say the eighth grader deserved a whipping. Judge Franklin has had that child on probation for some time. However, nobody is going to mention this to the judge. So don't worry about that."

"What am I going to do with him?" Mama demanded, glaring now at Terry.

"Let's wait until after the hearing Thursday, Mrs. Calder. A few more days out of school won't make that much difference with Terrell at this point."

Mr. Hammond stood, paused awkwardly, then patted Mama's shoulder before leaving.

Mama sat, a wet handkerchief showing between her fingers.

"Terrell, I want you to stay in this house. Don't go outside. Is that clear?"

"Yes ma'am."

She looked at him, her eyes reddened, cheeks puffy. "Terrell, why are you doing all this?"

"I don't know."

"Don't you see what is going to happen to you? They're going to take you away from us, Terrell. They are going to send you away. There won't be a thing your father or I can do to stop it. Don't you understand that?"

"Yes ma'am."

"Do you understand that?"

"Yes ma'am."

"Then why do you continue to do these things?"

"I don't know, Mama."

"Don't you love Daddy and Mama?"

"Yes ma'am."

She began crying again and tears rose in Terry's eyes too.

"I can't help it, Mama."

"What?"

"I can't help it."

Her expression was almost that of fright, looking at him, head shaking. "Terrell, if you can't help it, if we can't stop it, what's going to happen?"

"I don't know, Mama."

"Oh, God—" Mama pushed herself to her feet, holding her stomach with her hands as she walked toward the back bedroom.

"Mama!"

"What is it, Terrell?"

He was standing in the doorway, tears on his cheeks. "I'm sorry, Mama."

"Being sorry isn't enough anymore, son."

She went into the bedroom and laid down, weeping. When she turned, Terry was standing in the door, crying, watching.

"Mama. I love you, Mama."

Mickey rolled onto her side, her back to him, and closed her eyes without answering.

Gerald listened impassively as Mickey told about Terry's fight and the principal's comments. Terry sat at the dinner table, food unserved, hands in his lap. His eyes large, he watched every muscle in Gerald's face, awaiting a verdict.

"Do you know what you're doing to your mother, Terrell?"

"Yessir."

"I don't think you do," Gerald said coldly. "If you truly knew, and if you did it anyway, I would find it very difficult to forgive you for it, Terrell. You see her crying. You see how disappointed and upset she is. But what you don't see is what she feels inside. She is ashamed to talk to her friends. Everybody knows the trouble we've been having with you. Our friends feel sorry for us. But after a while, our friends, and Judge Franklin, and the principal and everybody else begins to wonder what could be so terribly wrong in this family. What could be so wrong that a boy would do what you've been doing over and over again?"

Terry's head dropped, eyes down.

"Look at me, son."

Terry lifted his eyes.

"What is wrong, Terrell?"

"Nothing."

"That can't be true, Terrell. If nothing was wrong, why would you continue to get into trouble?"

"I don't know, Daddy."

Gerald sighed heavily and stared at the dinner table. "How long has it been since we had a meal without tension? My stomach is in a knot, baby." Mickey stopped putting food on his plate and began serving Terry.

"Why do some people call you Terry?" Daddy asked.

"I don't know."

Wham! Daddy's fist struck the table and the silverware leaped. Terry jolted, his back pinned to his chair.

"Why do they call you Terry?" Gerald demanded, louder.

"I don't know, Daddy!"

"Why don't they call you Roscoe, or Charlie or Dick, then?"

"That's not my name."

"Is your name Terry?"

"No sir."

"Then why do you tell people that is your name?"

"I don't like it."

"You don't like the name Terrell?"

"No sir," trembling voice.

Daddy's tone altered suddenly. "Would you like for us to call you Terry, too?"

Terry nodded. Gerald looked at Mickey, and for a long time, nobody moved.

"Eat your supper, *Terry*," Mama said.

Terry began eating, hands shivering, the English peas

falling off his fork. He chanced to glance up, fork before an open mouth, and was stunned at what he saw.

Mama and Daddy were smiling at one another.

"They think that the boy you bit has rabies," Bucky said.

"Aw, they do not!"

"They sure do," Bucky reported. "Somebody said he was frothing at the mouth and snapping at his ma and pa. He bit a cat next door and the cat died!"

Terry laughed suddenly and Bucky's serious expression melted. "Spread that around awhile and I betcha nobody wants to take you on."

The two boys strolled the packing house platform. The guard approached them, scowling. "Your folks know where you are, Terrell?"

"Yessir."

The boy didn't run. He met the adult's eyes firmly. The guard yielded. "You boys stay out of trouble, you hear me?"

"Yessir."

Bucky put an arm around Terry's shoulder. "Do they really know?"

"Yeah. I told Mama I was coming over here. She gave me a quarter. I'm going to buy a hot dog. You got any money?"

"No," Bucky said.

"I have another quarter, too," Terry admitted. "I sold nine cigarettes this morning."

Bucky blinked his crossed eyes, arm squeezing Terry's shoulder. "I'm sure going to miss you, Terry."

"I'm not going anywhere."

"That's not what I heard," Bucky said, both of them chinning themselves up to the snack-bar counter so they could see the hot dogs being constructed.

"Well, I'm not," Terry declared.

"I heard tell you were going to Marianna Boys' School," Bucky claimed.

"I'm not, though. Judge Franklin told my mama everything was going to be all right."

"Hmm-m," Bucky accepted the hot dog, liberally salted it and, with a Nehi orange drink, followed Terry to a table. "You can't believe those high school kids, you know it? They'll lie to anybody. They said you went to jail and—"

"I did."

"You did!"

"Yeah. You want some peanuts to put in your drink? I have another dime."

"Sure! You really did?"

"Yeah," Terry said, without pride.

"Is it true they're going to lock away the old man?" Bucky asked.

Terry stopped eating. "Who told you that?"

"My pa. He said they were going to put him away for making you a delinquent."

"He didn't do anything to me!"

"That's not what they say."

"What'd he do to me?" Terry shrilled.

"Cornholed you, maybe, I don't know."

"He didn't do *any*thing to me!"

"Okay, okay, maybe I'm wrong. I was wrong about you going to Marianna, wasn't I?"

Terry ate his hot dog, sucking NuGrape from the bottle, teeth clenched to keep the salted nuts from getting by.

"Bucky, you think they can do that to Mr. McCree?"

"Hell, I don't know. If the johns get down on you, you might as well leave town, I can tell you that. They got down on my brother and they hounded his ass until they caught him down to Clewiston drinking and fighting. That's what got him sent to the road gang."

"Just fighting?" Terry was thinking of the eighth grader.

"Well, not just fighting. He hit a john in the head with a culvert pipe. That had something to do with it."

A man sat at an adjoining table and Terry leaned over. "Can I have a cigarette, please?"

The man gave him one.

"Could I have one for my friend?" Terry asked.

The man swore under his breath and handed over another Pall Mall.

"Thanks," Bucky said.

"Bucky, do you know what *committed* means?"

"We formed a committee once in class," Bucky dimly recalled.

"I don't think it means that. The judge said something about having Mr. McCree committed."

Bucky's head turned slowly as he shifted the emphasis of his gaze from the good eye to the bad one. "Yeah," he said, puffing his cigarette. "That does mean they're going to lock him up, I bet."

"I got to go, Bucky."

"Wait a minute, Terry! Where you going?"

"I got to go see Mr. McCree."

"You said they wouldn't let you in!"

"They wouldn't. But I got to go see him."

"Terry! Hell, if you can't get in, that's that, ain't it?"

Terry jumped off a loading dock and crossed the paved road for smoother walking along a railroad spur, feet touching only the creosoted cross-ties.

"Listen," Bucky reached the territorial limits he was allowed to wander and halted. "Terry, listen, I'll be waiting here when you come back, okay? Let me know what he says, okay?"

"I might not come back," Terry hollered.

"You better! They'll lock your ass up if you don't."

Terry began to run.

The nurse intercepted Terry as he walked fast down a tiled corridor.

"Whoa, young man! No children allowed in the ward."

"Please ma'am, I got to see my granddaddy."

"Who is your granddaddy?"

"Mr. McCree."

"How do you spell that?"

"I don't know." Terry was pulling against her grasp.

"Well, sonny, they don't allow visitors at this hour, even if you were grown-up. But children are never allowed to go into the ward."

"I got to tell him!"

"Tell him what?"

"Tell him about Grandmama."

"What about grandmama?"

"She died."

"Died!" the nurse gasped.

"She's home in bed dead and I need to know about feeding the dog."

"Jesus Christ," the nurse said.

"Please ma'am, let me see him." Terry began to weep.

"Whoa! Whoa! Hold it. I'll see what I can do."

Terry watched her from the sides of his eyes as the nurse telephoned someone, speaking in a hushed voice. She now turned to Terry, her tone sympathetic.

"The doctor wants to see you. But he's busy right now. He said Mr. McCree can come out into the hall and visit with you if he feels like it. How about that?"

"That's good."

The nurse indicated a bench where Terry could wait and she disappeared through the swinging doors of the ward. When she returned, she was holding Mr. McCree's arm and the old man was grinning, face shaved, wearing a faded blue robe over white cotton pajamas. He wore slippers that clopped with each shuffled step.

"Heylo, Little Hawk!"

"How's your arm, Mr. McCree?"

"Itches mostly. Slip over and let me sit with you."

"Is that thing heavy?"

"Not much. Bothersome, though. I keep bumping

people and things when I turn around. Can't say why they put it so my elbow sticks out this way."

Terry inched closer to the old man. "I told them you were my granddaddy."

"I know," McCree whispered.

Terry hesitated. "I told them I had to tell you Grandmama was home dead in the bed."

"Yes," McCree's eyes twinkled. "The nurse told me. I don't think she understood my laughing about it. I told her I never did like your grandmother too much."

Terry slipped his arm inside McCree's. The old man's sleeve felt empty of all except a little skin and bone.

"Mr. McCree?"

"What, Little Hawk?"

"I got us in a peck of trouble, Mr. McCree."

"How much is a peck, boy?"

"How many cups, you mean?"

"How many cups."

"Two cups in a pint, two pints in a quart, eight quarts in a peck—right?"

"Right."

Terry's fingers flicked against his knee. "Thirty-two."

"Pretty good," McCree said. "Little slow, but right."

"I'll practice it."

A man in white appeared and Terry looked up at a staff doctor.

"Mr. McCree, is this child your grandson?"

"You could say that," McCree said.

"He told the nurse—did you know—"

"Yes," McCree's face was suddenly sorrowful. "Terrible thing. So quick. She was all right yesterday. Isn't that what you said, Little Hawk?"

"She was fine."

"Is there anyone you'd like us to call, Mr. McCree?" the doctor asked, his voice gentle.

"No, no, I don't think so. What do you think, Little Hawk?"

"I don't think so."

"No," McCree said to the doctor. "We tend to our own, we do."

"Mr. McCree," the doctor scrutinized the boy and old man, "I'm sorry, sir, but I don't believe this story."

"It's a real shame. All right yesterday, Little Hawk?"

"Yessir, she was fine."

"Then this morning?"

"Dead," Terry intoned.

"In bed," McCree noted.

"Yessir."

"Mr. McCree, we have hospital regulations about children visiting. I really think this boy will have to go."

"I guess that's it, Little Hawk."

"I want to talk to you, Mr. McCree."

"I'd like that, Little Hawk. But the man says you're going to have to go. It's his hospital, not mine."

Terry stood, lips quivering. The doctor motioned to the nurse, and she came and took Terry's arm.

"When can I see you, Mr. McCree?"

"Oh, pretty soon, I expect."

"I need to talk to you!"

"We'll talk, boy."

"You little liar," the nurse said, voice low.

"Let go my arm."

"If you show up here again, I'll blister your gluteus maximus. Don't come back, little boy."

She pushed him toward the exit, Terry looking back as the doctor helped Mr. McCree stand.

"I should've known better," the nurse said, sharply. "Kids who lie go to hell, did you know that?"

"Little Hawk!" McCree's voice echoed in the hall.

The nurse halted, and Terry called back, "Yessir?"

"Don't try to bury her by yourself, son!"

Terry pulled his arm free of the nurse. "No sir, I won't—Granddaddy."

As Terry pushed through the door to the outside, he heard McCree chuckling.

18

Judge Franklin sat higher than anyone else, behind a polished desk. People being questioned sat to one side of the judge. When they brought in Mr. McCree, he was put at a table by himself, where he sat, elbow awkwardly jutting, listening to the proceedings.

A woman took the stand. "Mrs. Helen Osborn," the attorney asked, "do you know Jackson Cole McCree?"

"He comes into the health department once or twice a year for inoculations."

"What is the charge to Mr. McCree for these inoculations?"

"There is no charge. To him or anyone else. The shots are free."

Dr. Phillip Norman was called and he sat uncomfortably, constantly glancing at his watch.

"Dr. Norman, is Jackson Cole McCree a patient of yours?"

"Yes."

"How many times have you treated him?"

"Three that I recall."

"Why was treatment required, Dr. Norman?"

Dr. Norman put on eyeglasses and took a piece of paper from his pocket. He said, "Most recently, Mr. McCree was treated for a compound fracture of the right arm. About a year ago, he was treated for snakebite on the right hand. Several years before that, I treated him for snakebite, also."

"Poisonous snakes, Dr. Norman?"

"Yes, poisonous."

"Were they serious?"

Dr. Norman's eyebrows lifted. "Any poisonous snake-bite would be termed potentially serious. Particularly at his age."

"Thank you, Doctor. Oh! One other thing, Doctor. What kind of payment did you receive from Mr. McCree for professional services rendered?"

"He was a charity patient."

"How long has he been in the charity ward at the hospital this time?"

"About ten days."

"Who pays for charity patients, in fact, Doctor?"

"The county. Taxes."

"Thank you, Doctor. You may step down."

"Mr. Michael Elton, please."

A man walked toward the stand self-consciously adjusting his tie. He wore a new suit, shined shoes. It took Terry a minute to recognize him.

"Mr. Elton, what is your occupation?"

"I'm a security guard at the Blue Goose Packing Company. I work day shift, usually."

"Have you ever seen this man before, Mr. Elton?" The attorney pointed a pencil at Mr. McCree.

"Yessir, I have."

"Tell us about it, please."

The guard's hands kneaded one another. As he spoke, he gazed across the heads of everybody seated in the courtroom, his voice high-pitched.

"When I saw the old man come down that chute, I couldn't believe it. I mean, a person could get killed doing something like that. But there he went, zooming down the ramp into the washing machine, where he got soaked to the skin just like the kids. He got up and ran with them, like he was a kid, too."

The attorney nodded seriously. When Mr. Elton stopped talking, the attorney asked a question or two to reinforce the testimony, then, to Terry's surprise, the pencil pointed at him.

"Do you know the red-haired child, Mr. Elton?"

"His name's Terrell Calder."

"Yes," the attorney said. "Is Terrell one of the boys you saw with Mr. McCree?"

"Yessir. But now, I ought to tell you, I've seen the old gent a lot of times and this was the only time I ever saw him actually doing something wrong. Usually he comes around the packing house looking through scrap piles for crates, boxes and hampers that've been thrown out because they're damaged."

"Fine, Mr. Elton. But what we want to know now is was this boy, Terrell Calder, with McCree when they rode down the chute at the packing house?"

"He was one of them. Bucky Dallas was the other. The boy Bucky and this Terrell Calder run around together a lot."

"Thank you, Mr. Elton. You may be excused."

"Mr. McCree," Judge Franklin said, "you may question any of these people on your own behalf, if you wish."

"Can't think of anything I'd want to ask," McCree said.

"It's your right to cross-examine, Mr. McCree."

"Thank you, Judge," McCree nodded soberly. "If I think of something, I'll ask."

Judge Franklin looked at the prosecuting attorney. "Go ahead, Mr. Garrick."

Mr. Garrick called Eunice Washington. The black woman came from another room, passing through a door opened by a deputy. She hesitated, eyes darting, and the judge said, "Come over here and sit down, Eunice. We only want to ask a few questions."

Eunice avoided looking at Mr. McCree. She didn't seem to see Terry sitting between his mother and father on a bench, surrounded by other people the attorney planned to call.

"Your name is Eunice Washington?"

"Yessir." Her voice was surprisingly loud.

"What do you do for a living, Eunice?"

"Takes in washing."

"Where do you live?"

"Out close to Chosen."

"Do you live alone?"

"My Grandbaby she lives with me."

"What is her name?"

"LuBelle." Eunice pased. "Washington."

"Eunice, do you know Terrell Calder?"

"I knows him. Terry."

"That's right, Terry. How well do you know Terry?"

"He comes to play with my LuBelle."

"How long has he been doing this?"

Eunice lifted a shoulder, dropped it. "Couple years, maybe."

"Do you feed him when he's out there?"

"Most times he eats a little something," Eunice said. "If he's hungry. What boy ain't?" Several people laughed.

"Has he ever stayed overnight at your house?"

Eunice tensed visibly. She mumbled something.

"I told you before you came in here," Mr. Garrick said softly, "you are not in any trouble. We are trying to establish where the boy spent a week of his time. Just answer my questions honestly, Eunice."

"Yessir."

"Has he ever spent the night with you?"

"Two nights."

"When was this?"

"Week or two back."

"Didn't you think about whether he had people who would be worried, Eunice?"

"That boy lied to me."

"What did he say?"

"Says he don't have no people."

"Did you believe that?"

"No."

"Then why did you let Terry stay with you?"

Eunice shook her head.

"Come on, now, Eunice. Tell us. Why did you let Terry stay at your house overnight?"

"I didn't want to send him out to sleep in the swamps. I figured he needed someplace and I let him stay. I didn't meant to do him harm."

"We understand that, Eunice. Why did Terry finally leave your house?"

"I told him he couldn't stay. Told him to go home to his people."

"So you knew he was lying about being an orphan?"

"Yessir."

"How did you know?"

"That child comes to play with clean clothes. He gets a scratch and there's a bandage on it. He was too cared for."

"All right, Eunice. Now, do you know that gentleman sitting at the table by himself?"

"Mr. Cree."

"How long have you known Mr. McCree?"

"Oh, lawd. Long time."

"About how long?"

"Twenty, thirty years, maybe."

"What is your relationship with him?"

Eunice cut her eyes, warily. "What do that mean?"

"I mean, does he bring you laundry to do? Do you work for him? Does he buy from you, or sell things to you?"

"Oh, yessir. He comes on trading day. Brings fish and things I ain't got the time to catch, what with Lu-Belle to look after."

"What do you give him, for the fish and things he brings?"

"He stays to eat, mostly. I cooks. When he gets a yen for hot food, he'll stop by to take a meal with us."

"I see. He's been doing this twenty years or so?"

"About that."

"After Terry left your place, Eunice, where did he go?"

"To Cree's."

"When you told Terry he couldn't stay with you any longer, he went to Mr. McCree's?"

"So far's I know."

"No further questions, Your Honor."

Judge Franklin said to Mr. McCree, "Would you like to ask this woman any questions?"

"No. She said it right."

"Mr. McCree, are you sure you wouldn't like to engage counsel?"

"No," McCree said, his voice low.

Judge Franklin turned to Eunice, "You may go, Eunice. Thank you."

"Yessir, Judge. Can I say something?"

"If you wish."

"That white man is a good man, Judge. He looks after LuBelle and me. Comes to fetch firewood, brings us to town when LuBelle got the mumps, to see the doctor. He mended my roof after the hurricanes. Mr. Cree's a good man."

"Thank you, Eunice."

"Terry's a good boy, too."

"Thank you, Eunice."

"Him and that old man is two of a kind, they are."

"All right, Eunice. You may step down."

"Go home?"

"Yes."

Eunice walked out the side door of the courtroom.

"Sheriff Edward Lambert," the attorney called. The large law officer walked heavily to the stand. He sat, legs spread, one hand holding the arm of the chair, elbow out almost like McCree's, but without a cast to keep it there.

"Sheriff, are you holding a 1934 Ford pickup truck?"

"I am."

"Who is the registered owner of that vehicle?"

"It isn't registered. Mr. McCree claims ownership."

"Why are you holding it?"

"Operating without a license."

"When was it last licensed?"

"Apparently by the original owner, but not since."

"Any other reason why you'd hold it?"

"The taillights are faulty, brakes are bad, the muffler is no good. It's a pile of junk with a motor."

"Sheriff, has this man, McCree, ever come to your attention before?"

"Not to my knowledge."

"No arrests?"

"Not by my office, no."

"If he'd been driving around town, would you have noticed the lack of a tag?"

"Most likely."

"So he probably avoided downtown driving."

"I would guess so."

"Sheriff, do you know the child, Terrell, or Terry, Calder?"

"He's one of Miss Ramsey's truants."

"You were given orders recently to pick him up?"

"For running away, yessir."

"Thank you, Sheriff."

Judge Franklin looked at McCree and the old man nodded, then shook his head no.

"Step down, Sheriff."

"Thank you, Judge."

"I think we should take a break for lunch," Judge Franklin announced. "Everyone under subpoena is to return here promptly at one o'clock. Mr. McCree and Mr. Garrick, step to the bench before leaving." The judge struck his desk with a gavel.

"I need a dollar, Mama."

"What for, Terry?"

"For Mr. McCree."

"Not now."

"Mama! You promised!"

"Later, Terrell. Not now."

"Mama!" His voice made people turn.

"Mickey, what is this?" Gerald snapped.

"I told Terrell I'd pay for that rattlesnake he let go."

"Then for God's sake do it."

"Right now, Gerald? Right here?"

"You promised," Terry wailed.

Mama fished around in her pocketbook, face flaming. Gerald withdrew his wallet and took out a dollar bill. He gave this to Terry. Terry pushed through a swinging gate and walked toward McCree, who was talking in hushed tones with the judge.

"Mr. McCree, I insist you secure counsel. This is going badly for you. Are you aware of that?"

"Long as nobody lies," McCree argued gently, "what could a high-priced lawyer do?"

"Mr. McCree?"

"Yo, Little Hawk."

"When I went out to water your rattlesnakes, I let one get away because of Mama. She said she'd pay for it. I reckon it was about a dollar snake. It was one of the big ones."

"You keep the dollar, Little Hawk."

"No sir!" Terry pushed the bill into McCree's hand.

Mr. Garrick glanced at the judge and walked away. Judge Franklin spoke as Terry was returning to his parents. "Very well, Mr. McCree. We'll see you back here at one o'clock."

"Can Mr. McCree eat with us?" Terry asked.

"Absolutely not," Mama said.

"Mama, he can't find things to eat in town like he can out in the swamps."

"No!"

"Daddy?"

"I'm afraid not, Terry. Mickey, do you want to go to the drugstore?" They walked across the street, Mama holding one of Terry's hands, Daddy the other. They sat at a table which allowed Terry to see the courthouse door, up and down Main Street. Mr. McCree came down the broad white steps one at a time, slowly, looking at his feet. He stood uncertainly on the sidewalk, gazing first left, then right.

"Mama, please, let Mr. McCree eat with us."

"Terrell! No. Sit down and stop talking."

McCree moved slowly down the street. He paused again and again, looking through shop windows or up at signs overhead. Finally he went into the A&P.

Terry began to cry.

"Stop that, young man," Daddy said evenly. "Stop that, Terrell. This minute. Or I'll give you something to cry about."

After a while, Mr. McCree emerged from the grocery store, a small sack in hand. He shuffled back to the courthouse and found a bench in the shade of an oleander bush. Terry watched as McCree, with slow, deliberate movements, opened a can of vienna sausage, a package of crackers. He sat on the bench, pulling sausage from the can, chewing crackers, staring into space.

Burrell Mason entered and came to sit with them. "Gerald, did you get the good news?"

"No, Burrell. What?"

"The House of Representatives passed an antistrike bill by a vote of 252 to 136. Maybe we won't have that rail strike Sunday after all."

"Thank God for that," Gerald said.

"Gerald, it's almost one," Mickey noted.

"Burrell, we have to go, I'm sorry." They all stood except the publisher.

"Hey, redhead," Mr. Mason said, "you didn't touch your sandwich. Anything wrong with it?"

"No sir."

"What?"

"No sir!"

"Well, I tell you what, I'll give you a dime for it."

"Plus a nickel for the drink?" Terry questioned.

"Terrell!"

"Sounds fair to me," Mr. Mason said, ignoring Mama. He gave the coins to Terry and winked. Terry winked back, pocketing the money.

"Gerald, why did you let this child get away with that?" Mickey demanded, as they crossed the street.

"It was his sandwich," Gerald said, tersely. "It was his sale, Mickey."

Terry broke away and ran across the courthouse lawn. "Terrell!"

He reached McCree as the old man was putting the empty can and cracker wrappings into a paper sack.

"Mr. McCree?"

"Yes, Little Hawk?"

"I'm sorry, Mr. McCree."

"No need to be."

"I caused you all this trouble." Terry's lips twisted and he began to sob. McCree pulled the boy to him, his good arm enveloping Terry as he patted gently.

"I think your pappy wants you, Terrell."

The use of his name shocked Terry. "I'm sorry, Mr. McCree."

"I told you. No need to be, Little Hawk."

"Terrell, don't ever run across the street like that again," Gerald commanded, harshly. "You didn't look left or right."

He took Terry's arm. McCree's hand slipped away. Daddy's grip was very strong, Terry's arm throbbing from the pressure as they walked fast toward the courtroom.

Mr. Hammond told of meetings with Mrs. Wright, Terry's teacher, and with the parents. Meetings Terry had never known took place. Mr. Hammond spoke of the day he had Terry in his office for putting frogs in Mrs. Wright's desk. Everybody laughed except Terry, Mama, Daddy, Mr. McCree and Mrs. Wright. Mr.

Hammond didn't mention that Mrs. Wright had taken off her clothes in class.

Mrs. Wright spoke of Terry as bright but difficult. She said she was a friend of Mama's. Terry listened numbly as Mrs. Wright told of seeing Terry bolt from the school yard, refusing to answer her call. He heard himself described as intelligent, perceptive, well-mannered, but a paradox.

He didn't understand the word *paradox* but soon decided that it meant he wasn't truly intelligent, perceptive, and well-mannered.

Miss Ramsey sat, knees together, neat and professional in appearance and demeanor. She told how many days Terry had attended school, how many days he'd missed. She said she had chased him from cane fields to packing houses to Lake Okeechobee. She said he was her most persistent truant.

"Now, Miss Ramsey," Mr. Garrick questioned, "tell us what you've discovered in the past few weeks about Terrell Calder."

"He's been drawn to the man McCree," Miss Ramsey said. "Mr. McCree seems to wield some sort of control over this child. The old man is colorful. His house is a shack in the swamps with no electricity, no sanitary facilities. He has no way to bathe. The day I went there looking for Terrell, I found an unbelievable mess in the shack itself. If there was a bed, I didn't see it. Junk of all kinds litters every inch of space."

She described the burlap sacks, snakeskins, hampers of seeds and the lack of screens to keep out insects.

"The boy had gone out with Mr. McCree many times, I learned."

"In your opinion, Miss Ramsey, as a professionally trained social worker, did Mr. McCree exert a favorable influence on this child?"

"No sir, he did not."

"In what way, Miss Ramsey?"

"They ate what they could find, scavenging for seeds

and roots, which they cooked or ate raw. They slept in the open during the time they were out, under a makeshift thatched shack McCree constructed from palmetto fronds. The boy was covered with axle grease, which they'd applied to smother red bugs; they had smeared mud on themselves to attain some protection from insects. Nevertheless, Terrell was a mass of bites, some of which were festering and becoming muck sores.

"Under the spell of the old man, Terrell invented fanciful tales, resorted to lying—as, for example, saying he was orphaned. McCree not only ignored this, he seemed to condone it. He told the Negro washerwoman, Eunice Washington, he did not question Terrell's stories, accepting them as truth.

"In an interview with me, the first day McCree was in the hospital, he admitted Terrell drove the truck out of the swamps, bringing McCree in for medical care. He said the child had been allowed to steer the truck on other occasions. When they are together, McCree almost always takes advantage of the child, using him as a laborer to gather the seeds, cones and berries which McCree sells. They had both been climbing trees in search of air plants the day Mr. McCree fell and broke his arm. If McCree had died out there in the swamp, it is a virtual certainty that the child would have perished, also. As it is, McCree readily says, if he hadn't been with Terrell, he, McCree, would surely have died. He was incapable of getting back to town, by his own admission.

"I asked Mr. McCree if he had given any thought to the welfare of the child, why he wasn't in school, for example."

"What did Mr. McCree tell you?"

"He said it had never occurred to him."

"Miss Ramsey, you have given this case a good deal of thought, haven't you?"

"Many many hours."

"What, in your professional opinion, has been the

problem with Terrell Calder? What can be done about it?"

"The problem is, as I see it, Terrell has been mesmerized by Mr. McCree. He was a lonely child and the old man was lonely. Each served a need to the other. Mr. McCree is, apparently, incapable of assuming a responsible position in society. He appeals to Terrell's rebellious instincts, fosters them, in fact."

"And what can be done about this, Miss Ramsey?"

"First, the child should be separated from McCree."

"No!" Terry screamed.

"Terrell!" Mama snatched him back down onto the seat.

"No!" Terry yelled.

"Terrell!" Judge Franklin was hitting his desk with the wooden mallet.

"Terrell, be quiet!"

Terry subsided into sobs. Miss Ramsey continued, "In my opinion, Mr. McCree is incapable of looking after his own welfare. Much less that of a child under his influence. The boy has learned some unfortunate things; he has attached himself to McCree and developed very poor value judgment. He resents the restrictions of society, yearning to live a life like McCree's. To a six-year-old boy, that is a life of uninhibited freedom, moving around without ties to anybody or anything except himself."

"Thank you, Miss Ramsey."

Mr. Garrick whispered to Judge Franklin and the judge leaned across the bench. "Mr. and Mrs. Calder, we would like to have Terrell on the stand."

19

Judge Franklin spoke softly. "Terrell, do you know what it means to swear to tell the truth?"

"Yessir."

"What does it mean?"

"If I lie I go to jail."

"Yes. But it means more than that. It means, before God, you promise to tell the truth."

A man held out a Bible and Terry did as he'd seen the adults do, placing one hand on the book, the other hand raised.

"Do you swear to tell the truth, the whole truth, and nothing but the truth, so help you God?"

"Yessir."

"Sit down, Terrell," Judge Franklin said.

Mr. Garrick smiled at Terrell. "Terrell Calder is your name?"

"Yessir."

"Some of the people in this court also call you Terry, is that right?"

"Yessir."

"Which should I call you? Terrell, or Terry?"

"Terry."

"All right, Terry. Are your mother and father here?" Terry pointed at them.

"Do you love your mother and father, Terry?"

"Yessir."

"But you've been getting into a great deal of trouble, haven't you?"

"Yessir."

"You are causing your parents much worry."

"Yessir."

"Why have you been doing that?"

"I don't know."

"Well, maybe today we can find out why. Would you like to know why?"

Terry looked at Mr. McCree. The old man returned his gaze without smiling.

"Terry, do you know Mr. Jackson Cole McCree?"

Terry nodded.

"Please answer yes or no, son."

"Yes."

"How did you meet Mr. McCree?"

"Out at LuBelle's."

"That's your little colored friend, the granddaughter of Eunice Washington?"

"Yessir."

"How long have you known Mr. McCree?"

"About—two years."

"Do you like him?"

"Yessir."

"Why do you like him?"

"He's nice to me."

"How? What does he do that's nice to you."

"He takes me with him when he goes hunting things."

"Things like what?"

"Australian pine cones, cocoons, air plants—"

"So you work for him?"

Uncertain, Terry mumbled a reply.

"Did you say yes, Terry?"

"Yes." Pause. "Sir."

"Do you get paid for your work?"

"No. But he teaches me things!"

"Oh, such as what?"

"How to charm birds and catch fish with no bait."

The attorney laughed. "I'd like to know how to do that. How do you catch fish with no bait?"

"You sit real still, staring at the water. You have to mix bubbles in your spit and let it fall. If you move too fast, or too slow, the catfish gets away. So you move your hand out when you see the fish come up and put your hand in the water with your fingers together. Then you just pick him up."

"Just pick up the fish."

"Yessir. Pick him up."

"You've seen Mr. McCree do this?"

"I did it too."

"You did!"

Terry's eyes narrowed suspiciously. "Yes."

"Tell us about charming birds, Terry."

Terry told of the day McCree called the birds until there were dozens flying around and lighting on the old man.

"You saw this with your own eyes?" Mr. Garrick asked.

"Yessir!"

"What else did Mr. McCree teach you?"

"I don't know."

"About rattlesnakes?"

"Yessir."

"Mr. McCree isn't afraid of anything, is he?"

"No sir."

"Have you ever seen him pick up a live snake?"

"Sure! He does it with his hand, no stick or anything."

"Did you ever try that?"

"No."

"But when you and your mother went out to McCree's, you were going to pick up a snake that day, weren't you?"

"I was going to put him back in the tub."

"Did the snake strike at you?"

"Yes. He missed."

"Fortunately. Why did you let the snake go?"

"Mama said she'd pay for it."

"That's the only reason you didn't pick it up and put it back in the tub?"

"I guess so."

"Terry, let's talk about the day you and Mr. McCree went to the packing house together."

"With Bucky?"

"Yes. What were you doing there?"

"We went to eat tomatoes. Bucky had a box of salt."

"Did Mr. McCree eat tomatoes, too?"

"Sure."

"Did you pay for these tomatoes?"

"No sir."

"You just helped yourselves?"

"Sure, everybody does it."

"Well, not quite everybody. If everybody did that, the packing houses wouldn't have very many tomatoes to sell, would they?"

Terry considered this. "I guess not."

"Then you decided to ride in a packing crate down a spiraling chute. That's what Mr. Elton the guard said. Is that true?"

"Yessir."

"You did that?"

"Yessir."

"And Bucky?"

"Yessir."

"Mr. McCree rode one, too?"

"Yessir."

Mr. Garrick nodded. He held a ruled yellow pad of paper with notes scribbled on it. He turned a page.

"That was something, driving Mr. McCree's truck, wasn't it?"

"Sure was."

"Exciting."

"Yessir!"

"How many times have you done that?"

"I don't know."

"Many times?"

"I guess."

"When Mr. McCree fell out of the tree and broke his arm, where were you, Terry?"

"Up another tree. Getting plants."

"Tell us what happened after Mr. McCree fell."

"The bone was sticking out of his arm and there was blood on his shirt, so I knew it was broken. I helped him get to the chickee."

"What's a chickee, Terry?"

"That's what the Seminoles call it. It's a hammock with palmetto for a roof."

"Did it rain that night?"

"All night."

"Was it cold?"

"Yessir."

"Did you get hungry?"

"I sure did."

"What did you have to eat?"

"Nothing."

"Did you get thirsty?"

"The next day. Both of us."

"What did you drink?"

"We left Mr. McCree's sassafras tea because he was hurting so much. We didn't drink anything."

"How did you manage to drive the truck?"

"I stood between Mr. McCree's legs, steering. He helped me get it started and the throttle made the gas go."

"Did you go fast?"

"Yessir! We would've gotten stuck if we went slow."

"That must have been exciting, too."

"I was worried about Mr. McCree. He kept falling asleep."

"Is that right? When he did that, it was because he was tired?"

"Because he was hurt."

"Passing out. What did you do while he was unconscious?"

"Drove the truck."

"Terry, the hospital staff says you told them Mr. McCree was your grandfather."

Eyes down, voice almost unheard, "Yessir."

"You told a nurse that you had to see your grandfather because your grandmother was home dead in the bed, is that correct?"

Terry answered over laughter from the people listening. Mr. McCree was drawing circles on a piece of paper with a pencil they had given him.

"Terry," Mr. Garrick leaned nearer, "you really love that old man, don't you?"

Terry glanced at his parents. Mama's eyes were frightened. Daddy sat holding her hand.

"Yes."

"What did you say, Terry?"

"I said yes."

"You'd do almost anything for him, wouldn't you?"

"Yessir."

"You worked for him for no pay, you ate little or nothing and without complaint, isn't that so?"

"Yes."

"In fact, you saved his life, didn't you?"

"I don't know."

"It sounds as though you did."

"I don't know."

"Terry, did Mr. McCree ever tell you to go home? Ever?"

"No sir." Terry swallowed hard. "He drove me to the camp at night."

"Oh, he did?" Mr. Garrick turned and looked at Mr. McCree. "So he did know where you lived, then?"

"Not really. I always got out at the bridge."

"All right, Terry. Unless Mr. McCree has some questions, you may go back and sit with your mama and daddy."

Mr. McCree shook his head without looking up.

Mr. Garrick said, "I now call Mr. Jackson Cole McCree."

Mr. McCree's chair scraped the floor as he rose. His arm oddly postured, he walked slowly to the seat Terry had just vacated and sat down. He took a long, deep breath and exhaled noisily.

"State your name, please."

"Jackson Cole McCree."

"What is your occupation, Mr. McCree?"

"I sell seeds and things."

"Seeds and what things?"

"Wildlife, raccoons, possums, snakes, moths, whatever folks want to order that I can catch."

"Do you make a living at this?"

"I get by."

"But you don't seem to pay for anything, Mr. McCree. Your medical treatment, for example."

"No. Never did."

"How much money would you say you make in a year, Mr. McCree?"

"Couldn't rightly say."

"Five hundred, a thousand?"

"Sometimes, maybe."

"Let's go at this another way, Mr. McCree. How much did you pay in taxes last year?"

"I don't recall paying any."

"The year before?"

"No."

"In the past ten years? Twenty years?"

"Don't recall any."

"You have, in fact, never paid taxes, have you?"

"No, I reckon not."

"Do you know what Social Security is?"

"Yessir."

"Do you qualify?"

"Don't rightly know. I never asked."

"How about insurance, now or ever?"

"No sir."

"Of course, so long as you get medical care free, you would be throwing your money away to buy insurance, I suppose."

McCree's eyes followed Mr. Garrick as the attorney strolled across the room, talking.

"Mr. McCree, did you know there is a law requiring that all motorized vehicles have a license tag?"

"Yessir."

"Why haven't you bought one?"

"I used to bring my horse to town," Mr. McCree said. "They told me I'd have to stop that. So, for a while, I'd leave my horse to the edge of town and walk the rest of the way. When the horse died, I bought that truck of mine. I never come to town in it, either, except passing through. Always leave it at the edge of town and walk in, just like I did with the horse."

"Do you know there's a law about such things as registration of vehicles, faulty lights, brakes and muffler?"

"Nobody ever told me that."

"Ignorance of a law is no excuse in the eyes of the law, Mr. McCree."

"They keep telling me that the last day or so."

"Did you know there are laws prohibiting the use of child labor—with or without pay?"

"Me and the boy never rightly thought of it as work."

"You sold what he gathered, didn't you?"

"I did."

"You make your living gathering things from the swamps to sell, don't you?"

"Yessir."

"So you know the value of what you gather?"

"Most times, yessir."

"You did not pay the child, is that correct?"

McCree nodded, eyes lowered.

"Have you been apprised of the charge against you, Mr. McCree?"

"Yessir."

"Contributing to the delinquency of a minor. Do you know what that means?"

"I think I do. It ain't true."

"It isn't? You wouldn't say you have encouraged this boy to stay away from school, run away from home, and lie?"

"I didn't think so, no."

"How about stealing? Did you encourage the child to steal?"

"No. Never stole in my life, sir."

"Who paid for the tomatoes you ate with the children, Mr. McCree?"

"Well, sir, about the tomatoes—"

"Mr. McCree, do you have a hunting license?"

"No."

"Fishing license?"

"No."

"You do hunt and fish and trap, do you not?"

"I do."

"Do you have a license to ship animals and plants across state lines?"

"No."

"Any kind of business license?"

"No."

"How about a driver's license to drive the truck with no tag?"

"No."

"Have you ever had a driver's license?"

"No."

"Where do you keep your money? Do you have a bank account?"

"No."

"Do you own property?"

Mr. McCree's head was down.

"Do you rent, then?"

An imperceptible shake of the head.

"Do you know who owns the property where you have your residence?"

"I never thought about that."

"Do you have a family, Mr. McCree?"

"No."

"No relatives that you know of?"

"Not to my recollection."

"How old a man are you, Mr. McCree?"

"Eighty-four come February."

"You fell out of a tree at the age of eighty-three. You were bitten by a snake—what kind of snake?"

"Crota—a rattlesnake."

"Bitten by a snake twice."

"Yessir. He slipped."

"How old were you?"

"When?"

"The first time you got bitten."

"About sixteen, I reckon."

"You've been bitten more than twice, then?"

"That was a copperhead, when I was sixteen. A moccasin got me a couple of times. You have to watch a moccasin, he relaxes and waits until you relax, then he snatches back out of your hand and pops you."

"I wouldn't know, Mr. McCree."

"The boy knows. I taught him that."

"Mr. McCree," Mr. Garrick's voice lowered, softened, "you don't eat too regularly, do you?"

"Regular enough, I reckon."

"Three meals a day? Two?"

"When I'm hungry."

"Do you often forget to eat, Mr. McCree?"

"Get busy now and again. I forget."

The attorney walked around the room a minute, studying his notes. He dropped the pad on a table. "Mr. McCree, tell me what you think of that boy." He pointed at Terry.

"That's a fine boy."

"He deserves an education, don't you think?"

"Be a shame if he didn't."

"Yes it would. You're fond of that boy, aren't you?"

"Mighty fond."

"He keeps you company."

"That he does."

"He did save your life, didn't he?"

"I'd of died if he hadn't got me back."

"If you had died, he would also have died, is that a fair assumption?"

"It's what kept me going."

"In other words, if Terry hadn't been there, you would have crawled off in the woods and died."

"Might as well as not. Couldn't make it alone."

"Your Honor," Mr. Garrick said, "I think we've pretty well established what the court needs to know."

"Yes, Mr. Garrick. Mr. McCree, is there anything you'd like to say on your own behalf?"

"Yessir." Mr. McCree turned, arm thrusting, and looked up at the judge. "I'd like to ask some questions, now."

"Mr. McCree, we have released some of the witnesses. I asked you, at the time, if you wanted to cross-examine."

"Those gone best be gone," Mr. McCree said. "I want to talk to my little friend."

"The boy?"

"Yessir. If you don't mind."

Judge Franklin looked at his watch, then a clock on the wall. "How long will it take, Mr. McCree?"

"I don't rightly know. I don't want to hurry none."

"Very well," Judge Franklin said, his tone slightly irritated. "This court stands adjourned until tomorrow morning at ten. Mr. McCree, you will have your opportunity to cross-examine the child then. Is there anyone else you want to be here?"

"The boy's fine," McCree said. He eased down from his seat.

"Gerald, does that mean we all have to come back here tomorrow?" Mickey whispered.

"I'm afraid so."

"Gerald, really!"

"Court's adjourned until ten A.M. Friday, December fifth, tomorrow," Judge Franklin stood, banged the gavel and walked out, frowning.

"Mr. McCree," Terry leaned over the rail separating them.

"Yes, Little Hawk?"

"I want to talk to you, Mr. McCree."

"Tomorrow, Little Hawk. We'll talk tomorrow."

20

Terry sat in the chair beside Judge Franklin's mahogany bench. An overhead fan whirled, blowing warm air down from the ceiling.

"You remember what you promised yesterday, Terrell?" Judge Franklin asked.

"To tell the truth."

"That's right." Then to Mr. McCree, "You may begin."

Mr. McCree gazed at Terry solemnly.

"How's your arm, Mr. McCree?"

"Itches something awful."

"I knew a boy with a broken leg once. He said his itched, too."

"Mr. McCree," Judge Franklin stated, "let us begin."

The prosecuting attorney slumped in his chair, thumping the tabletop with the eraser of a pencil. Mama and Daddy were in the front row of seats, the only ones present besides a deputy sheriff, who was opening casement windows with a long pole he used to crank the partitions apart.

"Yesterday," McCree said to Terry, "we looked kind of bad, you and me."

"Yessir."

"To hear them tell it, we broke about every law there is, Little Hawk."

"That's what my daddy said."

"Know something, Little Hawk?"

"What?"

"I don't feel that way about it. Do you?"

"No sir I don't."

"Your Honor, please," Mr. Garrick said. "Let's try to get to the point."

"I agree, Mr. Garrick. Mr. McCree, will you begin questioning the witness?"

"Now, You Honor," McCree said, smiling, "I didn't rush anybody yesterday. I sat by and listened to how I made this boy into a criminal. I didn't open my mouth one time. I'd appreciate the same from this gentleman. He's got a mighty bad opinion of me and I'd like to change his mind, if I can."

"That's what we're here for, Mr. McCree. But let's get on with it, shall we?"

"They mean I should start asking you questions, Little Hawk. Mind if I do that?"

"No sir."

"Good. First, I don't ever recollect you telling me how old you were. Did you ever tell me that?"

"No sir."

"How about school? You ever mention going to school?"

"I said I didn't want to go."

"Seems to me you said you were glad you didn't have to go. Is that right?"

"That's right."

"I forget what I said."

"You said, when the time came, I'd like it."

"I said that?"

"You said I'd learn lots of things."

"Like what?"

"About the world."

"Hm-m. More than you'd learn with me, for sure."

"I learned a lot with you."

"Oh? You don't say. What?"

"About how to find something to eat in the swamps."

"That's important, all right, if you're in a swamp. What kind of things did we eat?"

"Wild potato, bamboo shoots, lots of things."

"Good food?"

"Real good."

"Now, about those tomatoes we swiped. What kind of tomatoes were those?"

"I don't know. Tomatoes, is all."

"Were they green ones, or blue ones?"

Terry laughed. "Red ones."

"Good and ripe and juicy?"

"Yessir."

"Looked like they might spoil in a day or two?"

"If we hadn't eaten them they would have."

"Don't they usually throw out real ripe tomatoes?"

"Yessir, they rot in the hamper if they're too ripe."

"Reckon anybody minded us eating those real ripe tomatoes?"

"No sir."

"All right. Now, it's true we did shoot the shoot, didn't we?"

"Yessir."

"That was something, wasn't it?"

"It sure was!"

"You boys showed me how and I enjoyed it, let me tell you."

Terry wiggled in his seat, his hands resting on the partition that boxed in the chair.

"We didn't get hurt, did we?"

"No sir."

"Did we hurt anything? Tear up anything?"

"No sir."

"Listen, Little Hawk, about this business of working you for no pay. I didn't mean to cheat you."

"I didn't want any money."

"I know that. But you did help me, didn't you?"

"Yessir."

"How'd you help me?"

"Well . . ." Terry chewed his lip a moment. "We got three hundred bushels of Australian pine cones!"

"Three hundred bushels. I bet you don't even know what a bushel is."

"Yes, I do."

"What's a bushel? A basket?"

"Baskets aren't all the same size."

"That's true. So how many is a bushel?"

"Two cups make a pint, two pints make a quart, eight quarts make a peck, four pecks makes a bushel."

"You said that mighty fast. Could have memorized that. Let's see—how many cups are in a quart?"

"Four."

"How many in a peck?"

"Thirty-two."

"How about a bushel, do you know that?"

"A hundred twenty-eight."

"Not bad, Little Hawk. You say we got three hundred of these bushels? How many is that?"

Ten flicks of ten fingers. "Times three," Terry said.

McCree nodded. "What else did we gather, Little Hawk?"

"Cecropia cocoons."

"What's that?"

"You know what that is!"

"I do. These folks might not. What is it?"

"It's a kind of moth."

"About those snakes. What kinds do I catch?"

"*Crotalus adamanteus* and *Agkistrodon piscivorus*."

Judge Franklin interrupted, "What are those?"

"Rattlesnakes," Terry said. "One kind. There are seven different kinds. *Crotalus* means 'big rattle' and *adamanteus* means 'he won't back down.' He's the biggest of the rattlers."

"What was that other one?" McCree asked.

"Water moccasin."

"Little Hawk, let's talk about the day I fell out of the tree. You and me know I was doing poorly."

"Yessir."

"Broke arm, fever, pain like no pain I ever felt."

"You didn't cry, though."

"The truth now. I cried a little."

"Just a little."

"If you hadn't been there, I don't know what would've happened."

"But I was."

"Yes. I can thank my lucky stars for that. Let's say I got down and couldn't of got up. What would you have done?"

"You said go north."

"Yes I did, now that I recollect. North. Which way is north?"

"Left of east."

"Which way is east?"

"The sun comes up in the east and sets in the west. North is left of east."

"Which is your left, Little Hawk?"

Terry lifted his left hand.

"What if you'd got stuck out there at night by yourself?" McCree persisted.

"I'd build a chickee, like you did."

"You think you could do that?"

"Yessir."

"Tell me how you'd do it."

Terry told how he'd get only the fronds that were green, because the dead ones cracked and broke so easily. He explained the overlapping, like shingles, to keep out rain, and how the stems had to be interlocked to hold against the wind. He described the frame and, finally, the hammock that would keep him off the ground.

"What about mosquitoes?"

"Cover coals with moss to drive off mosquitoes."

"How about water?"

"Strain it and boil it hard. It doesn't always taste so good, but it won't make you sick."

"Food?"

"There's lots of food."

"Tell me."

"Swamp cabbage, *Daucus carota*—"

"What's that?"

"Wild carrot. Mama calls it Queen Anne's lace."

"Anything else?"

"Mr. McCree, you know I know that! Berries, nuts, most everything can be eaten if you know what to look for and how to cook it."

"Course you know how to fish with no bait."

"I sure do!"

"Caught one bigger than mine, didn't you?"

"Yessir!"

"With your bare hands! Reached right down and picked up that big catfish easy as you please."

"Yessir!"

"Did you tell your mama and daddy about that?"

Terry's smile vanished. "I told Daddy."

"Did he believe you?"

"I didn't tell him how I did it. I just said I caught a big catfish."

Mr. McCree nodded, looking at the floor. He propped his bad arm on the judge's bench, looking at Terry.

"How's Dog?"

"He's doing okay. I threw away the poultice and put camphor water on his bite."

Judge Franklin cleared his throat. "What is this?"

"My dog, Dog," McCree said. "Got bit by a rattlesnake and I haven't been back to tend to him. Little Hawk did it for me."

"Camphor water holds down on pain and soreness," Terry said to Judge Franklin. "We already put on boneset leaves mashed for a poultice."

Judge Franklin nodded.

"Little Hawk, if I asked you a straight question, will you give me a straight answer?"

Terry's eyes dropped. "Yessir."

"Do you love your ma and pa?"

"I sure do."

"You don't want to hurt them, do you?"

"No sir."

"You did, though. You might not have meant to, but you did. I saw it in your ma's face when Eunice told how you said you didn't have any folks."

"I'm sorry, Mr. McCree."

"I am too, Little Hawk. But let's see if we can figure why you said such a thing."

Terry had tears in his eyes, blinking fast.

"You have any friends, Little Hawk?"

"Aren't you my friend?" Terry asked.

"I am that. I mean, any other friends."

Terry thought a long time. "Bucky, I guess."

"You don't sound too sure."

"He's okay."

"What's wrong with him?"

"Nothing."

"You know how I judge who's a friend?"

"How?"

"By whether the other person will do the same for me that I'd do for him. Would Bucky do for you?"

"No."

"Who would?"

"You."

"Anybody else?"

"Mama. Daddy."

"Anybody else, Little Hawk?"

"No."

"Are your mama, daddy and I your only friends, then?"

Terry nodded, head hung.

"Nothing to be ashamed of, you know," McCree said. "Most folks don't have even one friend. But you have other friends."

"Who?"

"Eunice and LuBelle."

"Oh. Yessir."

McCree took his arm off the judge's bench and walked away, looking stooped. He halted before Mr. Garrick and looked at the attorney a long moment.

"When you was a boy, Mr. Garrick, did you ever want to take off all your clothes and go swimming?"

"I suggest you confine your questions to the child, Mr. McCree," Mr. Garrick said, not harshly.

To Judge Franklin, McCree said, "When I first came to the Everglades nigh onto sixty-five years ago, birds rose up on the wing, so many the sky turned dark for an hour. They don't have flocks like that anymore. 'Gators big as tree trunks were common as grass. Not many big ones left these days, and the day's coming when they'll all be gone."

McCree turned to Mama and Daddy. "Everybody's been worrying about why this boy wants to stay out of school. That's no mystery to me. He's a—little hawk. He needs to fly, soar, ride the air currents, before they clip his wings forever."

McCree looked at Terry, unsmiling, and a shimmer of water was in his eyes.

"Ya'll asked me was I fond of him?"

McCree paused, his lips twisting. "I said yes."

The old man brushed under his eyes, quickly, using a thumb for one eye, forefinger for the other.

"Truth is, he came to me like he was God-sent. This skinny little boy with a spirit yearning to be free as all outdoors. Me and him had something special, we did. From riding through the swamps, chasing old *Crotalus*, doctoring Dog's snakebite and even shooting the shoot! That was a lot of fun, wasn't it, Little Hawk?"

"Yessir, it was." Terry began crying softly.

"Now, you might lock up old McCree's body, 'cause my old body hasn't got many more miles to make it. But I pine for this boy the way I'd pine for a bobcat kitten in a cage who'll never know the smell of swamp water and the taste of wild food.

"If I'm supposed to be ashamed of giving this little hawk flight, I just can't find myself feeling it."

McCree came to Terry and put a quaking hand on the boy's shoulder, shaking gently. "We had us something special, boy. Something few men and boys ever know. Someday, I'm betting, it won't be learning to spell and add you'll think about, because you'll have them memory-locked. I'm betting you remember old man McCree."

McCree went back to his table and sat down. Mama and Daddy were staring at Terry, eyes moist. Judge Franklin sat a long time in a room silent except for the circling fan overhead.

"Monday morning, ten o'clock, December eighth," Judge Franklin said brusquely. "I'll deliver a decision then." The gavel struck the bench and Judge Franklin walked out.

Sunday, December 7, 1941, Terry was eating cookies and drinking milk while Daddy listened to the ball games on radio. Suddenly Daddy cried out, a sound so vivid and visceral that Terry would never forget it as long as he lived.

"What is it, Gerald?" Mama called from the bedroom.

"Mickey, Mickey, my God, Mickey!"

"Gerald! What is it?"

Daddy's face was starkly pale as he grabbed Mama, holding her, Mickey repeating, "What is it, Gerald? What is it?"

"The Japanese attacked Pearl Harbor, Mickey."

Terry saw her eyes go wide, frightened.

"That means war. Now. Today. Dear God."

They stood holding one another a very long time, Terry standing back, looking at them.

That evening the Japanese family in camp was attacked by angry, machete-armed laborers who, if it hadn't been for Daddy and Randy, might have killed them all.

Burrell Mason called and said he was retracting his editorial about the new camp. Terry watched Daddy talk into the phone in urgent, hushed tones—something about the President speaking tonight.

"They want me to join the International Red Cross," Daddy told Mama, hanging up from yet another long-distance call.

"What about the camp, Gerald?"

"War changes priorities, Mickey. They'll send someone else to manage the camps. I'll have to go to Fort Pierce for a day or two."

"The baby, Gerald."

"I know."

On Monday, the world looked the same, but all talk was of war. When Terry and Mama arrived in Judge Franklin's court, they and McCree were the only ones there.

Judge Franklin came in, looking older since Friday, and sat heavily, gazing down at a folder before him. He closed the folder and pushed it away wearily.

"Mr. McCree," Judge Franklin said, his voice strangely choked, "last Friday was a thousand years ago."

"Yessir."

"Somehow, today," Judge Franklin said, looking at Terry, "I think there are few people in the world who would begrudge the freedom of a little hawk."

McCree nodded.

The gavel hit the bench.

"Dismissed," Judge Franklin said.

"What does that mean, Mama?"

"It means they're going to forget everything," Mama said, standing. She winced suddenly, holding her stomach, mouth open.

"You all right, Mrs. Calder?" McCree asked.

"I think—I'm—"

McCree helped Mama sit again. A puddle of water spread across the floor.

"I'll have the judge call somebody, Mrs. Calder," McCree said.

In the hospital corridor, Daddy stood with Burrell Mason, doctors and nurses, listening to a radio. Mama was in another room trying to have a baby. Terry sat close to McCree.

"The vote was 388 to one for war," Burrell said, sharply. "Who the hell voted against it?"

"Jeanette Rankin, Republican from Montana," a doctor said.

Daddy and Burrell walked by Terry and the old man. "No need recriminating," Mr. Mason was saying, "we need that camp now."

Terry put a hand on McCree's knee. "Mr. McCree?"

"What, Little Hawk?"

"My daddy says we're moving away from Belle Glade."

"That a fact?"

"He's going to fight the war."

McCree nodded.

"Reckon I could come live with you in the swamp?"

"Reckon not, Little Hawk."

"Why?"

"Your mama ain't going to have a man around the house with your pa gone, Little Hawk. She's going to need you mighty bad."

"She'll have the new baby."

"She needs you all the more."

Terry blinked his eyes quickly.

"Summer's over, Little Hawk."

"This is December, Mr. McCree. This is winter."

McCree grunted. "Does it feel like winter to you?"

"No sir."

"The Seminoles used to say, so long as it's hot, it's

summer. When it's cold, it's winter. Seems reasonable to me."

"Yessir."

"Well, Little Hawk, you had a Seminole summer. Now it's past. Time for new things and new places. You got to be a man when your daddy goes to fight the war. You got to grow up some. Go to school. Understand?"

"Mr. Calder!"

"Yes?"

"It's a girl!"

Terry saw a strange mixture of expressions cross Daddy's face. "How's my wife? How's Mickey?"

"Fine!"

"Did you tell her it was a girl?" Daddy asked.

"Yes we did. She said, 'Thank goodness.' "

Daddy turned and grabbed Terry, hugging him too tightly. "We have a little sister in the house now. You'll have to help your mama look after her."

"Yessir. Mr. McCree told me."

Daddy had tears in his eyes, looking at Terry. He kissed the boy ever so gently.

"I don't know if I told you, Little Hawk. But I sure do love you."

Terry hugged Daddy. "I love *you*."

"Here comes the baby!"

"Look at that!"

The red-faced, fretting child looked like a prune! Somebody said, "Looks just like Mickey."

Terry turned to sit down, fuming. That baby looked like nobody. Ugly! Red! "Beautiful!" everybody was saying.

Terry looked for McCree where they'd been sitting.

The old man was gone.

Forever.